THE DAY AFTER YESTERDAY

AMANDA MACKEY

Serenade Publishing

MORE FROM SERENADE PUBLISHING

Songbird Series

By Sarah Williams

Songbird

Brigadier Station Series

By Sarah Williams:

The Brothers of Brigadier Station

The Sky over Brigadier Station

The Legacies of Brigadier Station

Christmas at Brigadier Station

Heart of the Hinterland Series

By Sarah Williams:

The Dairy Farmer's Daughter

Their Perfect Blend

Beyond the Barre

The Outback Governess

Primrose Series

By Tanya Renee

Prairie Sky

Prairie Nights

Prairie Fire

Prairie Hearts

Prairie Sound

Prairie Rain

With The Band Series

By Tanya Renee

Finding Direction

The Spring of Love Series

By Virginia Taylor

Forever Delighted

Forever Amused

Forever Heartfelt

The Tooth Fairy Chronicles

By Victoria Rocus

Tooth Decay With A Side Of Fae

Toothaches And Wedding Cakes

Baby Tooth And Tangled Roots

Wisdom Tooth And The Awful Truth

A New Page

by Aimee MacRae

It Happened in Paris

By Michelle Beesley

For more information visit:

www.serenadepublishing.com

ONE

Capri

My life will end tonight.

Of that, I am certain.

But I'll do it by my hand. On my terms. Not *his*.

I'm taking my power back. This one act is all I have left. I'm in control when for so long I haven't been. I've thought about it for the past week and there is no other way. If I leave, he'll find me. If I stay, he'll continue his torture. Death will be a blessing because living is far more atrocious when a monster is slowly stealing my soul.

It's one of those nights in mid-winter when the air is so cold it feels like a slap in the face, while the moon momentarily hides behind a small carpet of clouds. My breath billows out in swirling plumes with each calming exhale. I huddle into my cardigan, pulling it tighter around me, and step out onto the bridge extending across the river, the wind buffeting me from all sides. The corroded span is a lonely structure atop the muddy water below, silt churned up from the recent rains.

I haven't been here before, but I can tell it's no longer used. The one lane road is cracked and overgrown with weeds sprouting from the potholes. A newer version of the bridge has been built further down, which is the way the bus takes us to school. If I were allowed out on weekends like a normal teen, I would have discovered this abandoned relic years ago.

From this height, the impact into the water will be fierce, hopefully knocking me out first so that I'm unaware of anything else. It needs to be quick. I don't want to suffer. There's been enough of that in my seventeen years. Sure, there are faster ways to off myself, like walking in front of a train or truck, but the idea of someone finding me in pieces, traumatized for the rest of their lives is why I've chosen this location. At least whoever discovers my body will think I've simply drowned.

One would expect the isolated space to be totally silent, but it's alive with a chorus of sounds most don't hear unless they truly listen. A distant night owl hooting to its own rhythm. A whine on the breeze as it tunnels through trees and a constant chirping of crickets make the night come alive.

And yet, even though I'm calm, a sense of loneliness grips me in its black claws, squeezing whatever life remains out of me. I've been numb long before stepping outside my rickety home into the freezing November temperatures. Numb to life. Numb to pain and, most certainly, numb to my sadistic father. He's the reason I stand here, about to rid him of one less burden. The idea of doing him a favor doesn't sit right with me, but what other choice do I have? He's my legal guardian for another month, and that amount of time feels like a lifetime. I'm at my wits end. I can't do another minute in that house.

It's a miracle I escaped tonight, but God must have been watching over me. For once, my father forgot to lock my bedroom door because he was occupied with some cheap whore he hires on the regular. His mistake. It's the first time he's forgotten and thankfully he did because it's the only reason I ran. Normally, the windows and doors are secured tightly, like any maximum-security prison.

My pockets are empty from no job because I've never been allowed to stand on my own two feet. That would mean me leaving my tormentor and making a life for myself. He doesn't want that. He wants to keep me beholden to him so he can control me. It's all a power trip for him. He gets off on my pain. I see it in his steely gaze when I struggle. When I beg him to let me go.

I haven't been to school for the last two weeks because of the injuries sustained by him, and to say those long fourteen days have been a nightmare is an under-statement.

The bruising on my ribs is now a faded yellow, but the scars left on my psyche run deeper than blood. There is nothing left.

I'm simply a shell with no substance. Hollowed out. Dreams constantly crushed and the presence of fear which he created and continues to sustain. Simply put,

I've lost myself. I don't know who I am anymore. The me I used to be.

I'm so damn tired, right down to my marrow. Emotionally and physically done. I don't want to exist the way I currently am. I see others and know I'm not right in the head. They laugh, I smile to appease. They joke. I remain silent. They attend parties. I can't bear to be around my peers, drinking and enjoying themselves. It reminds me of how much I don't have. How sad I am. How screwed up my life is.

James Worthington. My legal life-giver. Ironic that he should create me and then, in turn, destroy me. Drunk. Angry. Evil. Once I'm gone, he will have no more power. The days will change, but he'll remain the same, except he'll have no outlet for his rage. Hopefully, he'll take it out on himself and do the world a favor.

I walk slowly out toward the middle and climb the railing, feeling each gust of wind become stronger and more powerful, until I'm standing precariously on the edge, looking at the turbulent waters beneath me. Tears trickle down my face, my mind full of memories from a black past and an invisible future I'll never know. Futures destined for most, aside from those who were never meant for anything except misery. Boyfriends. Marriage. Babies. A home with a white picket fence. Grandchildren. And most of all, happiness. A simple word so powerful in its delivery. Yet weak because it can be stolen so easily.

Standing here alone, for the first time in my life, a resigned sense of closure settles over me. The pain will end soon. I'll be free. Unshackled from the prison that is my existence. My soul cries out to be released from the confines of the heavy, cumbersome, broken body so it can soar.

The wind picks up, blowing my long brown hair into my face, momentarily blocking my view of my final resting place. I'll sink to the bottom and then eventually rise to the top, the motion of the river carrying me west. But it won't matter then, because I'll be long gone. My husk is the only remainder of a girl who never had a chance at life.

My two school friends will grieve for me but move on with their lives, the memory of me being nothing more than a pitiful one. Short-lived. Just a blip in time.

A noise to my left has me pivot, my balance precarious, the movement almost causing me to fall. The idea should please me, but I want to jump in *my* time, when *I'm* ready and not a moment before. For once in my life, this is all about me.

With the change of direction, the wind pushes the hair out of my face, and I let out a squeal as a figure stands about ten feet away, on the same ledge of the bridge I am.

Shock has me stiffen, a million thoughts spiraling through my mind as the full moon, now free of the moving cloud, highlights a male. Taller than me, perhaps six feet. His shaggy brown hair whips haphazardly around like mine. He's facing the river as if he too is about to jump, so my mouth speaks before my brain can catch up.

"What are you doing?" My eyes are huge, and my mouth remains open.

He glances my way, his features becoming more distinguishable under the lunar glow. His expression remains impassive.

"I'm about to jump."

Four simple words snare me like a fishhook and won't let go. They burrow deeper as I say them over and over in my head, wondering what the odds are of a boy appearing out of nowhere with the same intent as me. It doesn't make sense. Is he real? A mirage of my subconscious?

I stare, blinking a few times to ensure he doesn't vanish into thin air, a sign that I'm not in my right mind. But he remains, his focus on me intense, as if he too has the same questions.

Where did he come from and why didn't I hear him approach? We're secluded, but still. I would have heard footsteps approach. Wouldn't I? Or had I been too in my head to hear anything other than the water below calling me?

"You can't!" I shout as if I have any right. I'm about to do the same, so why do I care?

The idea of watching him plummet to his icy death is not something I want to witness right before I follow. Not that any of it will matter, but why does he want to end his life so bad?

Surely, he hasn't lived the same pathetic existence as I have.

"Give me one good reason, why not?" he asks, brushing some hair out of his face but failing as the wind carries it back to the same spot. He angles himself toward me a little, against the gust.

"Because you'll die." It sounds ludicrous after I've said it and he obviously thinks so too because he laughs. It's deep and husky, causing further goosebumps to litter my skin. All the other noises that seemed so loud earlier fade and all I hear is the rich baritone of a boy who clearly finds this whole situation amusing.

"That's the whole idea of it. Isn't that why you're standing here, too?"

Yes, but me jumping alone is different from me watching someone end their life first. Or even after, it doesn't matter. Should I be comforted by the fact that he wants to join me in the afterlife? No. In fact, it has the opposite effect. I don't want to see what I'll look like when I take the final step. Because then I might chicken out and become the coward I know I must be.

I watch him watching me, wondering what he sees. With him, I see a rebel. A guy who has witnessed too much. Done too much. But not someone about to end their life. What does that person even look like? Me? A smile can hide the deepest of pain. Some of us can mask our troubles behind quiet laughter or shy silence.

"I... yes, but I can't do it with you here. You need to leave. I don't want an audience. That's why I picked this spot. And this time of night."

It's midnight. Most people are in bed sleeping. Dreaming. Unconscious until their alarm wakes them up so they can go about their lives, not knowing a girl jumped to her death a mile away. They'll anticipate their future while enjoying a hot coffee and breakfast. Talking to loved ones the way I should have with my father. Except, you don't talk to men like him. You keep your mouth shut, hoping they leave you alone. Doing whatever is asked of you, simply to keep the peace, even if what is asked of you is everything you know you shouldn't be doing.

"Tough. This is where I've chosen, so either you jump

first, or I will." He's inched closer without me realizing. I was too busy thinking to notice such a small thing. But now that he has my attention, I can see his dark eyes. The glow from the moon bathes him in a pale blanket of light, his black clothing in stark contrast to his wishy-washy skin.

I glance back to the river, knowing I can't jump while he's here invading my space. What if, as soon as I hit the water, he jumps in after me and saves me? Because I know that if he launches into the air first, I won't be able to stand by and watch him surface and get swept away. I'll have to call for help on my cell, switched off in the pocket of my jeans.

"You're crazy." It's weak, but all I have. Spoken by a mouse of a girl who stands on the edge of a tall bridge, ready to become another statistic.

Five other teens have leapt from this bridge over the last three years. None of them survived. Another reason I've chosen this way. Death is inevitable.

I'm surprised he's standing so close. Boys never show any interest in me, let alone talk to me. At school, I'm seen as a loner, with only my two friends. We avoid most of the other students. We don't loiter in the halls. We get to class, keep our heads down and bolt for the doors when the final bell rings.

I've never had a boyfriend. Who would want someone so sad inside? I'm guessing it shows on my face because guys keep their distance, ignoring me most of the time. I don't have a type, but if I did? This guy might qualify.

Another laugh jerks me upright, my right-hand clinging to the railing now as if I'm attempting not to fall.

His voice is closer again, bringing about a bone deep shiver. My cardigan is barely keeping my torso protected against the bitter wind, while my hands remain exposed, not quite anesthetized yet. It's a weird feeling to be so desensitized inside but still able to experience the chill of the wind and icy temperatures on the outside.

"Stay back!" I cry, panicked. He needs to back the hell away. What is he doing? Is he going to pull me in with him?

"I just want to see you better, considering yours is the last face I'll see. And mine will be the last you'll see."

It's true. Two strangers sharing something so personal. Their last moments on earth. It's not how I planned this out. Not the outcome I'd envisioned. But here we are, fate working behind the scenes.

At least my father's face won't have been the last I'll see. This stranger is far more pleasant to look at.

He's making me stall, though. I should have jumped already. He's prolonging my demise.

The guy looks to be about my age. Maybe a year or two older. I wonder if he goes to my school. He's not familiar.

But now that he's within touching distance, I notice how exquisite his features are. Eyes that delve below my layers. Lips too shapely for a guy. A roman nose with a hint of a bump front on but as he gives me his profile, it seems to even out to almost perfect.

Our breaths are like low-hanging clouds hovering as we simply exhale and inhale for too many heartbeats, me wondering when he's going to jump, and will I be able to follow?

"Do you think it'll be lights out when we enter the water? Or do you think one of us will remain aware and experience the water entering our lungs?"

His eyes find mine after his question as he brings his hands to his mouth and breathes warm air into them.

I haven't thought about that. I simply assumed it'll all be over before I sink down deep. The idea of choking on fluid seems horrible. And yet, I've heard drowning is a peaceful way to go. I can't imagine the pain of my lungs filling with anything other than air.

"I, uh, don't know, obviously. This is my first attempt, and I don't know anyone who has survived to tell me." I've only thought of the relief of death itself, not of the journey there. Will it hurt? Will the suffering become greater than it already is?

"Hmm." His head angles my way, a frown marring his forehead.

"What? You don't think you'll be unconscious as soon as you hit the water?"

A swipe of his tongue over his bottom lip distracts me for a few seconds until he answers with a shrug, "There's always a chance."

It's my turn to glance away, not liking the conversation. It's putting my previous peaceful mood into an anxious one. Damn him for choosing tonight to come here. He could have picked any other evening. Why this one? Suddenly my brain is questioning my decision.

The guy must sense my newfound apprehension. He changes the subject. "Name's Atlas." He's holding out his large hand for me to shake as if we're not standing on the edge of a bridge, our lifespans having decreased from years to minutes.

My eyes rise to his as my hand comes up without too much thought to grip his surprisingly soft one. "Capri."

One of his thick eyebrows shoots skyward, "As in the island or the pants?"

My ice cracks slightly and for the first time in a long time, I let out a giggle, followed by a gasp. I'm so surprised this stranger has been able to pull such an emotion from me, it shocks me to my core. I school it away quickly and put my indifferent facade firmly back in place. I shouldn't be laughing at a time like this. I shouldn't be feeling a thing. To feel is to hesitate, and hesitation brings about doubt. Which makes me wonder if I'm truly ready for this.

He's grinning, but it falls when he sees my expression change. "You don't laugh much, do you?"

"I don't have a whole lot to laugh at. If I did, I wouldn't be standing here."

He hums in response. "Well, are you going to answer my question?"

I think about my name. Did my birth mother give it to me? Or was it my father? The second is doubtful. He's not that smart to come up with such a unique name.

My mother took off when I was eight. Apparently, she couldn't handle my father either. But she left me to suffer without her. Just disappeared to save herself and didn't give two hoots about her only child. Just another blow to my already shattered self-esteem. Not even one parent loved me.

Maybe she was beaten, too. Surely his cruelness didn't appear after she left. My early memories of him are vague, though. I've questioned why she didn't take me with her for years after. If he had abused her, why leave me there to suffer the same fate? What mother would do that to her only daughter? And why can't I remember my childhood before eight years of age? Perhaps it's the trauma of never seeing her again. The disappointment and anger of her quick exit from our lives.

What was she like? Did I love her? Did she love me? Obviously not enough to save me, too.

There's so much we don't understand about the brain. It's ability to compartmentalize events. To hide them deep in the subconscious to protect us. Maybe that's why I don't remember her. Because even an ounce of happiness in her presence would make me hate her even more for abandoning me.

Atlas is still staring at me, patiently waiting, so I appease him. "I can't tell you that. My mom shot through when I was young. I'm guessing my name was her choice, but I don't know the symbolism behind it, if any. Maybe she just liked the name."

"Fair enough." He nods and lifts his head to the night sky, leaving us in silence.

It's getting colder. I press my arms tightly across my chest to thwart off the freezing wind and look skyward, too.

The stars are brighter tonight, as if they've all come out for a last farewell, blinking. Waiting. Surprisingly, the silence isn't awkward. It's comforting. Having someone beside me, not judging or looking at me like I'm a freak. It's a pity we won't be around much longer. I feel as if we could hang out some more. The feeling is… nice.

"So, are you doing it first or am I?" he asks, causing a sliver of fear to manifest at the idea of this being it. I don't think anyone truly wants to die. They just want the pain to end. It's not like going to sleep and waking the next day. It's final.

The last little while has been unusually pleasant. I'm not quite ready to have it end. He's been different to me, unlike my peers at school. It's as if he cares.

"Uh. I don't want you to jump. But I'm not quite ready yet either." The thought catches me by surprise. Until he showed up, I was adamant. Now? I'm second-guessing myself.

I pivot slightly, careful to strengthen my grip, and face him.

He angles back toward me too, so we're facing each other. "Can I ask you something?"

I don't like questions. Not personal ones. So, I'm wary when I reply, "It depends on what it's about."

There's a pause. "If I hadn't come along, would you have jumped by now?"

Would I? with no doubt in my voice, I say, "Yes."

"Then I'm glad I came." His smile lights me up on the inside. It's scary but also as if a life buoy is floating nearby for me to grab on to. My heart stutters as we study one another, connected by the location and the reason we're both here. He gets it. And so do I.

"Me too."

Two

Atlas

I don't tell her my secret. The girl with devastatingly sad eyes. I'm just glad I turned up when I did. It brought back a flurry of emotions as she stood on the precipice of life and death. She appeared like a wispy, willowy ghost, her hair flailing about, the eerie mist teasing her.

For the initial first few seconds, terror seized me as memories slithered across my mind. One's I've attempted to bury but failed miserably. I couldn't show her my fear. Rather, I needed to act nonchalant, as if her standing perilously on a narrow ledge didn't strike up a near panic attack.

And now here we stand. Still alive. Strangely comfortable with each other. If I can keep her talking, hopefully she'll let me move her over to safety. I'll breathe easier once we're off this damn ledge. I can't let her jump. She'll regret it as soon as she lets go and begins free falling. But it'll be too late.

She's stunning and doesn't even realize it. Straight brown hair, I imagine glows in the sunshine. An upturned nose sprinkled with freckles. Lips that look bluer than pink at the moment because of the temperature.

And her eyes. Wow. Hickory in color, the shape of almonds and fringed by long, curled black lashes which don't appear fake. They tell such a sorrowful story. One I want to hear all about. I want to dive into their depths and uncover whatever it is that troubles her so. But I must tread carefully. If I come on too strong, she'll panic and jump. If I act like I don't care at all, she'll jump. She's watching me now and all I want to do is reach out and touch her delicate face. Let her know that it's okay. She is worth more than death. That no matter what has driven her to this point, someone cares.

Instead, I remove my jacket and place it over her cardigan, hoping to warm her up a little. Her eyes are wide as she takes in my short-sleeve T-shirt and the goosebumps that arise on my skin.

"No. Take it back. You'll freeze to death."

I bark out another laugh. "Ironic, don't you think?"

She smiles. Not fully, but enough for it to transform her face from somber to almost happy.

We truly need to get out of this weather, so I try for casual. "You want to hang out for a bit?"

"Isn't that what we're doing?" she asks, her brow scrunching.

"Ha. Yes, but let's move this over the other side of the railing. That way, one of us won't fall by accident."

"So, you're not going to jump?"

"I didn't say that. I'm just thinking that before we take the plunge, it'd be nice to chat with someone who understands."

She gives me her full attention, a myriad of emotions playing out on her face. A war within. She sucks her bottom lip in, clearly wondering what my end game is.

My end game is I want her away from danger. She might not know it now, but life doesn't stay the same. It's always changing. There's always hope. No matter the current circumstances, no matter her mindset, once she takes that step, there's no turning back.

I hold out my hand to let her know I've got her when no one else probably does. She's way too young to do this. My heart is beating an odd rhythm as I wait. It could go either way.

She stares at my hand and then back at my face.

"Five more minutes. That's all. We've already been here way longer than that."

Please say yes. Please.

On a large exhale, I receive a slight nod and then her soft, delicate hand entwines with mine. My grip automatically tightens so there's no way for her to pull free and then I'm stepping over the railing and onto the weathered, broken road with her, leading her across to the other side. To safety. A large tree rises from a grassy verge, so I drag her there before we both sit. Relief has my shoulders sagging and my breath leaving me. She's alive. For now.

There's only a short time to convince her she's worthy of life.

THREE

Capri

I'm not sure what's happening but being led from my death to a safe spot by a stranger was not part of tonight's plan. This hiccup has left me confused and guilty. Guilt from not following through. For hesitating. He's thrown me off my game. This boy who wants to talk.

No boys ever want to talk. I'm not very approachable at school. If he knew me beyond this evening, he'd soon see that he's wasting his time. I'm a lost cause. I have nothing to offer. My father has told me this repeatedly. It's ingrained into my psyche.

He doesn't hesitate to speak up. "So, Capri, how old are you?"

"Seventeen."

"You go to Milford High?"

"Yeah."

I'm not comfortable getting asked so many questions, so I decide to ask him some. "How about you?"

I notice goosebumps scattering over his toned arms, so I begin taking the jacket off.

"No. Keep it," he quickly says, putting his hand out to stop me.

"But you're cold."

"I'm used to it. I really don't mind." He grins, showing mostly straight white teeth apart from an incisor that sticks out slightly more than the others. Perfectly imperfect.

He hasn't answered my question, so I push. "How old are you?"

"Oh, sorry. I'm turning eighteen next month. And no. I don't go to high school. I work with my twin brother at a repair shop in town."

He brings a leg up and places his forearm on his knee as he glances away and then back at me. "Dropped out of school five months ago. I had some shit happen in my life and decided school was no longer for me. Killian offered me a job with him, and I took it."

It makes me wonder why he was here to end his life. Was it because of the shit that happened? It must have been severe to want to end it. I should know. Intrigue has me wanting to ask, but common sense prevails. Talking about something so personal to a total stranger is not going to happen. Just like if he asked me why, I'd clam up.

His eyes are clear. Not clouded like I imagine mine are from years of pain. To look at him, I'd think him a normal teenager.

And then he asks a question that totally throws me for

a loop. It's one I've asked myself over and over, but it always has the same answer.

"If you could be or do anything in the world and money or circumstance wasn't an option, what would it be?"

My insides splinter wide open as if his words are a sharp arrow let go from a bow that pierces the center of my heart.

A sound shoots from my mouth, which I quickly cover with my hand. And then he's moving closer and touching my back, which I barely feel through his thick jacket. Thank goodness, too, because I don't like being touched. It reminds me of *him*.

"Hey. It's okay. You don't have to answer. I'm sorry. I didn't mean to upset you."

Atlas is genuinely concerned, his voice raspy and soothing next to me. It shouldn't be such a hard question, and I feel silly for reacting the way I have.

God. He's going to see how ruined I am and think I'm pathetic. My face lifts to his, nothing but sincerity staring back at me.

I don't know why I do it, but my mouth responds without me having any control over it.

"A photographer." I brush strands of hair from my face and attempt a smile. After all, he's been kind to me. "If there was nothing standing in my way, I'd travel the world and take photos. Of people, places, and animals."

A frown line connects his eyebrows as his face falls for a moment. He sucks in a breath and then plasters on a fake smile. I've hit a nerve. "What?" I ask, curious and genuinely interested.

With a shake of his head, he swallows hard and then says, "Nothing. I uh, I happen to be interested in photography too."

"You are? Why so sad then?" I don't know why I'm feeling so brave around Atlas, but I want to know more about him.

"My best friend jumped from this very bridge six months ago. The fall knocked him out and then he drowned. We used to go take photos together all the time, but since then, I haven't picked up my camera."

Shit. Stupid Capri. Why couldn't you be all shy like you normally are? That was dumb.

"God. I'm sorry. I didn't know." I swallow harshly, hoping I haven't brought about any more pain for him.

"Of course you didn't. It's fine. It's getting easier."

Is it though? Is that why he wants to jump from the same bridge? Because of the grief for his best friend? That must be hard. Knowing he couldn't do anything about it. The what ifs and whys of it all.

How would he have handled watching me jump from the exact same bridge? If he wasn't already serious about ending his life, seeing me fall to my death the same way his friend did would gut him. Probably cause him to jump after me. I can't do that to him.

"Anyway, enough of the heavy crap." He rises. "I've taken up enough of your time. It's been nice meeting you, Capri."

He walks back over to the railing. For a minute I hope he'll turn and walk the way he came, but he doesn't. He's about to jump!

My body fills with adrenaline and a strong urge to stop him. He can't do this. I rise by instinct.

"Stop! Wait!" I'm running after him.

He pauses almost at the other side and turns to me, but doesn't speak. He's waiting for me.

"Don't. Please. Don't jump. I can't watch you do it. You don't need to. It's okay. You've got your brother to think about. You have someone who loves you. I have…"

"You have what?" he asks, stepping into me.

"I have no one. You have family."

His stare is unnerving, but he remains in the same spot. He bends his knees, bringing his tall frame lower, so our eyes are aligned. "You have me. That's someone, right?"

How can he say that? He doesn't know me. I don't know him. Not from an hour in each other's company.

"You don't know me well enough to say I have you. I don't." It hurts to say it out loud.

The truth. I don't really have anyone. Not even my two friends at school who hang around me because they are loners too. We sit in the cafeteria at lunch. Attend some classes together, but we never socialize after hours. I'm not allowed.

A soft, cold hand finds my cheek, and I jump at the contact. Not only the icy temperature, but I can't remember the last time fingers were gentle with me. Aggressive yes. But never like this. Dancing up and down my face like a feather. My breath stops. My eyes widen as blood whooshes in my ear. My skin tingles with the contact. It takes a moment for the chill to fade and a semblance of warmth to replace it. But I'm already pulling away by then.

"Maybe not yet. But you can. Get to know me, I mean. If you want. Here's the thing. We're in a bit of a predicament. You don't want me to jump first. And I don't want you to jump first. So, what do we do?"

He's right. And not only that. It's been an hour since I climbed onto that ledge. Since then, the desire to die has lessened somewhat. Since Atlas appeared. Since he's given me his attention. Since he's shown me he cares whether or not I live. Since he's opened up to me a little about why he's here.

How do I answer his question?

"I don't know." It's true. I don't know. There's no way I'm going home. I walked out of that house of horrors with the intent of never returning. But there's nowhere to go. I'm homeless, penniless, and jobless.

His umber gaze searches for something I may not be able to give him. It's unnerving but also exciting to have such focus on me. I'm not sure how to handle it, so I wring my hands together, nervously.

"You want to stay at my place tonight? You can have a hot shower and a warm bed and then tomorrow we can figure things out. My brother won't mind."

Why is he doing this? Offering me such kindness. He could be a psycho who wants to lure me home and keep me tied in a basement.

His mannerisms and my gut instinct tell me otherwise, though. I've learned to read people quite well. I'm no expert, but I've seen enough signs in my father to see them in others. Plus, why would he try to save me tonight, only to take me home and keep me a prisoner? Or worse. No. My instincts tell me I can trust him. He had every chance to push me off the bridge.

"I don't want to be a burden. I have nothing to offer you in return. I've been out of school for two weeks and I don't have a job."

While he hasn't offered me anything other than one night, I feel I'll be there longer. Or perhaps it's more hope. Something I haven't had. Ever. The night has taken a drastic turn. All because of him. All because he was here.

I don't even have extra clothes. I have nothing other than my cell.

"You won't be a burden. Promise." He goes to grab my hand again, but I pull away. He doesn't seem bothered by it. Instead, he says, "Come on. Let's get out of here."

A thought rushes into me. He's not going to die tonight. I'm not either, it seems. What is happening? Have I saved him the same way he's saved me? And does this mean I'm not going to jump ever? I'm not sure, but what I do know is for the first time, I have a lifeline. Even if it's temporary.

Four

Atlas

I've done it. Kept her alive. For now. A sense of pride washes over me as we walk to my truck. I parked a half mile from the bridge. Pride for her, choosing to walk away with me and pride I was able to convince her to leave.

If only I'd been quick enough for Jayden.

I had no intention of jumping tonight, but she had to believe I did. Kind of like reverse psychology. It worked, thankfully. Tomorrow is another day and hopefully, after a hot shower and a long sleep, she'll view things differently.

For so long after Jayden's death, I wanted to join him. The grief was so great. If not for Killian, I may have. He threw me a line, offering me a job with him. A way to focus on things other than my misery. For the first few weeks, I'd worked sixteen-hour days just to remain busy. With such long hours, I'd fallen into bed so fatigued, my mind hadn't been able to overthink.

Capri won't have that luxury. I somehow need to convince her that everything will be okay, and suicide isn't the answer.

My mom used to always say, '*Sleep on it, Son. Before you decide.*'

For the most part, it worked. I hope it works for Capri. Or perhaps she's already slept on it and still decided tonight would be the night.

I'm glad I showed up when I did. I couldn't sleep and came out to feel closer to Jayden. I do it a lot lately. Now that I'm not working such grueling hours, there are times when my grief catches up with me and all I want is to wind back the clock. To see the early signs so I could have intervened and got him help. Looking back, I realize how much he internalized his sadness, always putting on a brave front for me. When he should have let me in to help him. Sometimes, though, we push away those we love the most. Sometimes we suffer alone. I know that better than anyone. I show other's happiness on the outside, even though I'm bleeding internally. I don't like to burden anyone with my demons. Some days are harder than others, so it's a constant struggle, but mostly, I get through each day as best I can.

Suicide is a hard tragedy to grasp. Those left behind drown in a myriad of emotions. Sadness. Guilt. Anger. Helplessness. In no particular order. Questions forever unanswered. Especially when no last letter or note was written.

We reach my Ford pickup that I've restored, and I open the door and help her climb in. She's like a lost lamb, following me, glancing around as soon as she's seated. I shut her door and make my way to the driver's side and climb up, closing us off from the arctic air.

"Let's get the heater going. Tonight's a cold one." November in Maine is normally 30F-40F but tonight it feels below 0. I wouldn't be surprised if it snowed. They have been forecasting it, but we haven't seen any yet.

She watches me warily, and I can understand it. She's given me all her trust to look after her and keep her safe, and I fully intend to uphold that. The idea of her not having anyone saddens me. I need to know why, but not tonight. Tonight is about her well-being. Physical and emotional.

Once the truck gets moving, the heater kicks into high gear, warming us both up again. To be honest, I almost froze to death after I handed Capri my jacket, but better I freeze than her. Her lips were almost blue.

She's wringing her fingers together on her lap, obviously nervous. She doesn't know where I live or what my house is like.

"You, okay?" My gaze leaves the road for a couple of seconds as we turn onto the main street. Traffic is minimal, giving us a free run home.

Her head shifts up and down with a slight nod, so I attempt to make conversation.

But before I can speak, she's offering me a crumb of information.

"I've never been to someone's house." It's more a whisper than anything, and I barely hear it above the noise of the heater.

My head pivots right. "Are you serious? You mean, ever?" All kinds of thoughts are running through my head. Has this girl been a prisoner somewhere? Did she escape so she could kill herself to end her pain?

My stomach turns and anger grips me. I white-knuckle the steering wheel, but I don't raise my voice to her. Something tells me she's been around abuse. Her timid nature. The loss of light and joy in her eyes. Someone has snuffed that out and the idea of it makes me want to find whoever did this to her and end them. And out of me and my brother, I'm the least violent one.

Speaking of said brother, I'm not sure how he'll react to Capri's arrival. We're different in so many ways. He's a rebel with a short fuse and I'm tolerant to a point. Killian never forgives if you cross him, whereas I'm more likely to see reason.

Tough. He'll have to suck it up and deal with it. I'll make her my responsibility. This need to save her is overpowering. Failure isn't an option. I've already done that, and it won't happen again.

"I wasn't allowed."

The words echo inside the confined space and work their way into my marrow. *I wasn't allowed.* Jesus. Was she part of a cult? Who isn't allowed to visit friends at seventeen? She should be out shopping, going to movies and having fun, not confined to the four walls of whatever dwelling she came from.

Things are worse than I thought. No wonder she was about to jump. She truly had nothing left to live for.

Well, I'm going to change that. I'm going to show Capri just how good life can be.

FIVE

Capri

In ten minutes, we're pulling into a small, detached house in an older part of town. It's hard to tell in the darkness how well it's kept, but it's still better than my own decrepit home.

One thing I do notice is a black motorcycle parked in front of a large shed out the back. It must belong to the brother he mentioned.

Atlas parks in the driveway and climbs out. I don't wait for him to reach my door before I'm opening it and stepping down.

He places a hand on my back and gently urges me forward. "Come on. You can use the spare room."

My nerves amp up as I walk through the front door. Once it's closed and locked, I have no way of knowing if I'm leaving one prison and stepping into another. When I hear the click behind me, my heart thumps harder, my eyes inspecting my surroundings.

A small table lamp burns dimly, showing off a neat living room with a plain brown sofa, matching recliner and a flat screen television hung from the wall. Everything is surprisingly neat for a house shared by males.

A large beige rug takes up most of the floor space with a bare timber coffee table on top.

I jump when Atlas speaks. "You want a drink? Water or soda? Coffee?"

My shoulders relax a little. "Water is fine. Thank you."

He smiles and begins walking into a kitchen off the living room, flicking on another light, so I follow him.

Again, it's tidy. Dishes done and not much littering the space. It helps lessen my anxiety just a little, although even if Atlas is a murderer, it doesn't mean his house would be messy. Right? Killers can be clean too.

Under the strength of the fluorescent light, I see him clearly and my chest flutters at the sight. He's remarkably good-looking. The type of guy I'd avoid at all costs because I'd probably judge him for being so popular at school. And there's no way he would ever be interested in me. He's the kind of guy girls swoon over and gossip about in the bathrooms and in the cafeteria at lunchtime. Looks wise, he's everything I'd want in a boyfriend, even if he's unattainable. I've always wanted what I can't have.

Knowing he doesn't attend my school is oddly satisfying—knowing he's not a part of those who bully or ignore me because they think they are so much better. I'm simply a quiet girl who is an easy target.

His skin has more color in it from the car heater, his cheeks covered with a nice rosy tint.

Dark eyes capture mine and crinkle at the corners as he pulls a water from the fridge and hands it to me, our hands brushing. I jolt back at his warmth and the sensation of his touch.

"I'm sorry," he apologizes, stepping back, seeing my reaction. "You, okay? Do you want to talk for a bit or head to bed? It's late."

Surprisingly, I'm not ready to be alone in a strange room on my own yet. I welcome the company. Even though night will soon be morning, it's Saturday tomorrow.

I won't be attending school until Monday. If I go back. Tonight changes things. I don't have my belongings and I'm certainly not returning home to get them. My father would skin me alive for staying out all night. Now that I'm out of that house, I can breathe again.

"Sure. Talking would be nice."

He leads me back into the living room and we both sit on the sofa with a foot between us.

We just get comfortable when movement down the hall makes me stiffen.

"Bro, what are you doing up?" I hear a sleepy voice and then, "What the fuck?"

It's a deeper tone compared to Atlas, and one filled with hostility. It has me moving to the edge of my seat, ready to bolt. The malice automatically shoots adrenaline into my blood, and my fight-or-flight response kicks in.

"Kill, this is Capri. Capri, my brother Killian."

I turn to find a brooding guy, hair messy from sleep, boxers on, and nothing else.

My breath catches at the sight. I've never seen a male practically naked. He's a work of art, with tattoos dipping and rising among his muscles. A colorful image of a dragon breathing fire coats the entire left side of his torso and up onto his shoulder. He's got a nipple pierced with a small gold hoop.

My blood is whooshing through my arteries so loudly, I can hear my pulse in my ears.

I'm gaping like a fool and frozen to the spot. That is, until he says, "Not for sale. I'm not into my brother's sloppy seconds."

I jump at the harshness of his voice, my eyes connecting with pits of coal. They're dark. Black almost, highlighted by thick lashes I'm a tad jealous of.

His mouth lifts in a smirk and I finally look away.

"I..." There are no words. My feet should be moving. I should be out the door by now, running far away. But for some crazy reason, my mind hasn't caught up yet. And where would I go?

"Fuck off, Kill. She's not mine. I brought her here after saving her life," offers Atlas, his fingers clasping the edge of the couch, causing his muscles to bunch up.

Killian stares at this brother, then shakes his head as if in disgust. "Really, Bro? You brought a stray here? She's not staying. We're not an orphanage."

His words cut deep. He views me as a charity case. Just another guy who sees me as a shy little thing with nothing to offer.

My brain finally gets the memo to get the hell out. I'm up off the couch so fast and heading for the door with no destination in mind. Clearly, Killian is not happy with me being here, and I certainly don't want to cause friction between the two brothers. I know when I'm not wanted. I've lived the same scenario for years.

My hand grips the doorknob, but before I can turn it, I'm shackled around my arm by large fingers.

"Capri, stop. Don't listen to my dick of a brother. I pay half the rent on this place, and I'm the one who asked you to come here. Please. Just spend the night and we'll work something out in the morning. I want you safe."

I spin to face Atlas. He's pleading with his eyes. Totally the opposite to Killian. They are like chalk and cheese personality wise. His grip on my arm softens slightly, but he doesn't remove it.

"I don't want to be a burden. I know what that's like." Inside, I'm bleeding out at the idea of being kicked to the curb. For a small while, hope had bloomed that maybe I'd been too hasty in my decision to die tonight. But all it's really done is delay the inevitable.

Atlas narrows his eyes and pivots his head to where Killian still stands, watching us with an unreadable expression.

Idiot.

"She's staying in my room, so it's got nothing to do with you. Go back to bed."

I'm shocked at the tone he's using with his brother. It's different from what he's used with me. It brooks no argument and is growled into the quiet. I'm also shocked that he's setting me up in his room. He better not think I'm some easy hookup. What have I got myself into?

Kill gives me a momentary death glare before turning on his heels and calling out on the way back to his room, "She has until morning."

"That's all I'm asking," Atlas answers, waiting until his brother shuts his door before he turns back to me.

"Kill is a little… angry with the world. Long story. Don't take it personally."

How can one not, though? Angry men instill a sense of fear me in like nothing else does. When we arrived here earlier, my anxiety was lessening. Now it's at an all-time high again. I don't want to be here.

My head is shaking along with my hands. "I should have jumped."

"What? No! You shouldn't have. Don't you see? We crossed paths for a reason. Don't let my brother frighten you. Whatever you've run from, I guarantee, it's way better here. In fact, once you get to know Kill, you'll see that he's all bark, no bite."

Still, my insides are upended, the familiar nausea churning in my gut. My self-esteem is already at an all-time low. Why do people treat me as if I am the gum on the bottom of their shoes? I've been a good girl. I've always stayed on the right side of the law. Done my homework. Obeyed my father. And still, it feels as if nobody wants me around.

Atlas must see the uncertainty on my face because he bends at the knees to bring us to eye level. "Hey. You're safe here. I promise. I won't let anything happen to you.

Kill won't harm you. He might be a jerk, but he'd never hurt a girl."

There's always a first time. Plus, it's not even the fact that he might or might not hurt me. It's his whole vibe. The fact that he doesn't even know me. I'd never be rude to strangers. I'd give them the benefit of the doubt until they proved otherwise.

I remain standing with my hand on the door handle, warring with myself.

"Please? I'm not shy of begging, Capri. Don't go. I want you to stay."

"Why?" I still don't understand why he's so insistent. I've never had a person beg to me. I change my weight to my left leg and then back again, suddenly uncomfortable with his pleading.

"You're helping me as much as I'm helping you, right? I was on that bridge too, remember?"

I'd forgotten about Atlas's demons. Am I being selfish only thinking of myself? Even though he has his brother, perhaps I'm the one he can connect with because of how we met.

My shoulders slacken, as does my hold on the door.

It's only for a few hours, right? He seems sincere. Morning is only a few hours away. What can it hurt?

"Fine. Until morning, right? But can I sleep in a spare room or on the sofa?"

He eyes me strangely. "I'm not having you sleep on the sofa. The spare room has a few boxes in it and the bed isn't made up." He holds up both hands. "Promise I won't try anything."

He appears genuine, so I warily nod. "Are you sure?"

"One hundred percent. Come on. I'll find you something to sleep in." He visibly relaxes too, the lines on his forehead smoothing out.

It's funny how I feel at ease with him when his brother is an ass. We have connected over something so personal, as if each of us knows just how the other feels. For me, it's a first and not unpleasant.

So, I follow him down the hallway to a room with a queen-sized bed in it. It's wooden to fit in with the other earthy tones. A chair in the corner has a few clothes piled onto it, but apart from that, it's tidy. No surprise now.

"I can sleep on the floor. You take the bed. The bathroom is through that door. Towel is in the cupboard just inside the door. Feel free to use my shampoo and body wash. There's a new toothbrush in the vanity under the basin. I know I said earlier we had a spare bedroom, but I figured you might need the company tonight." His smile has me relaxing more, even though the idea of sleeping in the same room as a boy tweaks my nerves.

He's got it all organized and, for whatever reason, I do feel safe. At least with Atlas. He's been so kind to me.

I begin to move and then turn. "Thank you. For this. For everything."

His smile widens. "You're welcome." He takes a step forward and then stops. It looks as if he's going to say something else, so much emotion crossing over his face, his gorgeous eyes holding me hostage.

For a moment, my feet won't move, a strange sensation taking hold in my chest. It's been an odd night. One I never could have foretold the ending to.

My heart is cantering to its own rhythm, my throat dry. Why is he looking at me like this?

The need to lock myself in the bathroom is strong, so I about turn and do just that, not having a clue what I'm doing or what's going to happen next.

Six

Atlas

I leave Capri to her shower, walking out into the hallway to grab a pillow and blanket from the linen cupboard. I almost run smack-bang into Kill, who is clearly still angry.

"Why is she here?" he asks me, getting in my space.

My brother loves to intimidate others, but he should know I'm the exception. I'm the only one who knows how to handle him. The only one he doesn't scare.

"Settle. You don't get to dictate to me. Technically, I'm five minutes older than you. She was about to jump off Wilson's Bridge. I turned up just at the right time."

His eyes widen for a moment before returning to fire and ice. He was friends with Jayden, too. He grieved with me, although I took it harder. Even though we all used to hang out together, Jay became so much more to me. My entire world. A stab of pain grips my heart, but I will it away.

Kill squeezes his eyes shut as if to clear his head and then he's moving back. "So, what? You're just going to take her home in the morning? I know you, Brother. You're too nice for your own good. And the big question is, will she walk right back to the bridge and step off the edge?" His mouth tips up ever so slightly. He knows me and, to be honest, I've been thinking of how to broach the subject with him about Capri staying longer.

His question is valid and one I've been mulling over too. What is the purpose of tonight if she's going to end it, anyway?

I need to know she will be okay if I leave her.

"Give me more than tomorrow. I have to earn her trust and find out what drove her to absolute despair."

"We don't need her shit brought to our doorstep. We've got enough of our own to deal with."

"I know. I do. But what happened with Jay has eaten me away ever since."

He runs fingers through his dark hair, causing it to stick up like an old toilet brush. His fist tightens at his side. I'm not sure what he's going to say, and I know he's not happy I brought someone who might be trouble into our home, but I also don't want to be responsible for sending her away before I know she won't do anything stupid.

"Jesus, Atlas. You're asking a lot."

"You're right. But it's important. I think once she realizes she has a reason to stick around, then my job here is done. Please, Kill?"

It's the second time I've begged tonight. I don't like doing it, but desperate times call for desperate measures. He needs to agree to this. If she left here tonight and went to that bridge and followed through with her earlier mission, I'd never forgive myself. And I'd never forgive my brother.

He blows out a breath and grips his hair while staring me down. "Fine. But she's all your responsibility. Do not ask me to babysit or do anything else for her."

A smile broadens my cheeks as I pat him on the shoulder. "Thanks, man. You won't even know she's here."

A grunt is all I receive and then his back.

Tomorrow is Saturday. Killian will be at the shop till noon, so I'll be able to spend some time with Capri, making her feel comfortable. Or perhaps she'll sleep most of that time. The trauma of what she set out to do might catch up with her. Either way, I want to be here.

Once my brother shuts the door to his room, I hear the shower switch off, so I check the house is all locked up, making sure to use the key on the inside so she can't leave. Technically, we're keeping her prisoner, but it's for her best interests. I want to make sure she's still here when the sun comes up. It's hard to know how messed up her mind is.

I grab a few blankets and a pillow and set up my makeshift bed on the floor, then pick out a shirt and some sweats for Capri. She'll no doubt swim in them, but they are clean and comfortable.

I'm setting them on the bed when the bathroom door opens, and she steps out with just a towel around her.

Trying not to appear as a creeper, even though I bat

for the other team, I let my eyes do a quick scan of her body and then look away. "I… ah… there are clothes there for you to change into. I'm going to have a shower now."

My eyes remain straight ahead and all I hear is a quiet, "Okay," as I lock myself in the bathroom, my exhale long and drawn out.

I strip and turn the shower faucets on, then move to stand under the steady, warm stream. My mind is awash with all sorts of thoughts. Like how I'm thanking the heavens I drove to the bridge tonight. For if I hadn't, we'd have never met. The idea of that saddens me. What saddens me even more is the fact she would have jumped. Her words, not mine.

Perfect timing. Isn't that what happened? I was in the right place at the right time. And she was in the wrong place at the right time. Either way, the universe has put her in my path for a reason, and I intend to find out why.

When I'm done, I exit the bathroom and walk into my bedroom to find Capri snuggled up in my bed, her even breathing letting me know she's asleep. And rightfully so after the night she's had. I only hope she's having second thoughts about returning to the bridge.

Switching the light off, I lay on the hard floor, pulling the blanket over me, only to go over the night's events again, unable to fall asleep until the sun is almost rising.

The next thing I know, screams are causing me to sit upright, wondering what the fuck is happening.

Seven

Capri

Monsters aren't always made-up creatures in storybooks. Sometimes they are those we grew up with, those we trusted to keep us safe, dressed in normal clothing, hiding in plain sight, only coming out when you are alone or when it's dark.

I'm thirteen when I get to see firsthand how depraved my father is.

It's five in the afternoon when I arrive home from school after missing the first bus and having to wait for the second. I know he'll be pissed, but there's nothing I can do about it, so I brace myself for the fallout as I step through the front door.

He's standing in the middle of the living room floor, a tower of malice, his face furious.

I drop my backpack and watch him, hoping to appease him by saying, "Hey, Dad."

"Where the fuck have you been?"

Nope. He's beyond appeasement.

"I... ah... missed the first bus and had to wait for the second. We were late getting out of class." I'm not game to move, my heart rate kicking up a notch. You'd think I'd be used to the beast of a man, but every time he gets in one of his moods, my fear grows. I know how this ends. His black eyes are soulless. There's nothing remotely resembling kindness there. It's as if he's possessed.

"And you didn't think to call me?"

The scent of bourbon floats across the space between us, confirming my suspicions. I'm just not sure how drunk he is. His stance is solid, so he can't be too wasted. Just enough for the anger to take over.

"My phone died at lunch time."

He's on me before I can turn and run out the door. My arm is seized, and he's pulling me across the living room and into the hallway.

"No, please! I'm sorry. I should have charged it at lunch. It won't happen again."

My pleas fall on deaf ears as he drags me to the stairs, descending into the basement. A dark, dank space reserved for my punishments.

"I'm tired of your excuses! You know what time I expect you home. There are chores to do. You need to always obey me, you useless girl. When your bitch of a mother walked out, the onus became yours."

I attempt to pull from his grip, but it's as if I'm wearing handcuffs. His hold is so tight. My feet struggle to get traction on the old, rickety steps because I'm using all my might to stop him from pulling me further.

It becomes my detriment, though, when he yanks even harder. My legs fold from under me. My backside hits the timber so hard I feel it all the way up my spine, pain branching out from the point of impact.

"Ahh. Stop!" I'm crying, but it only spurs him on until I'm sitting on the moldy, cold concrete at the bottom.

The space reeks. You'd think I'd be used to the stench with the number of times I've been locked down here, but it always catches my breath.

"You need to learn your place. This is my house. My rules. You obey them or suffer the consequences."

He's a monster. How did he become so heartless? So controlling? There's no part of his heart that cares about me. In fact, I know he hates me with passion. I don't know why he doesn't just kill me and rid himself of such a burden.

A small lamp flares to life, coating the dungeon in a muted amber glow. Rodents scurry away in fright. The sounds of them hurrying into the safety of a pile of boxes in the corner is exaggerated in the silence that ensues my father's wrath. Pity I couldn't join them.

A sob breaks free at the sheer disdain I have for this man right now. He's everything a dad shouldn't be. Mean. Uncaring. Dangerous. Psychotic.

This is my reality versus other kids my age. I've seen their parents at school., Kind and welcoming. Funny. Is it wrong that I get jealous when I see how they smile at their children? How they hug them and show their love, while I fail to receive scraps of affection.

My knees scrape and bleed as he pulls me across the floor to the wall with the shackles.

I fight with all my might, wishing I was bigger and older so

I could overpower him. He's a coward. Picking on a young girl who can't fight back. That's why he does it. Because he can get away with it. He needs to be brought down a peg and given a taste of his own medicine. But I know of no one who could deliver that sort of justice.

A click sounds out as one of my wrists is manacled and then the other above my head. The cinder block wall is strong enough to hold me by the large constraints which were drilled in.

Fear claws its way into my throat as I scream at him.

"You can't do this! I didn't do anything. It wasn't my fault!"

He sneers back, moving my pee bucket closer as if the act is doing me a favor.

"You know the drill. Two days and nights down here. No food. Perhaps it will give you time to think about disobeying me."

He's mental. Seriously insane. Who does this? Panic has me screaming as he backs away and begins to ascend the stairs.

If I had a weapon right now, I'd use it. I wouldn't think about it. To have him at my knees begging for his life would give me the ultimate high. And power. I have none. He makes sure he holds it all.

Watching his back disappear and hearing the click of the lock, has me pulling on my restraints and yelling obscenities. It's the only time he lets me get away with it. Either because he can't hear me down here or I'm exactly where he wants me. I know it won't free me, but it helps purge some of my anger.

"Capri! Capri! Wake up!"

It's not my father's voice. It's deeper. Younger. And it holds concern. Definitely not my sperm donor.

I'm thrashing and then hands are gripping my shoulders, causing me to scream louder.

"Shh. Hey. It's Atlas. It's okay. Just a dream. You're okay."

Atlas? The boy I met on the bridge?

I'm confused for a minute. Until I open my eyes and my reality changes.

Large brown eyes are staring at me. Afraid. I'm pinned down. He's standing beside the bed, leaning over.

On instinct, I cry out, "Get your hands off me!"

He obliges, a look of shock on his face before it morphs into confusion and then a moment later, sudden understanding.

"I'm sorry. I didn't mean to scare you. You were having a nightmare."

Calming down somewhat, happy that I'm not in the basement, I breathe out harshly, embarrassed I yelled at him.

It's just, well, he had his hands on me. It triggered a different kind of memory. One I don't want to relive.

And now he's watching me like I'm some fragile piece of glass that might shatter at any moment. He's right.

I sit up and rub at my face, seeing the sky has lightened outside.

It's morning. I survived the night. I don't know how I feel about that. That I'm still here when I was so close to not being here. Thanks to the guy waiting for me to say something. But I don't, so he speaks.

"Want to talk about it?"

"No!" It's abrupt and way too loud, but sharing the circumstances that led me to the bridge last night is better kept behind my vault. Locked away forever. After all, Atlas has his own demons. Although, for someone who was going to take their own life like me, he seems almost... normal. Not suicidal.

I guess you can't judge a book by its cover, though. The saddest people have the brightest smiles, right? It's not always the ones you think who are hiding the deepest, darkest secrets.

He holds his arms up in a placating gesture. "No problems. We don't need to go there."

His hair is mussed, and his eyes are sleepy. Now that I'm properly awake, it's easy to take in his male beauty. I can't believe I'm even in the same room as someone of such caliber, let alone having just slept in his bed.

My face is probably puffy and lined from sleep, but it's too late now to worry about it. He's seen me at my worst.

There's a pregnant pause before Atlas says, "You hungry? Kill is cooking breakfast before he heads in to work."

My stomach groans for attention, causing me to smile. That's the second time I've shown a side of myself normally reserved for my two friends at school. And it's all been in the presence of Atlas.

"Come on," he offers, holding out his hand for me. When I hesitate, he lets it drop to his side again.

"Sorry. No touching. I get it." His eyes hold a sadness that defies his outward demeanor. Like he's hiding his own pain by pretending to be happy. I will file it away for another time. I'd like to learn more about what drove Atlas to the bridge.

I shuffle after him into the kitchen and pause when I see Killian, shirtless in a pair of low-hung jeans, cooking eggs over a pan. He glances up and when he sees me and fixes his scowl back in place.

"Smells good, Bro," Atlas says, patting his brother on the shoulder.

Killian grunts but doesn't reply.

I take a seat, nervous to be in their kitchen, especially when one of them has made it perfectly clear I'm not wanted.

Knowing I don't have anywhere to go yet, it makes sense to eat a big breakfast because I'm not sure when I'll get food again.

Technically, now that I've run away, I'm homeless.

If I don't show up for school, they'll call my father, who will probably flip his lid and call the police. I'll become a missing person. They'll search for me and when they find me, they'll return me to him.

I need to remain under the radar until next month when I turn eighteen and then I'll legally be able to live on my own. December 26th. The day after Christmas.

I don't know how I'll manage school and living expenses without money coming in. Perhaps I'll need to look for a night-waitress job.

This thought alone surprises me. I'm not thinking of returning to the bridge. The fact is, I don't think I can go through with it now. Atlas is right. It's a new day. I'm focusing on a future I never thought I'd have. Has it been as simple as leaving the controlling regime of home? Now that I'm out, I do feel freer and that I might have a fighting chance. I can breathe again. I'm not sure how long it will last, but if Atlas is willing to help me beyond today, then maybe, just maybe, I can do this.

Is there a rule book on being suicidal? Am I supposed to still feel the need to end my life? And for how long? Or perhaps in some people it's a spur-of-the-moment decision when you feel like there's no other way. Which means, if I had taken the leap from the edge, I surely would have instantly regretted it.

A loud noise breaks my train of thought. It's my plate of bacon and eggs being dropped heavily in front of me by Killian, who looks annoyed he has to feed me.

Atlas gives his brother a dangerous look before sitting opposite me.

He nods at my plate. "Dig in."

It's hard to do so when you sense someone glaring at you. But my stomach grumbles again, so I ignore my watchdog and begin eating.

It's good. Really good. The eggs are done just right, and the bacon is crispy, just how I like it. I don't mean to moan, but it slips out.

My hand flies to my mouth mid chew and I glance up to see both guys watching me. Atlas has a smile on his face and Killian, well, Killian looks like he wants to murder me, veins popping on his neck. He compresses his lips tightly and storms from the kitchen.

Atlas turns to where his brother disappeared and then back to me. "Don't worry about him. Pretend he's not here. I do."

Easier said than done.

"You like?" he asks, pointing with his fork to my plate.

"It's great." I place another forkful of egg into my mouth. "He might be a dick, but he can cook."

"He likes it. One of the few things besides fixing cars

that he loves. My mom taught us both when we were younger, but Kill is the expert. I can make basic stuff, but that's it."

We finish our breakfast in companionable silence. It's nice to be sitting at a table with someone. Normally, I eat on my own at home or in my room while my father does. Who knows what? He prefers liquid meals anyway, so I've always cooked for myself.

"So, you're welcome to stay for a few days if you like. I've already spoken to Kill, and he agreed."

Surprise, has me asking, "Your brother agreed?"

Atlas glances down at his empty plate and then back up. "I explained the situation, and he eventually conceded."

Right. Not because he wants me here, but because Atlas insisted. What is the alternative, though? It might be nice to hang out here and keep my father guessing as to my whereabouts. Let him go without his punching bag for a while.

"Thank you. But I have no money to pay you. I kinda need a job."

"You don't need to pay us. It's cool. And I'm sure if I ask around, I could find you a part-time job. What can you do?"

I've had years of experience at keeping house, but apart from that, I'm not good at anything.

I whisper, "Nothing," because that's what my father has always said to me. I'm nothing and a nobody.

Atlas clears his throat, his hand clenching on the edge of the table. When he speaks, his voice betrays his emotions. "Of course you can. You just haven't found it yet. Leave it with me. I'll find something."

I truly look at him now. This boy who is willing to go out of his way for me and I have no idea why. It doesn't make sense. What is his agenda? Everyone has one, right?

Nobody does anything simply because they want to. There's always something in it for them.

"You don't have to. You don't even know me. Why are you being so nice?"

He leans back in his chair, his hands relaxing and falling to his lap. "Can't I just want to help you? Haven't you ever had someone do something nice for you because they want to?"

Does he want the honest truth? Because I've never had anyone make me a priority. Ever.

"No."

His brow scrunches up. "Never?"

I shake my head and drop my eyes.

"Jesus, Capri. That's sad. And that's why I want to help you. Everyone needs that one person who cares. I want to be that person. And no, I don't know you. But when you took a chance and stepped off that ledge with me last night, I knew you weren't totally one hundred percent invested in ending your life."

He's right. I could have jumped. I should have jumped. But after talking to him, a seed of doubt clouded my decision. I clung onto whatever crumb of compassion and attention he gave me. Like a stray dog in need of warmth, food, and shelter. Kindness.

What about him, though?

"Why didn't you jump?" I need to know. Did I have the same impact on him that he had on me?

His spine straightens, and he's about to answer me when Killian walks in again, dressed in a black T-shirt and shorts with the garage logo on it.

"I'm heading to the shop. You coming in today, Bro?"

He looks at me when he asks, as if I'm the reason his brother may or may not show up.

Goosebumps litter my skin at his stare. He's so attractive, it's a shame his personality lets him down. I guess looks aren't everything.

Atlas eyes me and then Killian. "It's Saturday. You good to finish the SUV without me? I was planning on getting Capri some clothes and necessities."

A flare of nostrils is the only sign he's not happy. "Fine. I'll be back later."

He remains staring at me for a beat too long. What does he see when he looks at me like that? A poor little lost kitten that they shouldn't begin feeding because then they'll never get rid of it. I don't want to be a charity case, but that's what Atlas has made me. If I'm going to stay here for a few days, I'm going to show him I will be pulling my weight.

The staring contest stretches out for too long, leaving me nervous. His eyes are the kind that pull you in and keep you there. They hypnotize me. But they also frighten me. Not the way my fathers did, but in a whole new way. Because I know if I got lost in them, I'd never find my way out.

I break our contest first, watching him spin and leave,

shutting the door a tad too loud. I jump, my heart stuttering at the interaction.

Atlas blows out a breath. "You want a shower to freshen up? I'll find you another shirt and some shorts that will have to do until we get you some clothes."

"Thank you. And just so you know, while I'm here, I'll clean, do laundry and whatever else you need. I'm not a freeloader."

Atlas stands, a smile showing off his white teeth, his eyes crinkling. "Whatever you need to do to make yourself feel okay. That's fine. Come on. Let's get ready to get out of here for a bit."

I grab the dirty dishes and load them into the dishwasher, turning it on and then follow Atlas down the hallway.

* * *

The mall is bursting with people. I feel self-conscious in the over-sized shirt and shorts, pulled in using a drawstring. People turn their heads and inspect me from head to toe as we pass, but I try not to let it affect me. It's only temporary. Plus, the scent of Atlas is ingrained into the fabric, helping to calm my nerves at being out in public.

If my father happens to be here and sees me, he'll drag me home kicking and screaming. It won't be pretty. And then Atlas will know just what sort of monster he is. Everyone will. Perhaps if I make enough noise, security will be called, and I can confess his sins while I have backup. But being a minor, what rights do I really have? He'll put on an act and make out that I'm mentally unstable and that he needs to take me home so I can take my medication. I know how his type works. He'll manipulate and lie to get his way.

Suddenly I feel as if I'm a sitting duck, waiting for him to call my name and come striding over to me, pulling me back to the house of horrors.

My head automatically lowers as I let my hair fall across my face.

Don't think of him, Capri. You're safe with Atlas. He won't let anything happen to you.

I know that with certainty. As hard as it is for me to grasp, if he wanted to hurt me, he would have. He's been nothing but wonderful. When I find a job, I'm going to pay him back for the clothing and anything else he has to buy me.

But I'm still on edge and he must notice because he asks, "Are you okay?"

"I'm fine," I mumble. He's not buying it and neither should he. I don't sound convincing, even to myself.

"Hey. Look at me." It's spoken softly. Non-threatening, so I comply.

When I find his chocolate eyes, so similar to his brother's, I find them filled with worry. "What's wrong? You look like you'd rather be anywhere but here." He bends his knees to lower himself to my level. The crowd moves around us, oblivious to my anxiety.

"Just hoping my father doesn't find me. He'll kill me for not going home last night."

"Can we call him and let him know you're okay?"

We haven't spoken about my family or lack-thereof. The reasons behind why I was at the bridge. Atlas hasn't asked, and I'm grateful for that. He must know how hard it is to talk about. After all, he was there too. Which reminds me. He didn't answer my question about why he didn't jump. We were interrupted by his brother. Now is not the time to bring it up, though.

"No!" I almost yell. "I mean, no. Please. We can't call him."

I'm pleading with my eyes that he'll leave it at that. If my tone doesn't give him a clue, then the fear I imagine is written on my face will.

He gets the hint and nods, allowing me to breathe out fully, my shoulders sagging in relief.

"Let's try in here." He places a hand on my back, gently coaxing me into a department store.

His touch elicits fear first and something else foreign. A nervous energy that stirs in my belly. When I drag in a breath, he quickly removes his hand.

"Sorry! I keep forgetting."

If I'm being honest, his touch is nothing like my father's. It doesn't compare and isn't unpleasant. I'm simply not used to the sensation.

"It's okay." I smile. One of my rare ones, which causes him to return it. He's so nice. Nothing at all like I imagined him to be when we met last night.

Inside, we walk to the clothing section, my legs carrying me straight to the jeans hanging on racks. I've always worn comfortable clothing such as jeans, shorts and T-shirts. Girls at school always dress up in what I call 'slutty' clothes, attempting to attract boys, but I'd rather lie low out of the spotlight, which I've managed to achieve thus far. I don't wear makeup, false eyelashes, or earrings. It's probably why boys don't even look my way.

As I'm browsing, Atlas wanders off for a bit, leaving me to search in peace. I'm not comfortable with someone hovering while I choose items. You never know if they are judging you or not.

I pick out two pairs of jeans, a denim pair of shorts, and three T-shirts. I don't want to appear greedy. Plus, I'll be paying him back when I begin earning money.

He reappears with his arms laden with clothes. I gape at him, wondering what he's doing.

"Um, what are all those?"

"They're for you. Dresses. Lingerie." He's got a cheeky smirk on his face, which causes my neck to heat.

"You've picked out lingerie for me?" How does he know my size or what I like? Going by the items I can see, they're not something I'd wear. I don't buy sexy underwear or bras. What's the point? No one ever sees them.

"Just try them on. I figured you'd go for the cheapest on the racks, but I don't want you to do that. I'm paying, so choose whatever you want."

He eyes the clothes I'm holding and frowns. "You're going with those?"

"Yeah. What's wrong with these?"

"They're fine. There's nothing wrong with them. I just thought you might like to try these on." His tone tells me otherwise, as if my choice is dull and boring. It probably is, but it's what I'm used to.

He's watching me like a hopeful child, his lip pulling into his teeth. I'm not really interested in being something

I'm not, but Atlas literally saved my life last night. I owe him everything.

With a sigh, I answer, "Okay. Just a couple."

His answering grin practically blinds me, so I follow him to the dressing room where I unload my pile onto the chair inside and take a green halter dress and a short skirt and midriff top. These are just like the clothing the popular girls at school wear. I don't want to be like them. But I'll humor Atlas for now.

I leave him holding three other dresses and the lingerie. As I'm about to close the curtain he pipes up, "You're not trying any underwear?"

I need panties and bras, but the ones he's chosen are tiny scraps of things. Not exactly the style I'm used to. But he's trying, so I snatch two pairs and throw the curtain closed.

"No peeking." I offer as I stare at myself in the mirror.

"Promise." He chuckles. "I'll return these to the racks and then I'll be back if you want to show me. You know, the dress."

Well, I'm certainly not parading my lingerie for him.

The girl in the mirror doesn't look like the girl I feel like on the inside. Those passing me on the street or in this mall would never know the struggles I've had to endure in my life.

My eyes might hold some hint of trauma, but they've always been sad. Those eyes you look at and wonder what secrets they hold. Eyes you can't help but stare at because they're deep. That's what my two friends at school have told me, anyway.

"Caps, you always look like you're on the verge of tears."

"You hold all your emotions in your eyes."

"You're so easy to read."

Maybe that's what Atlas saw last night, under the full moon. A girl who was crying out for help. A girl who just wanted someone to have her back. Someone to truly see her and appreciate her. More likely, wishful thinking on my behalf. He no doubt felt sorry for me.

"You got anything on yet?" he asks, making me jump.

"Almost!" I answer, quickly stripping, before placing the bra on. I leave my own panties on because the idea of trying on underwear that others probably have too is not what I would consider hygienic, even with the plastic strip inside.

The green halter dress clings to my body and ends above the knees. It shows off my B cup breasts and slim hips. I've never worn anything like this before and I'm suddenly self-conscious about my body. Especially if Atlas is expecting me to show him.

"Come on, what are you doing?" It's said playfully, but I'm slightly annoyed he's asking to see it.

I inhale a deep breath and slowly pull the curtain aside, not knowing where to place my arms, so I cross them over my chest.

The deep V of the neckline shows a little of my below-average cleavage, but luckily, the bra remains hidden.

My eyes focus on the beige carpet, waiting on Atlas to say something. But there's silence, and I can't help but wonder if he hates it.

I wait for a beat and then decide to brave a glance at him.

He's standing stock still, his eyes wide as they move up and down me from head to toe and back again.

"What?" I ask, not really wanting to hear his answer.

"I… You…"

He's speechless, but is it in a good way? And why do I care?

"You look gorgeous." It's a whisper that causes my cheeks to heat.

A couple of girls browsing the racks nearby turn their heads and smile at me. But I don't react. Atlas' words have caught me off guard. That's not the reaction I was expecting.

"Remove your hands, Capri. Let me see the whole dress. And turn around. Do a spin for me."

I really don't want to. I suddenly feel as if I'm under a microscope and vulnerable.

He sees my hesitation and moves closer. "You don't have to hide from me. You're stunning and you don't even realize it." His eyes pleat at the corners and his lip quirks up at one side as he adds, "And if I wasn't batting for the other team, I'd be into you."

A gasp leaves me, along with disappointment. "You're gay?"

I never would have pictured him to be into guys. Not that there is anything wrong with that, but the way he's looked at me a couple of times, I wondered if he was into me.

"Yep!" He pops the 'p'. "My dad has disowned me. He's said on more than one occasion that no son of his is dating a member of the same sex. And if I want any inheritance, I'll quickly get over my 'fad'."

There's a certain level of disdain in his words and hurt in his eyes. I want to console him, but that would mean touching, and I'm not ready to instigate that on my own yet, regardless of how kind Atlas is. Part of me wishes he was into girls and that he was into me. For the first time ever, I feel comfortable with a guy. Whoever ends up with him is going to be so lucky.

My fingers itch to reach out, but I keep them close by my sides. Instead, I offer, "I'm sorry. He doesn't know what a great son he has."

It's true. The small time I've been around him, I can tell he's got a good heart. It shouldn't matter to a parent what their child's sexual preferences are. As long as they are good and treat others with respect. I've never understood anyone being homophobic. To me, that's their issue, not the gay persons.

My words appease him as he shakes off his moment of weakness and stands taller.

"It doesn't matter. I don't need his damn money. Kill and I are doing just fine."

Is that why he was on the bridge last night? His father drove him to almost ending his own life. We've got more in common than I thought. It saddens me to think he's got the same going on in his life as me. Perhaps not on a physical level, but on an emotional one, and sometimes that can be just as bad or worse.

Deciding to step out of my comfort zone and appease him, I do a twirl, watching him nod. "Girl, that's the dress. You need this. You may not wear it yet, but you need to have this in your wardrobe. You know, in case."

I'm not sure what 'in case' means, but I guess I could do with a special dress.

Before I can answer, he asks, "Did you try the lingerie on?" His eyebrows flicker up and down, causing me to giggle.

A sound I've made more of in the last twelve hours than I have in my entire life.

"Maybe," I tease, turning and sashaying into the fitting room. I glance over my shoulder to see him roll his eyes at me, but he laughs, too.

I'm having a fairly nice time, my earlier anxiety at seeing my father disappearing momentarily. If only I could freeze time.

EIGHT

Atlas

The sight of Capri smiling and laughing hits my chest like an arrow would hit its target. I've put her happiness there. Given her a reprieve from whatever misery she carries on her small shoulders. It expands my chest exponentially. I need to give her more moments like these and hopefully if she experiences further happiness, she'll see how wonderful life is. That there are people who care. New memories she can create. A bright future.

Plus, focusing on her helps me forget about my own issues. My father giving me an ultimatum. The grief I still process every day about Jay's death. Taking her under my wing is just what I need as a distraction. Not only that, but I also actually like her.

Her earlier question about me jumping last night was thankfully interrupted by Kill. I'm not sure how she'll react when she finds out I had no intention of jumping. Will she think I deceived her, or will she be grateful that I saved her? It could go either way. Not that I haven't stood on that bridge many times, wondering if I should step off. I've always been able to talk myself down, knowing I could never go through with it. I'm too much of a coward.

She's happy now, so I'm not ready to spoil the mood by confessing anything.

When she's changed into a new pair of jeans and a T-shirt, we move to the cashier to pay, giving her the price labels on the clothes she's wearing.

"Would you like to grab a coffee? My treat?"

A look of indecisiveness crosses her features. "You've spent enough money on me."

"It wasn't that much. Plus, I've got a rewards card for the cafe near the entrance. It allows me to buy one, get one free."

She perks up at that. "Really? Sure. That would be nice, thank you."

And so, we take our bags and make our way to the cafe. It's busy, so we stand in a line to order.

As we're standing there and Capri is glancing all around, I see her shoulders stiffen and her energy shift. Her head is turned backwards, and she's focused rigidly on something or someone outside.

My eyes follow her line of sight to a cell phone store opposite, just inside the entrance. There are a few customers inside and one-man window-shopping.

"We need to leave," she stumbles.

"What? Why?" I'm attempting to garner what has her

so spooked but she's already spinning and walking back out the cafe.

Forgetting our place in the queue, I chase after her, watching with increasing anxiety.

Her face is filled with terror as I grip her arm. "What's going on?"

She's standing frozen, staring at the man opposite us. She knows him. But why is she reacting like this?

"Capri?" I ask, attempting to shake her out of whatever waking nightmare she's living.

The man opposite glances to the side, perhaps hearing us, and she visibly calms, her body deflating.

I'd guess his age to be forty-something. Carrying a little too much weight but not obese. Tall, dark hair slicked back. He's wearing khaki shorts and a green shirt. Just an average-looking dude.

She breathes out long and hard and rubs a hand over her face.

I grab her arm and drag her outside, the automatic doors closing behind us.

"You want to talk about what just happened? You looked petrified until the guy turned around. Who did you think he was?"

I have an idea, but I want her to tell me. Her story is coming together for me, and I know it's as I suspected. Daddy issues.

When her attention focuses on me, there's so much pain in her eyes. She clenches her teeth and grits out. "My father." Then she pulls her arm out of my grip. I keep forgetting she hates being touched. What the hell, though? Who has that kind of reaction to their dad? Just what sort of monster is he? Is that why she wanted to end her life? She almost shut down entirely, like the guy was her worst nightmare. I can only imagine what he's done to her.

Fuck. This is not good. I need to talk to Killian so we can figure out what to do.

"Come on. I'll make you a coffee at home."

The car ride is so silent I can barely stand it. I think back to the days and weeks after Jayden jumped, how I wish I'd delved deeper into his mindset. I thought I knew him inside and out, but it just goes to show. No one truly knows someone. They tell you what they want you to know and only show the side of themselves they choose to. Everyone has skeletons. Some are just more frightening than others.

"I know you don't want to talk about it, but trust me, it's better when you've got someone who will just sit and listen and not judge. Keeping everything bottled up inside only makes the burden heavier." I glance over at her staring out the window. Her hands are curled into tight balls on her lap. Clearly, the incident really shook her.

The thick energy in the car is palpable. Finally, when around a minute passes, she says quietly, "My dad is a monster."

The car swerves as I stare at her before focusing back on the road and correcting the wheel.

Not an asshole. A monster. That's way worse. Do I push for more?

I need to know.

"Does he beat you?"

She can't look at me, embarrassment evident in the redness creeping up her neck.

Her silence is all I need. My fingers grip the steering wheel hard. A surge of anger has me wanting to find out her address and pay the parasite a visit with Kill later tonight. Give him a taste of his own medicine. But until we get Capri's living arrangements sorted, I'll hold off for now. One thing I know for sure, though, we *will* be paying him a visit. He won't get away with whatever he's done to her.

The coward doesn't know how lucky he is to have a beautiful daughter like Capri. She doesn't strike me as being a problem child. Quite the opposite. She's quiet and compliant.

My brain is filled with images of what she could have gone through, but I'm sure it's not as horrible as the reality.

Jesus.

The questions I want to ask remain on the tip of my tongue, but I don't voice them. Not today. She's been through enough. To bring back our happy mood from earlier, I ask, "You like Ben and Jerry's?"

Her head pivots and a small smile puffs her cheeks out. A nod has me confirming that while ice-cream can't fix everything, it helps.

* * *

Later that day, when Kill finishes work and arrives home, I head to his bedroom and shut the door, leaving Capri to watch a movie on the couch after we'd both stuffed our faces with Chunky Monkey and downed two coffees. For now, she seems more relaxed.

"Ah, what are you doing?" my brother asks, eyeing the closed door skeptically.

"We need to talk."

He doesn't respond in typical Kill fashion, but merely shifts one eyebrow higher and stares at me with intensity. Since I can remember, he's always looked right into your soul. It's unnerving at times, the way he focuses, as if he's attempting to find out more than you're willing to tell him.

Girls love it. They're always telling him he has bedroom eyes, so he's never been short of a hookup when he wants one. But it always remains casual. I've never known him to have a girlfriend long term. He's never brought a female home. And since we've been so busy at work, we've both not had much time for anything else.

My brother is sprawled out on his bed, leaning against the headboard, shirtless as always, with a pair of boxers. He's reading a copy of Classic American magazine. Kill is in the process of doing up a '67 Mustang fastback. It's his pride and joy and is sitting almost complete at the shop as a side project outside of work or when it's quieter. The black mean machine is prettying up nicely with her fat tires and mirror finish.

I walk to the bed and sit. "I think I know why Capri was standing on the bridge about to jump last night."

Again, no reaction apart from a twitch in his right eye.

"Her father. She thought she saw him today at the mall and freaked the fuck out. You should have seen her. She went sheet white and couldn't move from fear. Then she proceeded to tell me he's a monster."

"So, she has daddy issues," the asshole says, not

garnering the seriousness of what I just said, turning a page instead of giving me his full attention. "Don't we all?"

"It's more than daddy issues. She wanted to kill herself, for fuck's sake. And I don't know what to do. One thing is for certain, though, I'm not sending her back."

He shoots me a damning look before finally setting the magazine down. He sits up and swings his legs over the side of the bed.

My brother is ripped. When he's not working and restoring his car, he's in the home gym. His dragon tattoo is a work of art and suits his bad boy vibe. I can see why girls swoon.

I don't have any ink but have thought I might get something small as a memory to Jayden, now that the grief is a little easier to tolerate. While we look similar in our facial features, hair, and eye color, I like to think that's where the similarities end. Kill is easier to enrage, whereas I put up with a lot to a point, and then my switch flicks. My brother acts before he thinks. I mull things over first. Weigh up my options. Unless I'm threatened. Then I'm all about the fight.

"So what, you're keeping her here? Christ, Atlas. First, we agreed to a few hours. Then it turned into a week. Now you want her to stay, permanently?" He's standing before me now, his muscles tense like he's gearing up for a fight.

"Where else does she have to go? And if she lives here, I can keep an eye on her. Make sure she goes to school. Keep her safe." Because if her father is the monster, she told me he is, he will find her. And it won't be pretty.

"Are you fucking insane? We don't know this girl. What if her low life father finds out she's living here and comes to pay her a visit? Shit will go down. Do you really want to deal with that?"

He's right. We've dealt with our fair share of crap from our father. Nothing like Capri, but Dad's not exactly a fan of mine. My mom is fine, but I don't see much of her anymore. The once-a-week phone call and that's pretty much it. I don't know if Dad will ever come around. If he can't support me one hundred percent, then I don't need him in my life. I have Kill and that's enough. Or so I keep telling myself. Deep down, the sting of betrayal and abandonment eats me up, but I cover it up well with denial.

"I'll beat him to a pulp, that's how I'll deal with it," I threaten, knowing it's true. Unlike Kill, I don't have an outlet for my emotions. While he pushes himself by lifting weights, I stuff all my feelings down to ignore them. I know it's not healthy, but everyone deals with things differently. One day I'll probably bust a gasket, but for now the lid is sealed tight.

Just the idea of anyone hurting Capri, though? It makes me want to take care of things. Him, namely.

Kill blows out a harsh breath before turning and heading to the bathroom that adjoins his bedroom. "Your responsibility. Like I said last night, don't get me involved. If she's staying here, she needs to get a job and pay her way. I'm not happy about it, but you've made up your mind. I can tell."

And with that, he's shut the door on me, a grin spreading on my face from ear to ear. I can't wait to tell Capri that she can stay as long as she wants.

NINE

Killian

With my head sagging on the tiles in the shower, I let out a curse. Just what does my brother think he's doing? Bringing a strange girl into our well-oiled machine. We are both finally doing okay with our lives, after the tragedy of losing Jayden and Atlas accepting the fact our father is homophobic.

And now? The girl with the eviscerating eyes appears out of nowhere to upend our lives, which makes me antsy.

She's going to be the third wheel. A chink in our chain. And most definitely a thorn in my side.

Atlas is too nice. Too caring. He thinks he can take on this world single-handedly and save everyone. He's always been that way. With the tiniest of creatures when he was young, morphing into humans when he got bigger. People are much harder to save as opposed to insects and cats or dogs.

Even at school, he took on the bullies for the unpopular kids, not caring about the consequences. He wore bruises like badges of honor for a while until he learned how to fight back.

Girls and boys alike. It didn't matter. He hated seeing innocents being hurt at the hands of another. And he's not violent by nature. Quite the opposite. Unlike me, Atlas is normally cool, calm, and collected. Until injustice arises. When first meeting him, you think he's sweet and charming, which he is, mostly. But I've seen another side to him.

Sure, it's noble of him to step up when others can't, but damn it, bringing someone home and expecting us to take her in permanently is a big ask.

I don't know what it is about this girl. The fact that she's hot just adds to the problem. How does he expect me to function if she's prancing around here in next to nothing?

He doesn't have that problem but I'm sure if I brought a handsome guy home, he'd be having something to say.

I rise and place my head under the hot spray, letting it pour over me for a moment before, grabbing the shampoo and washing my hair.

Mocha eyes appear behind my closed lids. Ones that bring about goosebumps when you first look at them and continue to haunt you long after.

Nope. Not going there. She needs to learn her place around here. And I intend to remind her every single day.

TEN

Capri

Sitting on the couch watching movies this afternoon is a rare treat for me. I'm normally studying or licking my wounds in my bedroom. Freedom is not something I'm used to, but I can honestly say that it's amazing. Not to mention the copious amounts of Ben and Jerry's Atlas and I consumed. I could get used to all this normalcy. But I know it won't last. Like anything good, it's fleeting. With every high there's a low.

Today, when I thought my father was at the mall, my panic levels had gone to an all-time high. The guy looked so much like him until he turned. My father wore similar clothes and was the same height and weight and even wore his hair the same.

Atlas now knows more than I would have liked him to but how should I have explained my almost meltdown?

Now that I'm staying a while, I owe him at least some of the truth.

"You like pizza?" Atlas asks, walking into the living room and sitting near me, ending my overthinking.

"Ahh..."

His eyebrows shoot up. "Let me guess, you've never had it?"

How does he know? And why am I embarrassed to confess that I have never been allowed pizza? I've always had to cook for my father for as long as I can remember, even if many times it ended up in the trash because he preferred bourbon or scotch. I enjoy it though. It's one of the times when I'm not being bullied and harassed by my life-giver.

"No."

His eyes squeeze shut and then open again, the cloudiness of anger clearing. "Well, you're in for a treat. How about we get a few so you can choose which one you like the best?"

With a nod I agree, hoping I like any of them after he spends his hard-earned money. That's another thing I'm frugal with. Not using anything in excess because I'll get beaten for it. I hated having to rely on my father for everything. Not having a job though, left me with no choice. Control at its best on his behalf.

There's so much I've never experienced. I'm aware of what people at school talk about. Holidays abroad. Lavish gifts. Sex. Expensive dinners. They're all things I'm not privy to but as today has progressed, I'm wondering if they might be things I can indulge in one day.

"Capri?"

"Hmm?"

"You with me?"

"Yeah. Sorry. Thank you. I appreciate it. I'm sure I'll love them all."

He smiles his breathtaking smile, so like Killian. Both brothers are gorgeous. I still need to pinch myself that I'm sitting here in their home with the offer of staying.

Fingers crossed I can find a job. With no experience I'll be at a disadvantage. Surely there must be something I can do. I'm willing to learn almost anything just so I can pay my way.

Killian saunters down the hallway as if to join us, wearing jeans and a singlet. I'm momentarily stunned again by his physique. His arms are sculpted perfectly as he walks to the armchair and picks up a black hoodie resting on the top.

His hair is damp from an earlier shower, falling over his brow in messy waves.

His eyes meet mine as he picks it up and puts it on causing me to shrink into the couch at his intimidating presence. His chest expands as he raises his arms to slip them through the sleeves, his focus still on me as he pulls it down.

"You good with pizza, Bro?" Atlas asks, obviously not noticing the sudden tension in the room and his brother's unwavering attention on me.

With a slight nod, Killian finally turns his head and asks his brother, "Any beers in the fridge?"

"A couple, I think," Atlas returns as he pulls his cell from his pocket and dials in our pizza order.

Kill walks out taking his attitude with him. Jesus, he's

terrifying. How am I going to stay here with the not-so-subtle tension?

"All set. You want a beer too?" Atlas asks.

With a shake of my head, I offer, "I don't drink."

He tilts his head. "Never had alcohol either?"

He's not judging but I can tell he's slightly shocked.

"No. I uh, wasn't allowed that either."

"So, basically he kept you prisoner and deprived you of all the joys in life?"

Hearing him say it out loud, truly brings home how screwed up my life is. Or was. It's embarrassing.

Before I can answer, Kill walks back in with his beer, handing Atlas one. He looks to me and says, "I heard you don't drink."

It's the first normal thing he's said to me and all I can do is nod.

"You want a soda or juice?" Atlas offers, being the kind brother.

"Juice is fine, thank you."

Suddenly realizing my cell is sitting uncharged and I haven't checked it since I left home, I ask, "Would I be able to charge my phone?"

Atlas stands. "Sure, I'll loan you my charger."

I rise and follow him, picking my cell up from a set of drawers in his bedroom where I slept last night.

We plug it in and just as I'm walking out the door, it pings. And keeps on pinging. I already know who has messaged me and I'm scared to check. My father will be insane with anger.

Atlas glances at me. "Gonna check those?"

With a shake of my head, I mutter, "Not yet. Let's just enjoy our pizza first."

What will be in the messages? I can only imagine. It won't be anything good. My heart rate kicks up a notch, a familiar ache in my stomach and chest. Just the very idea of my father induces such a reaction.

I should just check now and get it over with, but I know once I'm reading them, I'll feel so sick, I won't be able to eat any pizza. As it is, my appetite has waned.

It's another fifteen minutes before there is a knock on the door. Atlas and I have made small talk while Killian has sulked in an armchair, stealing glances at me every so often with his constant frown.

The pizzas are piled onto the coffee table and opened. "Help yourself," offers Atlas.

They smell divine so I choose one with chicken and vegetables and loads of cheese.

It's divine. I can't believe I've been missing out on this. Both guys are eating just as greedily as me and it's not long before there are only two pieces left.

I've tried one of each and enjoyed them all, my favorite being covered in meat, sauce and mozzarella. My belly is so full, all I can do is sink back into the couch beside Atlas and hold my stomach.

Shooting a quick look at both guys, my focus remains on a spot of sauce on Kill's full mouth. I want to tell him about it but I imagine swiping if off with my finger and seeing if it tastes any different having been on him.

My neck burns. He must feel me watching because when he notices, a tongue comes out to swipe across said lips, further inflaming my skin. He's cocky as anything, the corners of his mouth tipping up in a smirk, forcing my eyes front and center.

"What do you think?" asks Atlas.

"Hmm?" I ask, momentarily unable to remember what he said.

"The pizza? I'd say you thoroughly enjoyed it."

"Oh, yeah. It's so good. I can't believe what I've been missing out on."

Still not having my juice, I rise and go to the kitchen to get it myself, deciding not to ask. I'm more than capable of doing things for myself and starting right now, I need to learn where everything is.

When I walk back into the lounge room, Atlas notices and says, "Shit, I'm sorry. I was meant to get you that."

I sit beside him and say, "It's okay. I'm not an invalid. I don't expect you to wait on me hand and foot."

"You got that right," coughs out Killian, causing both Atlas and I to turn to him.

"Stop being a dick, Bro. Keep it to yourself. If you've got nothing nice to say then stay quiet," Atlas scolds, earning a glare from his brother.

His words cut into me when they shouldn't because I've heard worse, but coming from a stranger, they hit their intended target. So, I rise again. "I'm just going to check my messages."

"You need me to come with you?" Atlas asks, smoothing a hand over his hair as if it will tame the unruly mess.

"No. Stay here and spend time with your brother. I'll be fine." I know I won't be, but he's helped me enough already.

I've never relied on anyone and I'm not about to start now.

Heading into the bedroom where I've left my phone, I note it's already at thirty percent charge, so I unplug it and carry it to the bed, preparing myself for the backlash I know is coming.

You can do this, Capri. He's not here now. He can't hurt you. They're just words.

Still, as I open the first message and read, "Where the fuck are you?" I know I'm screwed.

Eleven

Atlas

"Can you at least pretend to be nice? She doesn't need your sorry ass giving her shit when she's already dealing with a mountain of crap as it is." I'm getting tired of Kill's attitude. He has no reason to dislike Capri. She hasn't done anything to him.

He swigs his beer and places it down on the small table beside the chair he's sitting on.

"I told you; I don't want anything to do with her. What part of that don't you understand?"

"I get it. You don't have to drive her anywhere. Look out for her. But I expect you to be civil. I'm not having this tension you've created in our home."

He tightens his upper lip and focuses anywhere but on me. Good. Let him think about it a bit.

I clear away the boxes trying to give Capri time to

herself but at the same time, if all the messages are from her father, maybe she needs someone there for support.

After throwing everything in the trash and making sure the front and back doors are locked up, I make my way to my room, not saying another word to my brother.

When I walk through the doorway, I slow my steps upon seeing Capri with tears streaming down her cheeks, sitting at my desk chair in the corner.

"Shit. I'm guessing they're no good?"

She sniffles, peeking a look at me before lowering her eyes back to her phone.

I close the gap and sit before her on the bed. "You want to share anything? I'm not trying to pry, but it might help if you unload some of the burden on me."

Capri rubs a hand over her nose, so I rush to the bathroom to grab the tissues, returning and holding the box out to her.

She takes some and blows into them. "Thanks."

"Were they all from your father? Is he pissed?"

Of course, he's pissed, douche. Otherwise, she wouldn't be so upset.

"He's going to kill me if he finds me. Or if I return home. Whichever one comes first."

"What the hell, Capri?" I hold out my hand, not expecting her to show me, but tentatively she gives me her phone, hand shaking.

When I read the barrage of psychotic messages, my rage is back. I'm gripping the phone so hard, my knuckles are white.

You fucking bitch! How the hell did you get out of the house?
When I find you, you're going to be so fucking sorry!

I'm going to kill you!

Did all your punishments not teach you a damn thing?

You're pathetic, just like your mother was.

I'm coming for you.

Don't think I won't hunt you down.

There's message after message. So many that I can only skim through the rest.

He's nuts. There's no way in hell I'm letting him ever get his hands on Capri.

"We should go to the police." This is serious. Child abuse should not be ignored.

She's shaking her head. "No. It'll only make things worse."

"How can anything be worse? They'll read these and lock the sick bastard up where he belongs."

Her sad eyes find mine, and it guts me to see her emotions bared for me to see. She's like an open book.

I sink to my knees and pull her in for a hug, not giving a damn that she hates being touched. She needs some kind of human affection right now.

She stiffens as I wrap my hands around her. "Atlas..."

"Shhh. I won't hurt you. Just breathe and relax. Let me be here for you. I know you feel alone and have probably felt that way for a long time, but you don't have to anymore. Let me in."

A sob breaks free. She's not hugging me back, her limbs stiff and awkward, but she's not pulling away either as her shoulders shake.

"I'm scared."

"I know. That's why we have to report him. So, you

don't have to be scared anymore. These messages are proof he's not a nice person."

She's too broken up to speak, so I offer, "Just think about it, okay?"

A timid nod. At least it's something.

"Do you need anything?" I ask, because what else is there?

"No. Thank you." She wipes her face, sniffling. "I'm sorry you had to see me like this."

Pulling back, I give her a smile. "You don't have to apologize. You have every right to be upset. Come. Sit on the bed."

She rises and walks with me, and we get comfortable against the headboard. I'm hoping she'll talk some more, so I wait.

But she changes the subject. "So, I'd like to get back to school on Monday. I'm falling behind after two weeks away. But my book bag is at my dad's. Everything besides my phone and the clothes you bought me are in my room there."

"You want to go and get it?"

She's shaking her head before I even finish the question. "No!"

"I'll come with you. I won't let your father hurt you. I promise."

"You don't know what he's like. He's evil. And I'd hate for you to get hurt because of me."

Unless he has a loaded gun inside, I know I could take the dude down. Kill and I learned to fight early on and can hold our own. I've got youth on my side and newfound anger over how he's treated his daughter.

"When does he leave the house?" Perhaps we can slip in and out while he's away. We can pack a bag for her and take whatever she needs. Hell, Killian might be persuaded to sit in the car as a lookout. Then again, he told me he doesn't want anything to do with Capri, so the odds are slim.

"I don't know. He picks up odd shifts doing maintenance work through the week while I'm at school. He... uh, goes out a lot to pick up women."

Her cheeks redden, and she lowers her eyes in shame. She doesn't need to be ashamed of that asshole. I'd expect nothing less after reading the texts.

My teeth grind, though, hearing about the scumbags' extra-curricular activities.

"Are you willing to go now and get everything? He may be out, but if he's not, I will handle him."

Her eyes immediately widen in fear, so I take her hand and link our fingers, noticing she doesn't pull away. "Trust me when I say he'll have to get through me first. Once we get your stuff, you never have to go back. It's either that or I can order you all new books for school."

"No! You're not doing that. You've already done way too much."

She breathes heavily, weighing up her decision.

Squeezing her eyes shut and then opening them, she nods, resignedly. "Okay. But if it looks like he's going to hurt you, we run."

"I won't let anything happen to you."

TWELVE

Capri

This is possibly the dumbest thing I've done in a long time, if ever. Going back into the lion's den. The only saving grace is Atlas.

There's no way I'd go back if he weren't with me. I don't think my father will do anything while he's there. He's a coward like that. It might be my only chance to grab everything I need.

He won't be happy, but when is he ever? I can only hope when he sees Atlas' size, he'll back down.

Killian, of course, turned down the offer to join us, as I knew he would. He's keeping to his promise of having nothing to do with me.

Honestly, I'm glad he's not with us. He seems like a loose cannon, and I'd be afraid of what would go down if he came across my father. As it is, Atlas will defend me physically if he needs to, but out of the two brothers, I feel he will be the least capable of murder.

Sure, I want my father six feet under, but not at the hands of two young guys who still have their whole lives ahead of them.

Dressed in an over-sized hoodie Atlas gave me, which smells just like him, we're bundled up in his truck, turning onto my street, my anxiety causing my breath to come out choppy. My legs are jiggling, and my hands are twisting.

"Hey." Atlas reaches across to touch my jean-clad leg. "Breathe. It's going to be okay."

"You don't know that. You don't know *him*." If only I had a crystal ball and could see the outcome of this visit. I'd hate to see Atlas hurt, or worse.

We don't park in the driveway, but on the curb. I want to bring as little attention to us as possible.

Atlas kills the engine, and we sit. I turn to him and notice him staring at my house with a fierce expression on his face.

"I don't need to know him to figure out what a piece of shit he is. And I certainly don't need to know him to want to protect his kind, beautiful daughter. He can try to take me down, but he'll have a battle on his hands."

I focus on the front facade of my house, too. The crumbling wooden structure is in disrepair. Neglected just like me. Normally you can't judge a book by its cover, but in this case, you can. The house itself looks macabre with its spire above the bay window, misplaced tiles on the roof and peeling paint around the windows.

The grass has turned into weeds that have taken over, a creeping vine winding its way up the mailbox.

What must Atlas think? It's the worst house on the street in what some would say is a lower-class neighborhood.

"You ready?" he asks, removing his hand from mine. The comforting loss is noticeable as I shake my head. I'm beginning to accept his reassurance. His touch. The non-threatening gestures I've never had. It's making me realize how much I've been needing safe human contact.

"I'll never be ready, but let's just get this over with."

He climbs out first and comes around to open my door. He reaches his hand out, which I grab onto like a lifeline as he kicks the door shut with his sneaker. I'm going to need every ounce of his support. He's wearing similar clothing to mine, with a pair of ripped jeans, a T-shirt and a black hoodie. We could be siblings; except he towers over my five-foot four height.

I let him lead me to my own front door. We attempt to be as quiet as possible. It's still early, so if my dad is awake, I want to take him off guard, so he's not prepared for my arrival.

He certainly won't be expecting me to rock up with a guy.

We take the two steps up onto the porch and Atlas stops me before we go inside. "Remember, don't let go of me until we get to your room. Don't let him intimidate you. This is the last time you'll have to deal with him. After tonight, you're free."

His words sink in. Truly sink in. In less than an hour, I won't have to be a victim anymore. I won't have to be afraid.

It's liberating. Like I'm a butterfly emerging from its

cocoon. I'll be able to spread my wings and fly. For the first time in my entire life. And I have Atlas to thank for it.

He's literally saved me.

Drawing in a deep breath, I steel myself for what is about to occur. I reach around him and open the door, fear still front and center.

The familiar smell hits me and I'm right back here, living what I already refer to as my old life. It doesn't feel like hours since I left. It feels like minutes.

The living room light is on, television going, but I can't see my father. For a moment, I breathe again, knowing not to get too excited. The front door was unlocked, so he's home. His car wasn't in the driveway, but he keeps it in the garage most days.

Maybe he's holed up in his room with another whore. I can only hope. That way he'll be too busy to worry about me.

Suddenly needing my lifeline, I grip Atlas' hand, watching his eyes widen in shock at my bold gesture and then I'm pulling him up the stairs to my bedroom, heeding his words of holding onto him.

We are almost at the top when my father comes out of the kitchen below, roaring, "Where the fuck have you been, girl? And who is this asshole? You screwing him? Is that where you've been? Huh? You a whore just like your mother?"

I can't move. My feet are frozen on the carpet. Just the sound of his voice almost brings me to my knees, but Atlas is holding my hand firmly. Squeezing.

He's gone rigid like me. I'm guessing his is out of anger and not fear.

Oh my God. I hate Atlas hearing him like this. It's embarrassing to be related to such a vile man. How did I put up with him for so long? Why didn't I try to escape sooner?

Easy. Because I didn't have an 'out' like I've been given now. I didn't know who to turn to. I don't have relatives I know of. They've all been hidden from me by the man downstairs.

Atlas moves to stand in front of me on the second last step, his arms and fists taut.

"Shut the hell up!" His tone is deep and raw. He's in protector mode, and my heart flutters slightly. If things didn't seem as dire as they are, I would focus on that fact more.

Before my father can react, I say meekly, "I came to get my things."

He walks to the bottom of the stairs. Atlas pushes me up onto the landing and follows me, probably so we have better footing against the madman.

"Oh, you think you're leaving, do you? Like hell! You're still a minor. I own you until you turn eighteen."

I'm sick with nausea. This is not going to go well, it's obvious. He's climbing the stairs and Atlas is backing me away. My room is only a few feet away.

When my father reaches the top, his face is bright red, an angry scowl turning his already somber features into something menacing.

"Don't come any closer," Atlas growls, taking a step back toward my father. I'm rooted to the spot, wondering what the hell is going to happen.

I don't want my savior in a physical fight over me.

"Oh, son. You think you're going to protect her? I'm her father!" He's shouting. "Leave, and I won't hurt you."

Why is he so horrible? How did he become like this? Was he born mean? He doesn't care who he hurts. I figured he'd be on better behavior because I had a friend with me, but obviously it doesn't matter.

"You take one more step and I'm going to re-arrange your face, old man. I know what you've fucking done to Capri, and it ends here. Tonight."

My father laughs, but it's not filled with joy. No, it holds terror. I've heard it before, and I know when he's about to snap.

"Atlas, don't," I warn, but he doesn't turn around. He's fully focused on his target.

I don't know what to do. Should I lock myself in my room? Grab something as a weapon?

No. I won't hide. I'm done with that. I won't let Atlas take on my father alone. Not when he's had my back for the last twenty-four hours.

"You're a pathetic kid. Just like her. You think you can take me?" He slides forward. Too close. He's too close. Memories burn the backs of my retinas, but I will not zone out. Not when Atlas needs me.

I can't breathe. My heart rate is thundering in my ears.

"Oh, I know I can. You think you can lay your hands on your daughter, you psycho? Big tough man? Do you always prey on women?" Atlas takes another step and there is only a couple of feet separating them.

My father's right eye twitches, his veins popping out of his neck. He glances at me with such hatred, it's still wounding. To know the person meant to love you with everything he has detests you in such a way, it destroys you.

Who is going to make the first move? This is not how I hoped the night would go. I've dragged Atlas into the pits of hell. He now knows the full extent of my nightmare.

"Come on, take a shot," Atlas goads.

No. No. Don't encourage him. Please don't fight him. I loathe violence. It's been a part of my life for so long, you'd think I'd be used to it, only the opposite is true. It makes me want to vomit right here on the carpet near my bedroom.

He rises slightly higher, as if it's possible. He's genuinely not afraid.

I'm watching on as if it's a movie and there's a jump scare about to happen. Too scared to look but unable to tear my face away. You know it's going to happen, but still scream when it does.

And then my father's arm rises to take a swing, only he doesn't get the shot in. Atlas intercepts it and grips my father's wrist so hard he's white knuckled. With his other fist, he strikes fast and hard, landing a blow to my father's nose, sending him reeling back. Atlas lets go and we watch as the 'old man' falls on his ass. His rage is clear even as blood pours down onto his thin lips.

"Get up!" Atlas roars. He's pumped and ready.

My dad appears shocked as he struggles to rise. Before he can get to his feet, a sneakered foot kicks out into his ribs, causing him to double over. In this moment, he looks weak and pathetic, so unlike the man who has overpowered me on so many occasions. He's not so tough now. I don't feel a thing as I stare at him. There is no emotion whatsoever. I'm sure if I were watching a stranger take a beating, I'd feel more. But watching the man who barely raised me, I'm numb. He's finally getting a taste of his own medicine. Oh, how I've longed for this. To have him know how I felt for as long as I can recall.

Atlas turns to me. "Go. Pack a bag. I'll stay here. Be as fast as you can."

I nod, jerking out of my stupor and running into my room to my closet where I reach up for a large bag off the shelf and begin tossing whatever I think I'll need into it. My school rucksack sits in the corner with some books I brought home with me to complete a couple of assignments. I've only managed to do a quarter of the work because I was recovering from injuries my father inflicted. I'll deal with the repercussions of that on Monday. For now, I'm whizzing around, grabbing toiletries, underwear, and anything else I can think of. My assigned laptop sits on my desk, so I grab it too with the charger and throw them into my bag, remembering my cell charger on my bedside table.

In a few minutes, I'm carrying my rucksack and bag out into the hallway.

Nothing has changed. My father still lies in a heap, facing the wall, Atlas standing guard.

"You ready?" he asks, taking a step toward me.

"Yeah."

"Good. Let's get out of here."

As we both walk away, my father shouts out, "This isn't over, girl!"

But as far as I'm concerned, it is. I'm leaving and I'm never coming back.

I don't even take in my home as we exit. There are no good memories here. Only sadness and pain.

We shut the front door. The cold night air is like a balm. I embrace it. I feel like I'm stepping into a new life. I'm leaving the cocoon and spreading my wings for the first time.

Thirteen

Atlas

I wanted to murder that son of a bitch. Luckily restraint is something I'm good at. If Kill were here, he would have gone psycho on the asshole. Jesus, I didn't realize how mental the guy is. He truly hates his daughter with a passion, and I have no idea why. His eyes were vacant and devoid of all humanity. I'm so glad I got her out of there in one piece. I can only imagine the horrors she endured while living there.

My knuckles are bright red and smarting but no skin broke, so there's no blood from me, only from him when I clocked his nose and probably broke it. I've learned how to throw an effective punch with as little damage as possible to myself. Her dad, however, might want to get his nose checked out. And his ribs will be hurting for a while. Hopefully, I let him know that he's not as tough as he thinks he is, and I'll be around to protect Capri. The maniac can live alone in his miserable filth until the day he stops breathing. I never want to see him again, and I'm sure his daughter feels the same.

"You, okay?" I ask as I turn the engine on in the truck and get the heat circulating.

"I am now," she whispers.

She's so strong it amazes me. When her face turns my way, there are no tears. Only relief. My heart explodes, knowing I've helped her escape sheer torture. Things will be okay. She'll be okay.

A smile forms on my face. "Can I show you something before we head home?"

Curiosity has her eyes holding mine for a long moment before she says, "Okay."

Kill is the only other one who knows my favorite spot. I don't take others there. It's where I go to mull things over. Where I went a lot after Jay passed. I'm not sure why I want Capri to see it, but I figure if it helps me, it might help her. I'm sure she needs it right now. While getting away from the house of horrors might be a relief, I know she'll be feeling a certain melancholy to be leaving a huge part of her life behind, the only one she's ever known. She's facing a new future, even if it is going to be so much better than her past.

On the outskirts of town, I turn left and begin the ascent into the hills that surround Bethel. I realize I don't know much about Capri, including her last name, so I ask, "What's your last name?"

She turns to me. "Oh. It's Lennon."

Capri Lennon. It has a nice ring to it.

"What's yours?" she asks, brushing a piece of her long cedar brown hair off her face.

"MacKenzie."

She nods, but I can see her repeating my name in her mind like I just did as her lips move, but no sound comes out.

"Have you always lived in Bethel?" I change down gears as the climb gets steeper.

"Yep. Born and bred here. I've barely left the neighborhood. I think we went on a school excursion once to the next town over, but apart from that, I uh… I've been kept on a tight leash."

I'll say. Well, that's going to change. I want to show her the beauty of our state. Maine truly is gorgeous. Fall came late. The trees are rich and vibrant shades of reds, yellows, burnt oranges, and bright greens. As we drive up the mountain road, leaves fall onto it in front of us with the breeze picking up.

"Well, you're in for a treat."

The smile she gifts me is like the sun emerging through storm clouds. Her entire face lights up. It's real and stunning. This girl doesn't even know how exquisite she is. No doubt because of her father constantly telling her otherwise. Bastard. He almost ruined her. Almost. But he didn't count on me showing up to steal her away and show her how to truly live. Capri Lennon and I are going to be best friends.

In another few minutes, we reach the top. The road plateaus out, houses scattered here and there, their backyards dropping away because of the sheer rock face in places.

I pull along to the lookout and park the truck. A sharp intake of breath has me glance over to Capri. Her eyes are like saucers, mouth agape at the stunning view of the town lit up.

The twinkling of lights against the black cape of the sky and the full moon is magical. Stars vie for attention and add to the fantasy. The night is clear and chilly.

"It's beautiful," she coos. "I've lived here all my life and never seen the town like this."

"Tonight is the first night of the rest of your life. You can be and do whatever you want to now. It's the day after yesterday."

She stares at me as if attempting to let my words sink in. I'm sure it's a lot to gather for her.

"I wouldn't be here to see this if it wasn't for you. I'd be a dead body, probably still floating up the river. Now that I've got hope, I don't want to die. I owe you everything."

I feel my eyes well up, but hold the tears at bay. It's been a night I never could have predicted, but one I wouldn't swap for anything. Not if it means getting her away from an abuser. There's so much she hasn't experienced. So much yet to see and do.

"I'm glad I was there at the right moment."

Capri clears her throat and peers out the front windshield before turning to me with a shy expression. "Uh, why didn't you jump? Were you really going to?"

And that's the question I didn't want her to ask, but she's smart. I was the one who asked her to move away from the edge to talk. I was the one who invited her back to my place and asked her to stay. If the tables were turned, I'd be asking the same question.

Will she hate me for lying? Or will she be able to see that I was simply trying to help her?

I blow out a long breath and give her my full attention. "Truth is… I wasn't there to jump."

"What?" Her voice is high pitched with a hint of disbelief. "You weren't going to jump?"

I'm shaking my head. "I saw you there and panicked. I had to come up with a plan and to gain your trust, I had to let you believe I was there for the same reason. I'm sorry if I mislead you. It wasn't with ill intent." Her head turns away as she whispers the words. "You lied to me. I thought we had something in common. Someone who understood." There's sadness in her tone that I hate.

Her door opens, and she's jumping out, walking to the edge of the expanse of stony gravel. Without thinking, I jump out in a panic, hoping like hell she's not going to follow through with her suicide mission.

"Wait!" I'm calling, watching her stand close to the edge, drawing her arms around her chest. It's freezing outside, but at this point I don't care. "Let me explain."

She turns fast, and the moon highlights tears falling down her cheeks like raindrops.

"I thought I could trust you. Why would you do that?"

"I didn't lie to hurt you. If I'd asked you not to jump, would you have listened? You didn't know me. I was a stranger. I could see the desperation on your face. All I could think of was Jayden jumping from that very bridge. I couldn't save him, so I was determined to save you. It wasn't a total lie. I've wanted to step off that bridge so many times. Just not last night." I added after a beat, "Please, just move back from the edge."

She scoffs. "What? You think I'm going to jump? I told you I didn't want to die now, and I meant it."

My shoulders sag with relief. At least that's one thing. A big thing at that, but there's still the issue of her not trusting me now. I'm back to square one.

Capri raises her face to the night sky and squeezes her eyes shut for a long time. I stand in silence, not knowing what to do or say. So, I remain quiet, letting her process.

Finally, when she opens her eyes and levels her chin, she turns on her heels and calls over her shoulder, "Just take me home."

"No! I won't let you go back to that monster!" I'm running after her. There is no way in hell I'm driving back to that neighborhood, let alone that house.

"Not my house. Yours." She opens the truck door and gets in, closing it a little too hard.

Oh. Good. My house. And she called it home.

FOURTEEN

Capri

Betrayal stings like a whip. When I was at my most vulnerable, I thought I had an ally. Someone who was in the same frame of mind. Someone who was about to do the exact same thing. I was wrong.

He simply made out that he wanted to jump to gain my trust so he could lure me away from the edge. Sure, I get why he did it, but at the same time, it was under false pretenses.

The sun is almost up. I've been tossing and turning all night, attempting to justify his actions. Perhaps he did the only thing he thought might work. Perhaps he was acting out of his own grief for Jay, but it feels as if the trust I am giving him is all for nothing.

It feels like manipulation to me. And it hurts.

Am I so sensitive to other's negative actions that I'm

simply being an ungrateful bitch? Am I searching for the skewed comfort it brings that my brain perceives as normal? Maybe I don't believe I'm worthy of anything better.

He told me he'd thought of jumping plenty of other times, so was it really a lie?

Ugh. There's no point lying here staring at the ceiling, overthinking every little thing.

Pushing the covers aside, I pull the long shirt I'm wearing over my panties and pad to the kitchen to make a coffee.

I'm sure to be quiet, so I don't wake Atlas or Killian. After we suffered a silent drive home last night, Atlas brought my bags to my room and left with a quiet 'goodnight.'

He feels bad and maybe I'm being too hard on him, but he needs to know that the way he went about saving me by lying cuts further into my fragile psyche. My distrust for people.

At the same time, would I have let him talk me out of it, if he hadn't told me he was going to jump too? Maybe. Maybe not. Either way, he did still save me, so I guess I should be grateful.

After switching the light on, I make my way around the kitchen, grabbing a mug and a plate for the toast I'll make to help fill my empty stomach.

The kitchen looks as if it's been updated in recent years with modern appliances and granite countertops. I can't help but wonder if the boys did it or if it was like this when they moved in. The high gloss cabinetry goes well with the earthy tops.

When the coffee is done, I spread my toast with peanut butter and fill my mug to the brim. I'm just about to sit down when a tousled, half-naked Kill bounds around the corner, probably not expecting to find me in his kitchen so early.

He stops dead, surprise lighting his features before he schools any emotion, replacing it with a cold detachment.

I don't miss his eyes roving over me from head to toe, though, causing embarrassment to ripple through me. I can't pull the shirt down any lower because I'm standing like a kid caught with their hand in a sweet jar, my eyes wide and mouth gaping, my plate and mug in each hand.

Words can't describe this dark angel. One would expect giant ebony wings to sprout from his back and for him to take flight from the back porch. His energy is far different to Atlas', even though they are twins. Although the glimpse of Atlas last night with my father showed similarities.

When Kill's tongue comes out and swipes his full, moist lower lip, I suck in a sharp breath at the sight of a silver stud on the end. He has his tongue pierced? Oh my. The very idea of getting such a sensitive piece of flesh speared with a needle has me shivering. That's two piercings now. Does he have any others?

Stop Capri. You have no right wondering that. You'll never find out.

A slash forms between his thick, dark brows. He's not saying anything, so I squeak out a "Hi." My eyes flick to his nipple ring, my wandering mind still hung up on any other piercings he might have.

He doesn't respond but moves to the fridge to grab a

water, undoing the cap and taking a long swig. I watch his back muscles bunch and coil, then he's walking out without a word, hands wound tightly into fists at his side.

I deflate slightly as I sit, wondering if he'll ever be civil to me. Maybe we're more similar than I think, and he doesn't trust easily either. I should be very wary of Killian MacKenzie. He's the silent, brooding type. But sometimes they are the ones you have to watch the most.

He storms to his room and appears a few minutes later, wearing a hoodie over his bare chest and sneakers on his feet. Without even glancing in my direction, he leaves through the front door, making me wonder where he's going. A run maybe? And then I chastise myself for even spending more than a few seconds of thought on Kill. He doesn't deserve my attention. If he's going to pretend I'm not here, I'll just have to do the same.

Easier said than done.

After breakfast, I decide to shower and then bake. I'd like to unpack, but Atlas said he'd prepare the spare room today for me, so I need to wait until he's up. Upon checking the cupboards, I find all the ingredients to make some chocolate chip cookies. Baking is therapeutic for me, so I'm happy to have what I need. Atlas did mention Kill enjoyed cooking, which I'm grateful for. I won't need to go to the store.

Dressed in my signature pair of jeans and a long sleeve shirt, I push the sleeves up a little and get to work.

It's 7 a.m. so I hope I'm not making too much noise as I measure and pour until the cookie dough is firm in the bowl. When the oven is hot enough, I spoon the mixture onto a tray and place them in.

As I'm shutting the door, a noise behind me has me rising to full height and spin. Atlas stands in the doorway, a grin on his face as his eyes scan the mess I've made.

"I… uh… I'm about to clean up. Did I wake you?" I feel a little guilty about the way I reacted last night now that I'm up and have thought about it. I hope we can return to being friends. At least friends-in-the-making.

With a chuckle, he moves forward and lifts his hand to brush some flour off my cheek. "Nah. I'm normally an early riser. I heard Kill leave for a run and came to see what you were doing. Um… what are you doing?"

It's not said with malice, but with mirth.

"I'm baking. Chocolate chip cookies. I hope you like them."

His head nods before his mouth moves. "I love them. They're Kills favorite."

That surprises me. A guy like Kill favors choc-chip cookies. "Oh. Okay. Well, they'll be ready soon. I'll just clean up here. Coffee's ready."

Atlas' smile broadens, his eyes crinkling. It seems genuine this time. "I think I'm going to enjoy having you around, Capri."

I return his smile, realizing that I'm feeling lighter, even after Killian's cool attitude earlier. I may very well like being here, too.

Seeing him not perturbed by my cool attitude toward him in the truck last night, I swallow my pride and say, "I'm sorry about the way I reacted to you telling me you weren't going to jump. I was surprised, that's all. I guess I overreacted."

He shrugs as if he's not bothered in the slightest. "It's

totally fine. I get why you were disappointed. I probably would have been too. It's just when I saw you standing there, I knew I had to do or say whatever I could to stop you."

I blow out a breath. "I know. Thank you. Truly. You've given me a second chance."

"Friends?" His eyes hold mine and I know he needs me to agree. We might just need each other.

"Friends." And just to cement the deal, we shake on it.

Fifteen

Killian

I'm pushing myself further than I ever have. The lactic buildup in my legs is extreme, but I'm not going to stop until I drop.

Walking into the kitchen this morning and seeing Capri fresh out of bed, wearing nothing but a shirt made me all kinds of antsy. I wasn't looking at her killer legs, wondering what sort of panties she had on. I also wasn't looking at her pouty mouth or the way she bit it as she eyed my naked chest. Nope. Not one bit.

She'd thrown me for such a loop, I hadn't been able to form words. Instead, I went to the fridge and grabbed a bottle of cold water to cool my heated blood. My initial reason for going to the kitchen in the first place was to enjoy a bowl of homemade muesli I make in bulk every two weeks. At such an early hour, there was no reason for anyone to be up, so imagine my surprise when I saw her standing there all wide-eyed and innocent.

Hence the reason I needed to get the hell out of there and put my body through its paces.

I've got my ear pods turned up full bore with Nickelback blasting out, so I jump when a car whizzes by me and blares its horn. I give him the middle finger, finally slowing down and moving to the curb.

My chest is heaving, and my knees almost give out as I stoop over and grip my thighs.

Sweat drips down to the freshly cut grass out front of a middle-class home in a leafy neighborhood. I'm miles from home, having zoned completely out as to my whereabouts because of my errant thoughts about our new houseguest.

If she's going to prance around in next to nothing, how am I going to cope? Not that I can talk, mostly going shirtless on my days off. But it is my home. I should be able to wear whatever I damn well please.

I can't with her eyes. I just can't. Whenever I'm brave enough to look into their depths, I find so much sadness it has me feeling all kinds of emotions I don't need to be feeling.

Not having an ideal relationship with my parents, I've learned the easiest way to get through life is to feel nothing. That way there are no disappointments.

Dropping out of school and taking over the repair shop my grandpa owned was not something my dad wanted me to do. If he had his way, I'd be sitting my bar exams and becoming a lawyer. Or attending medical school to become a doctor. He always wanted more from me than I could give. And so, I gave up attempting to please him, choosing instead to follow my dreams of restoring and repairing cars. It may not be the most prestigious of jobs, but I love it with passion.

I'd been working at the shop under my grandpa's watchful eye since I could remember. After school. Saturday's. Holidays. He taught me everything about cars there is to know. I loved those days with a man who had been more of a father to me than Dad ever was. They both had a tumultuous relationship, one I attempted to steer clear of. To this day, I still don't know the full story, but going by my father's attitude toward me, I can only guess who the villain is.

When Grandpa died and left me the shop in his will, I knew carrying on the business was my calling. To bring it back up to the thriving business it had once been. And with Atlas' help, we've achieved that goal.

On the rare occasion that I see my father, there's always disappointment in his tone when I talk about my business. He still gets in jibes about how I could have done better and didn't apply myself harder at school. How I'm wasting my life on a mundane job when I could be working eighty hours a week and stressed to the max just to be someone he can be proud of. Well, no thank you. I'd rather be working forty hours a week doing something that stimulates me daily and makes me want to get out of bed. Something I can leave at the shop and not think about again until Monday morning. I choose to work Saturdays if it's a job I've taken longer on than what I originally quoted. My work is second to none because I care about what I do. Customers know that and spread the word to their friends. It's why we're so busy.

The older you get, the more you realize you need to live your own life, not the life others have dreamed up for you. When you're a kid you do whatever is asked of you, but at some stage, maybe puberty, you begin to rebel against rules and regulations you don't agree with.

Atlas still has money from his inheritance. I got left the shop, and he received a nice tidy sum. I'm not sure what he's keeping it for but it's accruing interest, so he's in no hurry to spend it.

I remove my hoodie, leaving me in a just a singlet. The chilly air helps cool me down. The run home is going to be grueling, so for some of it I walk so I can steel myself against seeing Capri again. I want to hate her so badly, but the sheer intensity of her emotions that bleeds from her eviscerating eyes, bringing forth a sensation in my chest I can't name. Is it pity? No. Everyone has hard times. Everyone has their own demons. She's no different. Except whatever she evokes within me, it douses my anger. I just can't let her know that.

It takes a lot longer to get home. It's 9 a.m. when I walk through the door. I'm immediately overcome by the scent of home baking. So much so that I don't even head for the shower first. I quietly make my way into the kitchen, half expecting to see Capri still there, but it's empty, thankfully. Save for a plate of what looks like choc-chip cookies in the middle of the table. She baked? And made my favorite? What are the odds? Or did Atlas spill the beans?

Either way, I'm starving, having skipped breakfast, so I

snatch up one and shove it into my mouth, then go to the fridge and nab another bottle of water.

The sensation of the cookie almost melting in my mouth has me groaning and reaching for another one. They're good. Really good. And it's just the right consistency. Who would have thought the timid little kitten could whip up such a fine batch?

Noise travels down the hallway. Atlas and Capri are laughing. He likes this strange girl that he rescued. What is it about her? It can't be just her sad eyes and quiet demeanor. There's so much more to her than she shows. It's only into the second day of having her here and already my intent to have her hate me is softening.

I'm into my fourth cookie, washing them down with my water, when footsteps pad down the hallway. I pause mid chew as my brother and the girl in question enter. They both stop when they see me devouring the cookies. Suddenly, I feel like a kid with his hand stuck in the cookie jar.

"Oh," she says. "Are they okay?" The way her surprise has her expressive eyes widen and her full mouth open in shock has me shifting uncomfortably in my seat. A spark of awareness lights up between us as she regards me with unsure intrigue.

Atlas' face morphs from surprise to highly amused, eyebrows raised in question.

"They're alright. Not as good as mine." Liar.

She nods, accepting my answer, but Atlas doesn't buy it. "Bullshit. I've tasted yours and these are better."

He moves to the table and takes a cookie, eating it in

two large mouthfuls. All the while, Capri is watching us both, unsure what to think.

Rising from my chair, I brush past them both, throwing over my shoulder, "Next time you might want to cook them a little less. Some of them were way too hard."

I hear Atlas speaking to her quietly, probably reminding her what an ass I am.

Truth is that the cookies were better than mine. Cooked to perfection. If they hadn't disturbed me, I would have eaten the whole plate.

Point one for the girl.

Sixteen

Capri

I'm picking over each cookie, checking for burnt pieces or over-baked ones by turning them, but I can't figure out what Killian meant about them being too hard. It bothers me to think he didn't like them, although he still ate quite a few. They can't be that bad.

Atlas eats another one. "They are so good. Don't worry about Mr. Grumpy Pants, he's just being his usual defiant self. He'd never admit they're better than his."

Huh. Whatever. I think they turned out fine and there's only a dozen left, so at least they are being eaten.

He'd been for a run. His tight singlet stuck to every rise and fall of his torso from the sweat which trickled over his bare skin. His normally tousled hair clung to his forehead in wet strands, making him appear younger.

Sweaty guys aren't my thing, but oh my, he's got me

changing my mind. I picture him naked under the hot spray, imagining his entire physique and swallow thickly. What is wrong with me? I never fawn over a guy. But then, I've never been in such proximity to two devastatingly handsome ones.

I'm seventeen. My hormones are still roaring crazily through my blood. They have been since I got my period at thirteen. I'll never forget that day. Having to tell my father. The look of annoyance on his face at having to buy me pads. The embarrassment I felt when he threw them at me, telling me to wash my bedding if I'd stained it. Not the reaction I wanted, but one I expected.

I'm officially set up with my own room, which feels freeing. Not hearing my father in the house has helped calm my anxiety and relaxed me somewhat. Its weird being in a strange house, but Atlas has been nothing short of amazing. I feel close to him already and know he's playing a huge part in my new life.

Deciding to spend the day cleaning and earning my keep, I begin with the kitchen, going through cupboards, throwing away anything past its use-by date, organizing the pantry, cleaning the oven, and wiping every surface down. I move from room to room and when I'm done, it's the afternoon. I haven't stopped.

The boys left me to it, staying in the living room and playing Fortnite. Focusing on making the house gleam has given me a reprieve from my own head and made the day go by fast.

Taking a shower and changing into fresh clothing, I wander into the kitchen to make a late lunch.

Atlas intercepts me. "This place looks cleaner than it

ever has. Thank you so much!" He's gifting me with one of his supercharged smiles.

"You're welcome. It's going to be a weekly occurrence. I said I was going to earn my keep, and I meant it."

"Well, I'm taking you out to get food and then we can do a grocery shop and fill the cupboards with whatever you want."

"Really? You don't have to do that."

"Ah, yeah, I do. You haven't taken a break, and it's now two o'clock. Come on, my treat."

To me, the cupboards already look full, but maybe that's because at home, I always had to fight tooth and nail to get groceries so I could cook. Our cupboards were often bare.

He walks to the counter and grabs his truck keys. After our last outing and me freaking out about seeing a guy who looked like my father, I ask, "Where are we going?"

"Wherever you want." As we walk past the couch, I glance over to Killian, who is watching us with a frown. No surprise there.

"You want something to eat, Kill?" Atlas asks.

The broody brother simply shakes his head and turns back to his game. Not before giving me a death glare. Okay, well, he's back to that. I don't know why I figured he'd softened slightly. Obviously not.

I attempt to shake it off, exiting the house and heading to the truck parked in the driveway. The cold air hits me, but it's not horrible. It helps cut through the lingering tension I can still feel from the house. My jeans and jacket help stave off the bite of the breeze and once we're in the truck and on our way, the heater thaws everything out.

"So, have you decided where you want to go?" Atlas asks, a quick sideways flick of his eyes.

I think about where I've always wanted to go but have never been and it's a no-brainer. "Starbucks?"

His focus remains on me a little longer this time before returning to the road, a small smile tugging at his lips. "Another first?"

"Yeah. I hear kids at school talking about it all the time. If you want to go there, that is."

"Sure. I'm easy. Starbucks it is."

Both fear and excitement grip me. On one hand, it's like a prisoner experiencing life for the first time. Getting to do things they've never been able to. And on the other, I still hope we don't run into my father, although with how Atlas left him, I doubt he'll be out and about for a few days. My shoulders relax at that thought. Today, I'm going to enjoy myself.

The coffee house is busy, but we manage to find a small table in the back, which suits me fine. I will never enjoy being the center of attention, no matter how much I'm around hordes of people.

It's a hive of activity with barista's churning out drinks by the dozens and the clinking of China and chatter a steady chorus.

There's a buzz in the air and it's contagious. This is what I've been missing out on. Simple people doing simple things. Catching up with friends. Conducting business, or like the studious girl sitting at a table reading, perhaps just chilling with a book and a good coffee.

Life outside of my home is vastly different. Even school doesn't give me the full experience. The more time

I spend doing things I've never done, the more I am grateful I didn't jump two nights ago. Such a short time ago and yet I feel like I've already experienced so much. And it's all stuff most people take for granted.

Atlas orders a double shot of coffee. "What would the lady like?" he asks in a posh accent, bringing a giggle from me.

"Ahh, I've heard people talk about lattes, so I guess I'll have one. No sugar."

He rises to order. I watch his confidence as he strides to the counter. He's so sure of himself. Of his sexuality, even when his parents aren't. It must be so hard, not having their approval. Always knowing deep down that they abhor who you are. I know it pains him. I've seen his facade slip on a couple of occasions, although he does a good job at covering it.

It's a lucky guy who will get a chance with him, but at least I get to live and spend time with him. I can see us becoming besties real fast, and it warms my heart.

In the short time I've known Atlas, I feel closer to him than either of the girls I hang out with at school. Sure, they're nice, but once high school is over, I doubt we'll keep in contact.

When the drinks come, we sit and make small talk. "Are you looking forward to going back to school in the morning?" Atlas asks.

Am I? So much has happened. It feels like a lifetime ago since I walked the halls. To be honest, I'm a little apprehensive. I don't want to answer questions about why I've been away. Carly and Steph know that my dad's strict, but not to the extent he is. I've mostly been able to hide my injuries or explain them as being clumsy and falling over. Knocking into things. I'm not sure if they buy it all the time, but they don't push for the truth, which I'm happy about.

"I guess. I want to graduate and then I'm not sure. I've always just been attempting to survive and not thought too much about the future, but now that I can breathe again, I might consider doing something with my photography."

Atlas grins. "Yeah? I think that's fantastic. I'm sure some of the community colleges will have arts programs."

"That's why I can't afford any more time off. I need to keep my grades up."

"How are they normally? You look intelligent." He swipes a hand through his hair, causing it to stick up before he takes a sip of his coffee.

I've noticed both guys and girls watching him. He is breathtaking. It's hard not to notice someone so handsome. But he appears oblivious. Which makes me like him even more.

I smile. "Well, I try. Even with all the shit I've put up with at home, I've made studying a priority. Plus, it allowed me to lock myself in my room and not deal with my father. He always wanted updates on my grades, so while I loved studying, it was also essential I not let him down."

His face morphs into one of regret. "I'm so sorry you had to endure that. I wish we'd found each other sooner."

Me too, but what's done is done. I want to forget the past even existed. As far as I'm concerned, my life began when I walked into Atlas and Killian's home.

"At least we found each other, right? Or rather, you found me."

The time passes quickly and by four o'clock, we decide to head to the grocery store.

I'm cooking dinner and have opted for my favorite potato clam chowder. It's filling and super tasty. Hopefully, the boys will like it. Well, at least Atlas. Killian? I'm not so sure about.

When we arrive home, the living room is empty. Killian's bike is here, so maybe he's out back in the shed. We carry the bags of food into the kitchen and put everything away that I won't be needing for dinner.

I've no sooner begun preparing our food than there is a knock at the door. I wait for one of the guys to answer it, not wanting to overstep my boundaries and at the same time, hoping like hell my father hasn't somehow found me and is here to take me home.

It takes a moment before Atlas walks down the hallway and opens the front door. I hear a woman's voice.

"Hi, Atlas, how are you?"

"Hi, Mom. What are you doing here?"

"I have some news about your father. I'm hoping Killian is home, too."

There's silence for a heartbeat too long and even I feel awkward about it.

"Uhh, can I come in?" she asks.

"Ah, yeah. I'll go get Kill," Atlas replies.

Feet pad back down the hallway to Killian's bedroom door. There's a rap and then words are exchanged that I can't quite make out. It answers my silent question about where he is.

I startle when a forty-something-year-old woman walks into the kitchen. She's as surprised to see me as I am for her to wander in.

"Oh, hello," she offers. "I didn't know the boys had company."

I wipe my hands on a towel and move closer. "Hi. I'm Capri. I'm kind of living here for now."

The attractive woman with a blonde bob and way too much makeup raises her brows in question. "Are you now? Well, no one mentioned anything. Nice to meet you. My name is Caroline."

I'm not sure how to take her. She's trying to be pleasant, but at the same time, I can't be sure if it's genuine. Her eyes are dark like her sons. She's dressed in a pressed black skirt with a pale blue blouse and black jacket as if she's just left an office.

"That's because she's only just moved in, Mom."

Atlas moves over to me. "I see you two have met."

"Only just, yes."

There's another awkward silence before the woman asks, "Will Killian be joining us? I'd like to talk to both of you."

"Is everything okay?" Atlas asks.

"Can we move to the living room?" Her face falls as she glances to me and back to her son.

Whatever it is, is private, so when Atlas turns to me, I give him a nod. "I'll keep going with dinner."

They walk out and a moment later Killian joins them, sans shirt again. Hell, what is it with him and clothing? Not that I mind. If I were a guy and looked like that, I'd want to show it off too.

I try not to overhear or eavesdrop, but it's hard when Killian raises his voice. "And we're supposed to care? What the fuck has he ever done for us?"

"Language Killian! Show your father some respect." Caroline's voice is rising a few octaves, too. I don't like where this is heading.

"Respect? How about he shows his two sons some respect? He all but disowned us because we're not the perfect little replicas of himself he hoped to mold us into. When was the last time he called?"

"He's very sick. And you haven't called either."

"Because he told me I would never amount to anything if I kept the repair shop! He demanded I sell it! And when I didn't? He broke all contact. So, you know what, Mom? Fuck him. And fuck you for not sticking up for me!"

Kill is yelling. I can't hear Atlas and wonder what he's thinking. Internally, I'm cringing at the angry exchange. It's all too close to home.

Next thing I know, Killian is storming into the kitchen. He sees me and stops short. "Fuck!" With a quick rub of the back of his neck, he brushes past me and slides the glass door to the backyard open, hightailing it outside. The yard is decent, with a large shed in one corner. I watch him power across the grass, throw open the metal door and head inside.

Suddenly the kitchen feels too small, as if the walls are closing in on me. I feel like I've overheard a very private conversation I shouldn't have. It's obvious the boys have no relationship with their father. Something I can relate to. Maybe we're not so different.

Kill has issues with anger which may stem from not

being accepted by the one person who should be supportive. I know exactly how that feels. The rejection. Thinking you're not good enough. Overcompensating with everything to get in their good graces. Until eventually you resign yourself to the fact that no matter what you do, they just don't care. And then you give up trying.

Part of me wants to go out and attempt to calm him down, but I know he will hate me for it. He doesn't like me at the best of times, so right now, when he's volatile will only provoke an all-out war.

I hear the front door close, then Atlas enters the kitchen. His face is stoic.

I look away, pretending to focus on peeling the potatoes, when all I'm really doing is taking layers off the same spot.

"I guess you heard all that, huh?" he asks, taking a glass from the cupboard and getting some cold water from the fridge.

"Not all of it. I was trying not to listen, but Kill was kind of loud."

My gaze finds his and there's embarrassment there, plus a myriad of other emotions.

Atlas peers out the open sliding door and then back to me, moving to close it. "He hasn't ever had the best relationship with our father." After a large sip of water, he continues, "For Mom to make out that we should be calling him, regardless of the way he treated us, has added fuel to the fire."

I'm not sure if I should mention the fact that Caroline said he was very sick. I watch Atlas for a moment and then decide to go for it. "Your mom said he's ill."

"Cancer."

"Oh shit. I'm so sorry." What can you say to that? Placing the potato and peeler down, I turn fully to him and give him my undivided attention.

He's shaking his head. "Don't be. The idiot has smoked his whole life. We repeatedly told him it will end up killing him, and what do you know?"

He's deflecting. Perhaps in pain or perhaps like me, he just doesn't care. Under the walls he's built, though, I know he must be hurting. The same way I learned to hide my sadness at school to avoid talking about it with others. I only hope eventually Atlas will open up to me and talk about how he's feeling. I want to be that person for him.

A loud noise comes from the shed. It sounds like items breaking.

When I go to move toward the door, Atlas grabs my arm. "Don't. He needs to vent. That shed is Kill's space. He goes there when he's got too much anger. We keep old glasses and plates out there for him to throw at the wall. Once he gets it out of his system, he'll come back in."

Bloody hell. Maybe that's what I could have done with. A place to vent. I've never heard of having a space to throw stuff when you're mad, but it's not a bad idea.

Still, the idea of him out there suffering on his own doesn't sit right with me when we are in here listening. I know what it's like to go through stuff alone. Sometimes you just want someone to pick up your broken pieces. To know they care about you even if you don't care about yourself.

Seventeen

Killian

The last thing I needed today was a visit from our mother, informing us that our dear old dad has terminal lung cancer. Did she expect us to sob and bow down to him like we always used to just because he couldn't quit his pack a day habit?

The ass doesn't deserve an ounce of our compassion. He wiped his hands of us and made it clear where we stood as far as any inheritance went, so forgive me if I don't feel anything at the news. I don't want or need his money. What I do need is his love and support. But that's wishful thinking. It'll never happen now.

We've always had a volatile relationship, butting heads at every turn, and she has never done a thing to come to my aid by sticking up for me, choosing to take the side of her husband, even when she shouldn't have.

So, for her to show up here unannounced, attempting to guilt us into going to see him, when a simple phone call from her would have sufficed is what has set my inferno alight. It was always going to end in an argument because she fails to see things from my perspective. She failed both her sons in many ways by siding with him.

What's even worse is when I flew into the kitchen to see the little kitten standing there all wide-eyed, listening to our family drama, I wanted nothing more than to push her into the counter and give her a mouthful, but I know it's not her fault my mother turned up here without an invitation and proceeded to provoke me.

I pick up anything I can find and toss it against the blank metal wall of the shed. After every one of my outbursts, we go to thrift stores and gather more. Once I'm done here, I'll move over to the home gym and punish some weights until I'm feeling human again.

Damn it all to hell. Today was supposed to be a relaxing finish to my weekend, and it was heading that way until *she* showed up. The irony of it all is she thinks she's doing the right thing by Atlas and me. Can she not see by siding with Dad she's condoning his behavior? Mimicking it.

Just once, I'd have liked her to stick up for us in front of him. Or pull us aside and offer some support. But no. My brother and I supported each other. All our lives. He's all I have.

I throw a plate, watching it smash to smithereens, enjoying the satisfaction of hearing it shatter. There is China and glass sprayed everywhere and perhaps later I'll clean it up, but right now, I need this outlet.

Why have I felt like I'm never good enough? Why has he made me think I'm not?

I'm nervous as I enter my dad's study. What I'm about to tell him will go down like a lead balloon, but it's something I've decided, and I need to let him know.

A quick knock on the door and I push it open to find him on the phone. He looks up to see me and holds up a hand to stop me in my tracks.

"I don't care what you want. Get it done yesterday. I want a full report emailed to me by tonight." He slams the phone down. Okay, not a good sign.

"You got a minute?" I ask, moving closer, watching his body language.

"Make it quick, I've got another call to make," he answers gruffly, as if whatever I have to say will be inconsequential. Typical.

I heave in a deep breath to steel myself for an argument. Grandpa Joe died last month, and he left me the repair shop in his will. Dad is expecting me to sell it and pay for law school.

Dad peers at me, his mouth a thin line. "Well? What is it? I'm busy."

"Ah." I raise my hand to rub the back of my neck, a sign I'm agitated. "I've decided to keep the repair shop."

His face remains neutral. A trait I've learned so well from him. I never know what he's thinking.

"How are you going to find time to run that when you're at college getting your degree in law?"

And there it is. He's telling me what I'm going to be doing. Because it suits him. Because it's what he wants me to do. Not because I want it.

I need to just rip the bandage off quickly. If I stand here for too long, I'll turn my tail without telling him.

Just say it, Kill. Don't be a pussy.

"Here's the thing, Dad. I'm not going to college. I'm dropping out of school and running the shop. It's what I want to do."

He's up and out of his chair, rounding his desk, pointing a finger at my chest. "Like hell you are. I haven't raised a son to be a dropout. You'll finish school and go to college like we planned. I haven't busted my ass all these years and saved for your college fund, just to have you throw it back in my face."

His neck is red, eyes blazing. He's intimidating. "Is that all you came in here for? Because if so, this conversation is done."

Not this time, Dad. I'm not letting you steamroll me again. This is my life. And I'm owning it.

Rising higher, tamping down my churning stomach, I say, "I've never enjoyed school. In fact, I hate it. I only go because of you. Because you want me to get good grades and go to college. Well, guess what? I don't want the same things as you. I'm not you. I l love cars and I want to work on them as a job. A career."

He laughs, but it's not pleasant. "You think you're going to make it in this world by fixing cars? That's ridiculous and you know it. Tinkering with cars is a hobby. Not a career. You'll never amount to anything if you choose that path."

I'm shaking my head at his attitude. I don't care if I'm not rich. Wealth means different things to different people. I'd rather be happy.

"I don't want to be a lawyer. That's your dream. Not mine."

"Listen, you little punk, you live under my roof and while you do, you'll do as I say. I give you whatever you want, and you'll respect me by getting a career worthy of our family name!

God knows your homosexual brother has already disgraced us. You will not do the same!"

I growl. "You leave Atlas the fuck alone!" I'm fuming at his homophobic remark. He truly is a prick of epic proportions. "He's still your son."

"No son of mine is gay!" He's roaring now. It echoes off the walls. I'm not sure where Mom is, but last I saw she was in the kitchen preparing dinner. She must be able to hear us. Why isn't she coming in here, defending Atlas?

I'm done with this man. He'll never be what we need him to be. If I have to find an apartment and move out while I build up the repair shop, I will. I don't need his money or anything he has to offer.

As I turn and walk toward the door, he yells, "If you defy me and drop out of school, you'll never see another dime from me. You can kiss your inheritance goodbye."

I don't even turn back, just simply walk out, slamming the door.

"You okay, Kill? You've been out here for a couple of hours. I left you alone as long as I could, but I'm getting worried, man." Atlas' voice startles me, causing me to spin around, gaining my bearings again. I have a glass in my hand, ready to throw it but I've been too busy reminiscing about old times with dear old dad to throw it.

"Just peachy," I reply, walking to the wooden tool bench and placing the glass down.

"Her visit doesn't mean anything. We don't owe that man anything."

"It sure as hell did mean something. She showed up here at our home, making out that our dying father is the victim here. I don't care if he takes his last breath tomorrow. In fact, I'll welcome the day he's gone. Maybe then I won't feel like such a disappointment to him."

"I know. How do you think I feel?"

I stare at my brother, knowing full well he knows how I feel. Probably more so.

With a glance around at the mess I've made, I sigh. "Having little miss princess inside hearing everything didn't help."

"She's probably already forgotten about it. She was too busy cooking dinner. Besides, what she heard earlier is mild compared to what she's used to."

"Whatever, Bro. If she's staying here for a bit, I don't want her knowing too much. This is family business. She's already heard too much."

I turn my back on him, listening to him mumble something, but I choose to ignore it, picking up the broom to begin my cleanup before I begin my assault with some weights.

He leaves me in peace after a couple of minutes. I fear he's already getting too close to our new stray. A niggling feeling in my gut tells me she's not going to be leaving anytime soon. Not if Atlas has anything to say about it.

EIGHTEEN

Capri

Monday morning rolls around and I'm both excited and anxious about returning to school. There will be questions I don't want to answer. I've decided I'm going to say I've had the Coronavirus. That way the two weeks I've been absent won't seem strange.

Atlas is in the living room, waiting for me. He's going to work after dropping me off and he'll pick me up in the afternoon. I think he's worried about my father showing up, but to be honest; I doubt it. He's never been to my school. There's no reason he'd start now. I'm hoping we won't hear from him again after Atlas knocked him down.

With my backpack filled with everything I need; I head down the hallway to find Atlas in the big recliner. His face lights up when he sees me.

"You ready for your first day back?" he asks, rising and walking to me.

"I guess," I offer, throwing the strap of my bag over my shoulder.

"It'll be good to see your friends."

Yeah, the whole two I do have, I feel like saying, but instead I mutter, "Mmm hmm."

I'm dressed in jeans, a long-sleeved shirt and a denim jacket. My 'go to' attire. Outside, the air is icy, so we both walk quickly to his truck.

It's weird having him drive me to school. I've had the same routine for so long. Today feels strange. Normally I'd be sitting on the bus about now, wishing we'd hurry up and arrive because most of the students were noisy and obnoxious. To avoid much of the chaos, I choose to sit up behind the driver, who is always friendly to me and chatters away during the drive.

When we pull into the parking lot and find a spot, my stomach lurches at being back. So much has happened. I feel different now. Kids are walking in or standing in groups chatting, not even aware that I wanted to die two nights ago. It hits me then. Life goes on the same as it always has. The sun rises and sets. People go about their lives. Sure, they don't know my circumstances, but even if they did, nothing would change.

"You, okay?" Atlas asks, making me pivot my head to him.

"Yeah. Just nervous."

"You'll be fine. I'll be waiting here to pick you up this afternoon. We can grab coffees if you want."

He's so nice. Always trying to put me at ease. For

someone with their own demons, it's remarkable that he should care about my state of mind.

"You need me to walk you in?" he asks, glancing around at the students milling about before finding me again.

"Nah. Thanks, though. I'll be fine." I take a deep breath and slowly let it out, opening the door and jumping down. "I'll see you later."

He gives me a wink and a smile that steels me for my day ahead and then I'm out and walking in to my first class.

First up is math, where I find Carly when I enter the classroom. She looks up from the book she's reading and blinks for a moment, probably not believing its me. Then she's up out of her chair, racing over to me.

"Oh my God, Capri. You're back. Are you okay?" The slightly overweight girl with freckles and auburn hair genuinely seems worried. I've had many days off in the past because of my injuries sustained at home, but this time, her eyes offer me newfound warmth.

"Yeah, my first bout of Covid. I'm good now." I smile and move to the desk beside hers. Everyone else seems to have had the virus, except me. Probably because, besides school, I don't go out. When the school board shut classes down because of lockdowns, everyone studied online and kept the virus from spreading like wildfire to all the students.

"You get sick a lot," she says, not snidely but merely an observation. Truth is, I haven't been sick in a long time, but no one at school knows that. They must think I have a poor immune system with the number of days I'm absent.

I wish I could tell them the truth, but now that I'm out of my situation, what's the point?

"Mm hmm." It's all I can say as the teacher, Mr. McIntosh, walks in. He spots me and smiles.

"Miss Lennon. Welcome back." He places his briefcase on the desk before opening it and taking some papers out.

"Thank you," I offer quietly.

"Feeling better?" he asks, slanting his eyes my way before pulling his chair out.

"Much better."

"Good. Please stay back after class so I can give you some work you need to catch up on."

Great. Now I have double the load. All because of my angry father. Didn't he ever realize by hurting me and having me miss so much school, I'd be at risk of failing?

The very thing he hasn't wanted to happen.

The rest of the class files in and before long, the bell rings and we're sinking our teeth into algebra. I've always been pretty good at math, so the class is one of my favorites. And Mr. McIntosh is nice.

A few students stared at me when they arrived, but other than that, I'm back to being a nobody. Insignificant and mostly invisible.

By lunchtime, I'm back into the swing of things.

Upon entering the cafeteria, we line up and grab plates of food. I've opted for a healthy salad and juice. Carly gets the lasagna and a coke.

Steph waves us over when we turn and look over the sea of faces. We sit at our own table, other students avoiding us, choosing to stick to their cliques. The noise level is almost deafening as laughter and talking fill the large space.

"Hi," offers Steph, a little less enthusiastic than Carly. She's got jet-black hair, tied up in a messy bun and mascara and eyeliner way too dark. Her nail polish matches her hair color, which in turn makes her skin appear even paler. But somehow, she manages to pull off the goth look.

"Hey," I say, placing my bag and tray on the table.

Once we're all seated, Steph leans across the table and whisper shouts, "You weren't on the bus this morning."

Normally, we ride to school every day. She gets on after me, but I always save her a seat.

"I had to sit next to Daniel Walden." She glances around, making sure no one can hear her. "He smells. Bad body odor. Someone ought to tell him he needs deodorant."

I chuckle at that. I can imagine her with her hand covering her face the whole way just to block out the nauseous aroma.

She's not finished, "Becky Harper told me she saw you get out of a guy's car. A very handsome guy. Do tell."

Carly drills me with a stare so hard, I don't even have to turn fully to get the full effect of it.

What do I say? Do I tell them I've left home and I'm living with two brothers?

If I say nothing, they'll think I'm dating Atlas.

Knowing I need to give them some rope, I leave out the part about him saving me from jumping off the bridge and instead opt for, "I ran away from home. I'm kind of staying with Atlas and his brother for a while. Until I figure out my next move."

Steph is all eyes and lifted brows. "You ran away?"

"Yeah, ah, things weren't good at home." No need to elaborate. I'm sure they'll get it.

"So, where did you meet Atlas?" I have their full attention. I think they're shocked, not only by the news that I left home, but the fact that I'm living with two guys. After all, we avoid them like the plague at school and they do the same to us.

I've never had a boyfriend. Whilst most of the girls in our grade are boy crazy and a lot are dating, we three are virtuous singles.

"We've known each other for a while. We met through my father." Liar. Liar. Pants on fire.

They each eye me skeptically but don't push it, thankfully. I hate lying, but I can't give them the truth.

"Why did you want to move out?" asks Carly, suddenly interested in my private life.

I place my fork down and take a sip of my juice, steadying myself for another revelation.

"My dad isn't a nice man." I glance up to find them nodding at my answer, but they don't get the full gravity of my statement. They probably think he's just a little too strict. If only. I could handle him if it was simply a case of an overprotective parent. God. At least I'd know he cared. But he has no heart or compassion. I know no love from the man. Only hate, anger, and abuse.

"My dad pretty much lets me do what I want, and so does my mom. I have a curfew, of course, but I'm allowed to go to the mall and do stuff on weekends if I want," Carly pipes up.

"I'll probably still be living there in my twenties." She laughs and I feel envious of her. I shouldn't because most of the kids at this school probably have similar parents. It's normal.

"Mine isn't home much. He works away," admits Steph, scrolling through her phone.

"Well, I say, good for you. If you're happier, then we're happy for you." Carly is smiling at me. I'm grateful to have their support. They've accepted my situation, which means when Atlas picks me up and drops me off, there won't be further questions.

"Yeah. What she said. Maybe now you'll come to the mall with us?" Steph adds, offering for the first time in ages. My response was always no, so she gave up asking, keeping our friendship distant because of it. Maybe now the three of us can become closer.

As much as I had a meltdown when I thought my father was at the mall when I went with Atlas, I'd like to think I could go and be safe with my friends. I want to be like a normal seventeen-year-old. Finally. After never being allowed out.

"I'd like that."

The rest of lunch and the day go by quickly and soon, I'm walking toward the school gate, finding Atlas standing just outside it, like a parent picking up their small child. He grins when he sees me and I have to admit, it's nice to be greeted in such a way. It's also nice not having to catch the bus.

"Hey, girl. How was your first day back?" He grabs my bag as we walk to his pickup. A few students watch us and whisper, but I don't mind. Let them talk. It's nothing I haven't had to deal with. Plus, I don't mind gossip about Atlas and me, even though I know he's gay.

"It was better than I thought. I've got a bit of homework to catch up on but other than that, it was uneventful."

"Well then, let's go get that coffee I promised you."

Once we're settled at a table with our coffees, Atlas rubs his neck and appears a bit sheepish as he says, "So, I kinda have a date tonight."

I cough loudly as I nearly choke on my drink.

"What?"

He watches me carefully while I internally freak out because if he has a date; it means I'm going to be left alone with Killian. And we all know how that will go.

"I'm going to dinner and then bowling with a guy I met recently who came into the shop."

I should be happy for him. I am happy for him, but all I can think about is not having him around tonight. He's become my security blanket in such a short time.

"Oh. That's great." My attempt at being happy for him fails as my voice falls flat. I haven't heard him mention anyone besides Jayden.

"Hey. What's up?" His head bounces around, attempting to hold my gaze.

It's silly for me to feel this way. He owes me nothing. I can be alone with his brother for a few hours, right?

I'm shaking my head. "It's nothing. I'm fine. Really."

My eyes lower to my coffee as I let my hair fall into my face.

"You can't fool me, Capri. Tell me what's going on in that mind of yours. Do you want me to cancel my date?"

Yes. "No!"

"Then why are you acting like your favorite pet just went missing?"

"It's silly. I'm being silly."

"Look at me." It's not a demand but more of a soft coaxing.

Raising my eyes, I only find compassion. And concern. Something I've never had a lot of.

"I'm just nervous about being left with Kill."

A knowing smile appears on his face. "You're scared of my brother?"

"Not scared. Just uncomfortable." It's true. He puts me on edge with his disdain and attitude whenever I'm around. Atlas is the happy medium between us.

"I'll have a word to him before I leave to make sure he's on his best behavior, okay? If he's not playing nice, you call me, and I'll come straight home."

He'd cut his date short for me? I can't believe he would, which makes me feel stupid for acting like a child. I'm nearly eighteen. I've been through the ringer at home. Surely, I can be in the same house as a broody guy for the evening.

"That's okay. I'm sorry. I can handle Killian. You go and have a great time. We'll be fine."

The words are a lie. I don't think I'll ever be fine around the handsome ass.

NINETEEN

Killian

"You're leaving me with your foster child?" He expects me to babysit when I've specifically said right from the get-go that I'm not going to have anything to do with the girl.

"Quit being a dick. I'm going out for a few hours, which I don't do often, so I need to know you're not going to frighten her or jeopardize her safety. She's beginning to settle in and trust me. The last thing I need is to be talking her down from that bridge again because you can't find it in you to be civil."

I knew it would happen. I just didn't expect it to be so fast. She hasn't even been with us for a week and already he's thrusting us alone together, expecting me to watch out for her.

I eye him as he throws on a clean shirt to match his

black pants. While I'm happy that he's going on a date, the fact that he's leaving me with a female whose eyes incinerate me with their sadness leaves me antsy. She makes me nervous. A timid flighty little kitten who I don't know how to act around. A part of me can relate to her deep-set pain, but it's too familiar to my own. It reminds me of the volatile relationship I have with my father. The way she carries herself. The emotions leaching out of each furtive glance. Her attempt at being brave when I know she's anything but. I used to be like her. Before I toughened the fuck up and decided I wasn't going to become a victim. I've taken control of my own destiny and it's freeing. I hate the fact that as soon as she entered our home; it stirred up unhappy memories.

But Atlas is the only true family I have, so I need to suck it up and get through tonight without going to the shed and raging again.

"Fine. I'll behave. But you owe me."

He smiles, moving to the bed and bending down to put his black shoes on. "Name it."

Pfft. I know I won't get him to honor the favor, so I say, "I'll get back to you on that."

Turning his wrist over, he checks his watch. "Shit. Gotta get moving. You good?" he asks, standing and patting me on the shoulder.

"Yep."

And then he's moving into the hallway, heading for the kitchen where I know Capri is cooking dinner, a spark in his eyes I haven't seen in a long time.

I scrub my hand over my face. This night is going to suck.

When the door shuts a few minutes later, the atmosphere changes in the house. Perhaps it's my state of mind, but when it's just me and her, I feel it. The tension. The awkwardness. We don't know anything about each other apart from past trauma. We're strangers.

What do I do? Do I hole up in my room all night? Totally ignore her? No. This is my home. Why should I have to? If Atlas' date works out, there's going to be more nights like this.

Plus, my stomach rumbles at the smell brewing from the kitchen. It's wafting through the whole house.

I'm going to attempt to act normal.

After finishing work, I'm showered and wearing a pair of basketball shorts and a white tank. It's six o'clock.

Normally I'd play a few rounds of Fortnite and chill with a beer. So that's what I'm going to do. Why change my routine for her?

Padding down the hallway, I steel myself for the sight of her. She's been in her room until a little while ago, doing schoolwork, so I haven't seen her all day.

When I round the corner, I stop in my tracks. There are pots boiling on the stove alongside a pan of what appears to be a Bolognaise sauce. She doesn't see me at first, so I remain still, watching her in her element fussing over the meal. Her hair is in a messy bun, tendrils falling around her face and at the back of her neck. That's not what drags my eyes up and down her body, though. It's what she's wearing.

A Linkin Park black rock shirt with a pair of extra short denim cutoffs. Damn, her legs are milky white, long and super smooth. Her shirt grabs my attention for an extra heartbeat. The band is one of my favorites. I can't believe the mouse of a girl would be into their music. She comes off as a Taylor Swift fan.

A gasp and squeal catch my attention as she turns her head to find me ogling her. She drops the spoon, covered in tomato sauce, onto the tiles and brings her hand to her throat.

"Oh, you scared me!" She's all wide-eyed, frightened innocence. It stirs something inside me that it most definitely shouldn't. And when she catches me in the pools of her emotive eyes, I'm free-falling. It feels like jumping off the highest cliff, your stomach left far behind. You know, for a moment, an excited exhilaration will take over before the anxiety kicks in. Knowing at the bottom there's going to be nothing left of you.

I feel her sadness like it's my own. It's disconcerting. I've never normally been affected by a chick's eyes before. I'm more of a breast guy. But this girl's stare pierces you right beneath the ribs.

My eyes blink as I move to the fridge to grab that beer I wanted earlier, not game to speak. If I find those eyes again, I might do or say something I regret, so instead, I crack open the top, take a swig and saunter out to begin my game of Fortnite, finally able to take a breath.

I feel her watching me the entire time. What does she see? Hopefully, it's a douche because that's what I want to remain to her. No, I *need* to remain that to her. It's easier. Then I don't have to confront buried emotions within myself that she mirrors with her own fucked up shit.

I know I'm being a dick. The chick's done nothing to

me other than show up. I've made up my mind about her without getting to know her. I'm being judgmental. But she's not permanent here. She's going to be moving out soon, and then Atlas and I can get back to normal.

Twenty

Capri

After cleaning up the mess on the floor because Killian startled me, I take a couple of plates from the cupboard and begin dishing up the spaghetti bolognaise I've cooked. I'm not sure if he will want to eat my food after he so clearly ignored me earlier, but I'm living in his house, so I need to be courteous. I need to show him that his attitude doesn't bother me, which it most certainly does. The way he just appeared in the doorway, wearing a tank that showed off his toned physique, has my heart galloping like a wild steed with a rock settling in my throat.

He openly stared at me. I can't figure him out. No doubt he saw my worn clothes and came to his own conclusions like so many of the kids at school. Poor little girl without money who lives in poverty.

Well, if my father didn't drink his money away and

provided for me, I wouldn't have to accept hand-me-downs from Carly or Steph. On the rare occasion I asked my father for new clothes, and he left me fifty dollars. I always shopped at thrift stores to make the dollars go further.

When I've got dinner served, I walk into the living room and call out, above the din of the game he's playing, "Dinner's ready."

His head tilts slightly and his shoulders stiffen, but apart from that, it's as if he hasn't heard me. Well, screw him. He can eat it cold.

On a sigh, I walk away and sit down at the table to eat mine. I wonder how Atlas' date is going. I want to see him happy but at the same time, I kind of hope it doesn't go well so I don't have to suffer through another icy night like tonight. And I'm not talking about the outside temperature.

I finish my meal and clean up, walking back out to find Kill in the same spot. I don't bother expending energy by speaking. Instead, I head to my room to do some more catching up on schoolwork. It helps keep my mind busy.

After about ten minutes of working on an English assignment, I hear the rattle of cutlery in the kitchen. A smile forms on my lips. He's eating my food. Even if he did wait until I left. He likes my cooking. It shouldn't bring warmth to my chest, but it does.

Atlas arrives home late. I'm still poring over books at ten o'clock when the front door opens and closes. Mumbles down the hall let me know Kill is still awake, too.

I decide I've done enough homework for the evening and I'm putting my books in my bag when there's a knock at my door.

"Come in."

The door opens, and Atlas walks in smiling.

"I take it your date went well?" I ask, glad to see him happy, but my earlier fears of having to spend more time alone with Killian resurface.

He floats across to my bed and sits. I can almost see the stars in his eyes.

"He's super nice. We hit it off straight away."

"That's great. When do we get to meet him?" I finish stashing my books and zip up my backpack. Rising, I walk to the bed and sit beside him.

"Soon. I'm seeing him again this weekend."

Even though the idea of being alone with Kill again disturbs me, I don't let Atlas see it. Rather, I plaster on a grin, turning my head to him.

"So, what's his name?" I offer, in my cheeriest voice.

He's buzzing. "Coby. He's 19, and he works in the cafe close to our repair shop. It's on the same road, about 200 yards up. That's how we met."

"Oooh. Nice. You can see him every day on your lunch break."

Atlas blushes. Something I haven't seen him do yet, but it's sweet. "I'm planning on it. I'm also going to ask him if he has any positions available if you're interested. They're so busy. You could do afternoons. I think they shut at five, which would be perfect because Kill and I finish then too."

"Really? That would be fantastic. Anything is a bonus." The idea of getting my own money is exciting. I want to pay my way somewhat and be more independent. I'm genuinely excited.

"I can't promise anything, but I'll talk to Coby tomorrow."

"Thank you. Once again. You're going above and beyond."

He rises from my bed. "You're very welcome. Everyone needs a leg up sometimes. This is me giving you one." He moves toward the door. "I'm hitting the sack. You should too. I'll see you in the morning."

"Goodnight."

He leaves, gently closing my door. My mind is not going to be able to shut down for sleep. It's already alive with thoughts of getting a job. It will mean doing homework at night, but that's okay. I'm not normally in bed before 10 p.m. anyway.

I get changed and turn my light off. In bed I lay on my back, shutting my eyes, but I don't fall asleep. Instead, I focus on a broody dark-haired guy who dislikes me. The issue is with him. I hope Atlas' words of Kill coming around and warming up to me are true. For so long, I've lived with conflict and negative energy. I don't want that anymore. This is a new start for me. A chance to turn my life around.

My insides flutter at the memory of him scanning me from head to toe in the kitchen earlier. Even if it was because he didn't like what he saw, he's got the X-factor in spades.

He's the type of guy my dad would warn me about and perhaps that has something to do with my curiosity about Killian MacKenzie and not the fact that whenever he's in the same room as me, I'm a hot mess.

Ugh. Stop thinking about a guy who would send you packing in a heartbeat if his brother didn't want you here so much.

I roll onto my side, fluffing my pillow, attempting to zone out and think of nothing, but it's futile. At midnight, I'm still wide awake.

Throwing the covers off, I get up, deciding to go to the kitchen and heat a glass of milk in the hopes it will help me fall asleep.

Instead of turning the overhead light on, I opt for the small bedside lamp. It offers a hazy glow and isn't as harsh on the eyes.

With my sleep shorts and tank on, I quietly shuffle down the hallway, not expecting to find anyone hunched over their phone in the dark. Kill is sitting at the table wearing nothing but his signature boxers. He sits up when I enter. Even though it's dark, apart from the glow of his cell, I can tell he's giving me a once-over.

"Hey. Sorry, I didn't know anyone was up."

A grunt.

I reach for a glass from the overhead cupboard before moving to the fridge to get the milk.

"Can't sleep either?" I ask, hoping I'll get at least a one-word answer.

He brushes a hand through his already messy hair before lowering it to the back of his neck and squeezing.

He doesn't reply, which, for some reason, really gets my temper flaring. Normally I'm not a hothead, but enough is enough. I'm trying to be nice. The least he can do is answer me.

I slam the fridge door shut and turn to him. "What is your problem with me? I've been nothing but nice to you. Are you always going to ignore me?"

He pushes his chair out so fast and is in my face in an instant. I move backwards until my back is against the counter.

He towers over me, smelling of a musky aftershave which is odd considering he hasn't shaved for at least a few days, judging by his stubble.

Both hands come up to the overhead cupboards, essentially caging me in.

My breath falters. I'm too scared to look up and see the anger on his face. It's bringing back horrible memories.

I squeeze my eyes shut and grit my teeth, waiting for the backlash. His breathing is choppy, his chest rising and falling. I'm waiting, but nothing happens. He stays like this for way too long before pushing off, leaving the chill of the air to grip me with icy fingers.

When I open my eyes again, he's gone, leaving me wondering what the hell just happened.

TWENTY-ONE

Killian

I was all set to tell her exactly why I would continue to ignore her, but when I noticed her shaking and cowering like the small kitten she is, I couldn't do it. She was genuinely frightened of me. I'm not a guy who hurts girls. The way she folded in on herself lets me know she's been a victim of physical abuse. It's clear as day that someone hurt her. Repeatedly. One doesn't have that reaction without the body being conditioned to it. A natural response. Without a doubt, I know it's her father. Atlas told me he's apparently a monster. Who else would it be? The very idea of it sours my stomach. I've had issues with my own dad, so I know how deeply it cuts to not have the love and support of someone who is meant to put their kids first. But for a grown-ass man to prey on his daughter brings about an anger in me like no other. Was it sexual abuse too? Acid rises into my throat.

I can understand Atlas' reaction of wanting to take matters into his own hands. Even though I don't want the girl living with us, it's got to suck to have gone through that.

Seeing her walk into the kitchen in those skimpy pajamas had me almost lose my shit. And when she grew some balls and called me out on the way I've been treating her, I wasn't sure if I wanted to yell at her or run my hands down her phenomenal body. I'm sure she doesn't even know how stunning she is. But she's more damaged than I am, so I need to keep my distance. I don't need to be friends with someone with so much baggage. It'll only drag me down. I'm getting my life together. I don't need her drama.

Despite all that, I eat her food. She's a good cook. I consider myself decent, but the spaghetti bolognaise she whipped up is to die for. The one serving I consumed earlier wasn't enough. I have a second helping before throwing my plate in the dishwasher and turning it on.

Okay, so maybe there are some perks to having a female in the house. It means I don't have to cook every night. Not that I don't love it but on long days at work, the last thing I feel like doing is making something that takes forever to prepare.

In my room, I undress and lie under the covers, thinking about the little stray. What is her full story? She must have decided to off herself because she felt there was nothing else left for her. I can't say I haven't wondered if I'd have been better off dead in the past when my own life-giver failed to accept me for who I am and what I want out of life. Things that don't fit his agenda. And seeing the way he treated Atlas had me questioning everything.

He's a bastard. Plain and simple. One who now wants our support when we never had his. It's a hard pill to swallow. A part of me still hopes that by pushing aside my disdain for the man and seeing him before he dies, he might utter the kind words I've longed to hear my entire life. And the other part has already cut the ties that bind and doesn't give a hoot about him.

All I've ever wanted was a dad like the kids at school who showed up to parent day. Who took them to the park to play ball. Who encouraged them when they felt like they never fit in.

Atlas took over that role. He's been my parent and sibling in many ways. And I've been his.

It's not meant to be that way, though. We're still practically kids. We shouldn't have to shoulder the role not meant for us.

I must sleep for about four hours because when the alarm goes off at seven, I feel mildly energized. I can survive on a few hours a night. Always have. Don't get me wrong, I'd love to be able to hunker down for a solid eight, but I guess it's just not in my makeup.

After a piping hot shower to revive me, I throw on my work shirt and shorts and head into the kitchen to find Atlas and Capri already at the table, sipping coffee.

"There's some left for you if you want," Atlas says on a yawn, nodding to the coffeepot.

Liquid gold. I give Capri a curt nod, noting her

surprise as I move to grab a cup and fill it with caffeinated goodness. Go me. I may officially stop ignoring her completely after feeling relatively sorry for her last night.

Even after sleep, guilt festers. I don't need to feel the emotion I carried with me since I was younger and worked so hard to get rid of, after telling my father I was dropping out of school and taking over the garage. So, I'm swallowing my damn pride and putting in mild effort.

"Are we starting on the F250 this morning?" my brother asks, finishing some lame ass cereal he buys for breakfast.

I'm an eggs and bacon guy, so I prepare enough for myself, wondering if Capri has eaten. Which I shouldn't be. She seems to know her way around the kitchen, so if she wants anything, she can get it. I'm not normally so selfish, but I don't want her thinking I'm trying to be BFFs.

She gets up to put her mug in the dishwasher and I can't help taking a peek. She's wearing a pleated short skirt with a polo top, as if she's about to play a round of tennis. My eyes zero in on her long legs, noting how smooth her skin appears. Atlas clears his throat to garner my attention and when I turn my head to him, I find his eyebrows reaching skyward in a 'what the hell' gesture. He's caught me ogling his pet and no doubt I'll be in for an earful later.

What does he expect? I'm a male. I notice these things. If a hot dude was in our kitchen, wearing skimpy clothes, I bet he'd be in full pervert mode.

In a huff, I turn back to my breakfast, turning the egg once.

"You ready to leave?" Atlas asks Capri.

I see it's almost eight. I need to get moving.

"Yeah, I'll just go grab my bag." She saunters off, leaving me with a quiet brother. I can feel him grilling me with his stare, even though I'm facing away.

Sure enough, when I turn, he's glaring at me. "What?" I ask, knowing full well what he's referring to.

"Don't go getting any ideas," he whisper-shouts. "I saw you drooling before. Don't even think of it. She doesn't need you ogling her. And what gives? I thought you were ignoring her?"

There's no time to answer because the girl in question strides back in with her hair tied up into a high ponytail and a smile on her face.

"Ready," she sings, only glancing at me for a second before addressing Atlas.

"We'll talk at work." He's picking up his keys from the counter and walking out. Before Capri leaves, she utters a quiet "Bye" to me.

All she gets in return is a grunt, which I still consider progress.

Twenty-Two

Capri

A week passes by way too quickly, but thankfully without incident. Kill ignores me. Atlas hovers.

We're in the truck on our way to my school when Atlas speaks up. "So, I asked Coby if there were any positions at the cafe he works at and there aren't."

"Oh," I mumble, deflated.

"But the office at the repair shop is in dire need of someone to organize files and to answer phones so I'm going to run it by Kill today. He can't say no. We've got to where we are so busy, neither of us can keep up with all that stuff. I can't believe I didn't think of it earlier."

My pulse speeds up. I don't want to get my hopes up, but the idea of working with Atlas pleases me. "Really? That would be great. Even though I've never had a job."

"Don't stress. We'll show you the ropes."

We, as in him and Kill. As if his brother will want me at his place of work and his home. He can barely tolerate me, although this morning and during the night, I could almost sense a shift. Or perhaps it's wishful thinking that we may get along.

"It'll be hard to convince your brother."

Atlas indicates, and we turn right. "Not if you see the state of the office. I can be very persuasive when I need to." He angles his head and smirks at me.

I laugh. "Like the night you talked me off the bridge?"

His face changes to something far more serious and the air thickens with unspoken words.

"Do you regret it?" he whispers, wiping his left hand over his mouth and chin.

Do I? No. I'm glad I didn't jump now. Being away from the house of horrors has allowed me to see the world through fresh eyes. Eyes that don't have to watch for the constant threats I dealt with daily.

"No." I half-turn in my seat toward him. "I'm glad you were there."

He relaxes again and grins back. "Me too."

We reach the school soon after, and Atlas finds a parking space in the lot. Kids scramble off the bus I used to catch, and others get out of cars as parents wave goodbye.

"I'll take you to show you the office at work after school. You can see for yourself what a nightmare it is."

I'm hoping it's not as bad as he's making out. If I'm only working weekday afternoons, it will take me forever just to sort things out. I pray I can keep up with that and do homework.

At least it will keep me busy and stop thoughts of my father coming looking for me at bay. I glance around for any sign of him and thankfully come up empty. His injuries inflicted by Atlas will be healing. Enough for him to leave the house now. He'll always have me peering over my shoulder. Will he forget all about coming for me when I turn eighteen? God, I hope so.

Atlas obviously picks up on where my mind is. "Don't worry about your dad. I'll wait until I see you walk into the building before I leave. He won't get close to you, Capri. I promise."

I'm grateful for his oath, but I know he can't watch me 24/7. I'm sure if my father wants me, he'll find a way. It's unsettling, to say the least. All I can do is pray he's been taught a lesson and keeps his distance.

"What if he calls the school one day soon and orders me home? They'll make me go with him because he's my legal guardian."

Atlas turns and looks out the window, watching the students walking in. He blows out his breath. "You need to talk to the guidance counselor or the principal and let them know what has gone on. Surely, they'll be understanding."

I'm shaking my head. "I can't. I don't know where to begin. It's embarrassing and shameful."

"Hey." His hand reaches out and stops to garner my reaction. When I don't pull back, he touches my arm. We're way past the no touching rule, but it's nice that he still lets me decide. "Do you want me to call them?"

"No!" I cry out. It's said with too much bite, so I contain myself. "I mean, no. Thank you though. I'll be fine. If I get called to the office because he's here to pick me up, I'll speak up then, but I don't think he'd do that. To risk being found out."

"Hmmm." It's all Atlas says in reply. I know he isn't convinced, but I open the door and begin getting out.

"I'll see you here after school, right?"

"Yep. Have a great day. And stay where there are plenty of people."

I nod, closing the door and walking in, hoping like hell I don't get a call to the office.

The day drags on. Although I'm constantly on alert every time the intercom goes off, thankfully I don't get the call.

I attempt to immerse myself in my work. I've just about caught up on assignments and reading from when I was away, which eases some of the pressure. The idea of having an after-school job with my own money brings about a sense of excitement. Being able to buy whatever I want, whenever I want, is a freedom I'm not used to.

And then a thought suddenly hits me. Atlas will pay me, right? What if he expects me to work for free because I'm living with them and not assisting financially? I'm paying my way via chores, but perhaps working at the shop for free is part of me living under their roof and giving them more in return.

No. He knows I want a paying job. He wouldn't expect me to volunteer.

Would he?

I walk into my last class. English. Carly and Steph are already there when I arrive.

"Hey," I offer cheerily, taking my seat in the middle of them.

"Hey yourself. How's the cute boy you're living with?" Carly asks, picking at her nails and giving me the side-eye.

Steph pipes up. "Cute boys, plural."

Placing my backpack on the floor and digging around for my notebook and pen, I sit up and reply. "For starters, one is gay. And the other one is a douche, so all is peachy."

Both girls laugh, but it's Steph who continues. "That doesn't stop you from banging brother number two." She bats her eyelashes and smiles seductively.

"Ahh, no. I wouldn't touch him with a forty-foot pole. He despises me anyway."

She doesn't give up on that. "A little hate sex, they say, is what every girl needs." Carly is nodding and I simply shake my head at both girls, knowing they are both still virgins like me. And since when have they become interested in boys? Have they suddenly become obsessed while I've been away like every other girl in school?

"Not going there. Not interested." I face the front, feeling the lie on my tongue. When Killian hedged me into the counter, towering over me, I felt *everything*. If he had grabbed me and kissed me, I probably would have let him. His scent and aura of danger had my body disobeying my mind. I can see why girls get into trouble with the rough-and-ready types. There's an allure. And that he is so darn handsome has even more of an impact. But there hasn't been a repeat since.

The teacher walks into class and places his briefcase down. "Good morning class. Today we're going to split up into pairs and look at different organisms under our microscopes."

Half of the class groans and the other half gives off some excited chatter. I'm fairly neutral when it comes to this class, so I remain quiet.

I don't get to work with my friends, instead I get partnered with Chase, a cool guy who is on the football team. We both meet at the side benches lining the perimeter of the class and sit down together in front of a microscope.

"Hey mouse. Haven't seen you around for a while." He's six foot something with a blonde crew cut and rippling muscles. Anyone who doesn't know his age would peg him for twenty-one, not seventeen. He's as cocky as they come because of his status, which makes me anxious. I've never been drawn to the popular guys.

My nickname at school is mouse because I'm quiet and don't mingle with anyone other than my two friends. I'm not part of any popular crowd or clique, so they assume I'm a timid little thing. In many ways, I am. That's the way I like it and that's the way I want to keep it.

He checks me out from head to toe. "You been away sick or something?"

With a quick peek at him, I answer, "Or something." Even though I've been back at school for a week, Chase has been absent. I don't care to ask why.

He nods, understanding that I don't want to tell him, which gets me off the hook. "Yeah, me too."

"Okay. You have six slides, each with…"

I tune the teacher out as Chase leans into my ear and whispers, "Why haven't I noticed you properly before? You're cute, mouse."

He's too close. A familiar sense of panic grips me. My blood roars in my ears as fight-or-flight mode kicks in.

"Get away from me!" It's said louder than I would have liked.

"Miss Lennon and Mr. Rubeck is there a problem?" the teacher asks with a frown on his face, his lips forming a slash on his face.

"No sir. Just getting to know my partner," Chase drawls, earning a few snickers from classmates. Two who are his friends.

I'm embarrassed and want to run out of the room as all eyes are on us. I don't do well with attention on me. My hands sweat. I wipe them on my skirt and attempt to focus on the task at hand.

Thankfully, after a chuckle, Chase moves back, obviously amused at my freak out. He'll know just who I am after that. I'm not someone who will swoon and gush over him.

Mr. Jackson continues to watch us sternly until we bring the microscope toward us. "After you," I offer, needing class to be over. I bite into my lower lip, fingers tightened into fists.

His grin is smarmy and unattractive to me. I don't get why females throw themselves at him.

"I'd love to break you in and watch you bleed." It's whispered in a husky voice. Upon a quick scan of the classroom, I find everyone focused on their task. All accept one girl. Michaela Gibbins. Head cheerleader. She's staring daggers at me. I can almost see her invisible claws coming out, ready to scratch my eyes out. She's been wanting Chase's attention all year and failing, so she obviously thinks I'm a threat now that the object of her desires is whispering to me. If only she knew. Can't she see the turmoil on my face? This very reason is why I don't mix with the cliques and prefer the company of Steph and Carly. There is so much school drama going on, I'm happy to be an outcast.

I focus back on my notepad and with shaking hands and a tremble in my voice, I almost cry, "You'll never find out."

Chase pretends to act offended, placing a hand on his chest. "Oh mouse. You wound me."

I squeeze my eyes tightly again, counting to ten in my head, over and over. It's been a coping mechanism over the years. Focusing on the numbers and not my fear.

One. Two. Three. Four...

Finally, after gathering myself, we get down to work, but I don't miss the grazing of his hand against mine every so often, which leads to me jerking away. He knows what he's doing. He's goading me and enjoying seeing my reaction. He's sick like my father.

After an eon, when the class is finally dismissed, I practically run from the room, ignoring the laughter as I exit. At my locker, I quickly stash the books I won't need overnight and grab the ones for homework. Then, I'm briskly walking out the door to find Atlas, almost throwing up on the way.

With my fingers working overtime, I send a quick message to Carly and Steph, explaining I had a migraine. Hopefully, it will be enough. They already rib me for being 'sick' all the time.

TWENTY-THREE

Atlas

When I see Capri fast-walking out, I'm immediately on guard. Something has happened. I can tell. Her face is downcast, and her right arm is swinging so wildly, she clips another student with it as she passes.

I'm out of my truck, walking to the gate before my brain can catch up. All kinds of scenarios run through my mind and none of them are good.

She practically plows into me as she exits.

"Hey! It's me." I grip both her shoulders to prevent her from falling, causing her to jerk upright with a horrified expression and then step back.

When she comprehends it's me, her shoulders deflate. "Oh, hey. Sorry. You scared me."

"Because you had your head down, looking like you were all set to break into a sprint. What's wrong?" If one of the students has been harassing her, I'll knock them for six.

Or even worse. Has her father been on campus? Suddenly my heart is kicking up its tempo, my muscles tensing further.

She knows it too because she offers me a calm, "It's okay. Just a stupid classmate asking me why he's never noticed me before. He was flirting, and I panicked."

I turn to her and ask, "A guy noticed you? Does that make you uncomfortable?" Given her history, I understand she has demons, but I'd think someone giving her attention would be good. Perhaps it's the wrong kind of attention, though. I wait for her answer.

Shaking her head, she replies, "It's silly now. One of the popular guys paid me attention, and it made me uncomfortable. I know it's irrational, but he's got a reputation around school."

"Do you need me to have words with this dude?" We climb in and buckle up. He starts the engine and pulls out of the lot.

"No! It's no big deal. Seriously. I doubt he'll even talk to me again."

I watch her to see if she's lying, but she has such a good poker face side on, I can't read her eyes.

"Well, just give me the word and I'll set him straight." I mean it. She's quickly becoming someone I want to nurture and protect at all costs. I want to give her what she's never had.

After we're on the main road to the repair shop, she whispers, "Thank you. No one's ever offered to stick up for me before."

"I've got your back now, Capri. You don't need to face anything alone."

With a smile and a nod, the conversation is over, and we travel in silence the rest of the way.

I park in our reserved spot at the shop and walk Capri inside. I can tell she's nervous, so I say, "Relax. I've spoken to Kill. He's on board for you to do some hours here."

She glances at me in disbelief, adjusting her backpack. "Yeah, right. I'm sure. Tell me what he really said."

In all honesty, he was a hard cookie to crumble. We almost had another argument over her, but after I convinced him we needed someone and she would stay out of his way, he reluctantly relented. After a few choice words, of course.

The office is warm compared to outside. I installed a wall heater which has been going all day. Outside, the wind has kicked up, causing the temperature to feel below zero, even though it's not.

Kill is under a Buick, so he hasn't noticed our arrival. He's got music playing and is oblivious to anything else apart from what he's doing. That's one thing I give him credit for. He's fully focused on the job at hand and is darn good at it. He doesn't get distracted easily.

We've got to wait on parts for the F250, so while we do that, we'll get other jobs done.

In the office, Capri looks all around. It's a mess. I notice her wide eyes and gently say, "I know it looks like a mammoth task, but you don't have to do it all at once. Small baby steps."

I move to the files sitting on top of the desk. "These here all need to be put in that filing cabinet, in alphabetical order. Use the last name. Once you've done that, come and get me and we'll move on to the next thing."

"Oh, okay." She places her bag on a chair. "That is easy enough."

"You good for a bit?"

"Sure. I'll come get you when I'm finished."

And so, I move into the large adjoining industrial shed to help Kill.

"How's it coming along?" I ask, only seeing his legs from under the vehicle.

He rolls out, face with spots of oil on it. "It's got a cracked intake manifold. Coolant has leaked dry." My brother stands and wipes his hands on an old rag. "I'd better call the owner and tell him."

When he moves toward the office, I decide I need to warn him. "Capri is in there tending to some filing. Just thought you should know."

His back straightens, fingers curling into balls. I expect more rebuttal, but he simply begins walking again. Should I go with him?

I'm about to walk after him, then stop myself. No. If she's going to be doing some afternoons every week, they need to get used to each other.

Twenty-Four

Killian

I will not let her affect me. I'm not. But as soon as I step over the threshold into the cluttered workspace, she's there. An armful of files, standing at the cabinet, stock still when she sees me. Her sad, sensational eyes grind me to a halt, too. The afternoon sunlight streaks in, dappling her in a halo. We're both frozen.

My eyes move with no effort, roving down her long legs in that freaking pleated skirt. They remind me of fine porcelain, all delicate and flawless. Moving up past her waist, which tapers in perfectly, her chest expands and fills out her polo shirt like a second skin.

I'm staring.

Her voice has me raising my eyes north to her face again. "Hi."

It's like a sweet melody. Or the softest lullaby. For a

second, I remain rooted to the spot, gawking. She blinks while waiting for me to either say something or ignore her.

I want to do the second. I truly do. Because ignoring her means less interaction. Less hearing her voice. Less drowning in her sadness. But I grind my teeth and gather all my humanity, knowing if I'm a dick to her here at work, Atlas will be on my case big time, and I don't need the tension here as well.

"Hey." There's way too much silence and awkwardness. If I simply walk off, I'll still look like an ass, but I don't know what to say to the meek girl.

"Did you want me to make you a coffee? I can do this in a moment. Atlas might like one too."

She's trying hard. Too hard. It takes me back to my thoughts about her father. I'm guessing to stay in his good graces if that were even possible. She needed to be at his every beck and call. I don't want her feeling like she has to do that with us.

So instead, I say, "You don't have to. I've got a phone call to make and then I can make us all one. You drink coffee, yeah?"

Her brown eyes expand in shock, and I even surprised myself. It's not an unpleasant thing. Being nice to her. But I'm not throwing her the whole bone. I'll give her scraps. For Atlas.

"Yeah. White with no sugar." Her cheeks are instantly a rosy pink as she watches me. Probably waiting for me to tell her I was joking and to get it herself.

I nod and pick up the phone, dialing the customer and telling him how much his repair is going to cost.

Then I'm in the kitchen, wondering what the hell I'm doing, as I grab three cups and pour coffee into them.

When I return, she's all but finished the pile of files. A fast worker. Hmm. Maybe she can get this office back into shape. It's just been so busy here lately that everything has piled up and by the end of the day, my brother and I are both too exhausted to stay behind to catch up.

I place her drink down on the desk.

"Thank you," she says, moving over to pick it up. Watching her blow on it with her pouty mouth and then take a sip has my dick hardening, so I make a quick exit out to Atlas with his drink.

This is not good. My body is betraying me already. I knew the second I laid eyes on this girl, she was going to be my downfall.

TWENTY-FIVE

Capri

He spoke to me. More than one sentence. Is that progress or just a fluke?

For a few brief moments, we stood in a bubble. Nothing else around as we focused on each other. I wasn't expecting him to walk through the sliding door from the workshop so soon after my arrival. And Lord, my heart fluttered wildly when he stopped to check me out. It's a far different reaction to the way Chase had acted in class today. For some insane reason, when Killian stares at me like he just did, my body reacts. Not in a horrible way, either. He's got an allure about him. Maybe it's the fact that it's Atlas' brother and I know he can't be all bad, even though he's been rude and arrogant to me so far. Plus, he's not cocky like Chase. Dark, but not cocky. He's got a different air about him. One I can't yet pinpoint.

This afternoon has been a nice change. Like perhaps he's finally accepting me into their world for however long I plan on staying. I'm not going to hope for too much though where he's concerned. He's just as likely to ignore me again later.

Time flies by and as I stand back and look at my progress, a sense of pride fills me. There's still a lot to do, but I've made a dent. Atlas showed me how to answer the phone and take messages, so between that and organizing, I'm surprised when the boys come in and say it's time to leave.

"Wow! Look at this place. We can see the desk now," Atlas beams.

Killian's gaze scans the office before settling on me. A flicker of something resembling 'good job' shimmers in his dark eyes before it leaves and is replaced by his indifference.

"I think a couple of pizzas for dinner sounds good. What about you two?" Atlas glances between Kill and me.

With a nod, I reply, "I'm easy."

Killian coughs before mumbling under his breath, "I bet."

When I find his face again, it almost appears as if he's sorry for what he said. As if it's a habit and he didn't mean to say it. But it's too late.

I immediately go on the defense. He's back to being nasty, and it's only been an hour. "Excuse me?" My voice is whiny and out of character.

Atlas chimes in before things can escalate. "Kill, stop being a bully. Look at this place. You should be thanking her, not shooting off snarky comments." He shakes his head in disbelief at his brother, who stalks outside to the car.

"I thought we were doing better today. He spoke to me civilly." I pick up my backpack and wait for Atlas to lead the way. I'm not walking out without him by my side.

After locking up, I climb into the back, feelings of anger and disappointment flooding me. I can't work out why he changed his attitude toward me so fast. Being near him is like being on a roller coaster. You never know what he's going to say or do or what mood he's in. I should never have thought his improved mood would stay.

I sit and watch the scenery go by, a tense silence in the front. It isn't until we're turning into the parking lot at a pizza takeout that Atlas asks, "What do you like on your pizza, Capri?"

Not daring to say, 'I'm easy' again, I answer with, "Anything without olives and I'm good."

"Kill?"

The broody brother mumbles, "Meat lovers." Of course, he'd choose a typical guy's pizza.

"Okay, I'll be back soon. You two try not to tear each other's heads off." Atlas turns the car off and is out before I can argue with him to stay and send Killian.

Great. Now I have to be in a confined space with the dude. This is going to be the most uncomfortable fifteen minutes of my life.

He adjusts himself, trying to stretch his legs but failing because of his height, so instead he sighs and places his head back on the rest.

The tense silence is so strong, I allow a few minutes of

it to go by before I can't stand it anymore. I blurt out, "I'm not easy. I've never even had sex."

Why I need to clarify that with him, I'm not sure, but I certainly don't want him thinking I put out for any guy. He doesn't know me at all, so for him to assume is very childish.

I watch his fingers tighten on his thigh.

"Whatever. I really don't care." His voice is gruff. Gone is the person from earlier who I hoped I could have some kind of amicable relationship with. Not friends, but not enemies either. It appears he just doesn't care.

Part of me wonders why. Does he feel threatened by me? Does he think I'll take Atlas away from him, even though they are twins? But that's so crazy. They have a bond between them that far outweighs anything I could establish.

"You've made that abundantly clear." I don't know if he hears me or not because he's back to ignoring me.

For the first time in my life, I choose to voice my opinion rather than keep it to myself, and I'm not punished. It's the exact opposite. I get no response whatsoever.

Deciding to leave him alone, I open my backpack and pull out my laptop so I can focus on my social studies homework. The jerk in front has no intention of making conversation and I don't care to sit in the uncomfortable silence without something to do.

I settle in, attempting to focus, but all I end up doing is re-reading each sentence three or four times on the screen.

The guy sitting in the front passenger seat is stealing

all my attention by simply being there. The scent of oil, grease and a hint of cologne lightly perfumes the air. It's not horrible. It's distracting though.

Killian's cell peals out into the deafening silence, making me jump. He pulls it from his shirt pocket and answers it.

"Mom."

No 'Hey, Mom' or 'Hi, Mom.'

"Yep."

Okay, very terse. Is this how he speaks to her all the time? Suddenly, I don't feel like I've been singled out. It's not just me.

"That's not my problem. I'm not going. I told you that." His leg jiggles and it's easy to determine he's getting agitated, so I decide to go into the pizza restaurant to wait with Atlas so Kill can have some privacy. He glances my way when I get out with a frown on his face. Our eyes meet for a split second before I turn and shut the door.

There are quite a few cars in the lot, so it must be busy. As I'm walking toward the entrance, I notice a man to my right, out of my peripheral vision. Without too much thought, I turn my head further and then freeze.

Every atom inside me reacts in an all too familiar way. My heart begins jack hammering, my skin prickling, and a deep-seated fear brings about nausea and sweating. I can't move even if I try. And as if the man senses me gawking, his evil eyes find mine.

Everything spirals. From the moment his grin forms in the sick way it always has until his legs begin a new course toward me, I'm transported back to the prison I've escaped.

"Well, well, look who we have here. You didn't do a very good job of staying invisible, did you sweetness?" His voice has me gag. The very sight of him makes the past few days seem like a dream I've just woken up from. Evidence of the beating Atlas gave him shows via the bruising and swelling on his face. It brings me a small amount of joy to know he must have been hurting. I wonder if he went to the doctor and told them or if he lied like he always does.

"Cat got your tongue? That's no way to greet your father." His hard features and black, soulless eyes only show a glimmer of what he's like on the inside.

My head tilts so I can keep an eye on the front entrance, hoping at any moment Atlas will walk out and see us.

Where the hell is he, anyway? It's surely been longer than fifteen minutes.

When I don't answer, he closes the gap and grips my arm. Hard. "Still need to be taught some respect, I see." He shakes me, causing my head to jiggle and pain to shoot through my shoulder. "When I speak, you answer me!" His voice raises, instilling an icy dread to wash through my veins. This is the point where he gets aggressive. I know him so well. His tells. "I don't need to answer to you anymore." It's my meek voice I've almost stopped using altogether these past few days, but give me one second in his presence and it's back.

"You're wrong. I'm still your father. Just because you've been gallivanting around like a whore with that boy doesn't mean I'm not going to drag your ass back home where you belong."

My breath stops. No. He wouldn't. A couple walk past and watch, but they don't stop to intervene. Even when I meet the woman's eyes and plead silently.

"I'm not going with you." Surely out in public he won't really haul me to his car. And my attempt at defying him surprises me. I wouldn't have done it before I left, but living with Atlas and Killian, even for a short while, has given me enough breathing space to know that how I was treated was disgusting. I'm not going back there. I can't. If I have to scream blue murder, I will, because if he gets me in that car, there's no way I'll ever be able to leave again. He'll keep me tied up in that basement forever.

"Oh yes, you fucking are." He pulls on me as a thick, deep voice speaks from behind me.

"Let her go."

Killian.

My father spins with a surprised expression. "Who the fuck are you?"

Kill steps in front of me and right into my monster's face. He's taller than my father and has puffed himself up to look equally as menacing. "I'm the one who is going to put you on the ground if you don't walk away."

Every muscle in his body is taut, ready to fight if he must. I'm shocked he's sticking up for me. He's the one I thought would be happy to see me go, regardless of the way I went.

Now I've had both brothers come to my defense.

My father laughs. He clearly is deranged if he thinks he won't be beaten up again by someone younger, considering the lingering marks that prove the first time.

I truly hate him. Most people think 'oh, hate is a strong

word', but I absolutely one hundred percent loathe him. There's not an ounce of pity, love, or compassion toward him. I don't care if he lives or dies. Preferably the second, because only then will I have true freedom.

"Oh, you think you can take me, punk? You'd have to grow some balls first."

Clearly, he has a death wish because even from behind I notice the moment everything changes.

Kill growls and grabs my father by the front of his shirt, pushing him into a nearby car. Hard.

"Oh, my balls are just fine, but judging by the color of your face, yours haven't dropped yet. Now tell me, you scumbag, why were you picking on a defenseless girl, huh? Is that your thing? You can't pick on a male because you know you'll lose? So instead, you go for someone smaller and weaker?"

I'm not sure how I feel about him calling me weak, but now is not the time to question it.

At that moment, Atlas walks out the front door, carrying three pizza boxes. His face changes from happy to 'what the fuck' in a fraction of a second when he zeroes in on his brother and the very man he protected me from.

His eyes pivot to me, and he's practically running across the pavement. "Here. Take these. Go get in the car, Capri. Now." He's fishing his keys out once I take the boxes.

Only, I don't want to go. I want to watch what happens. It's almost like they're giving me some retribution. Some revenge. I'm not missing it. Not for a second.

I shake my head. "I'm not moving. I need to see this."

He stares me down, pleading with his eyes, but when he sees me standing firm, he gives a quick nod, turning to the ruckus, which has already attracted attention.

My father's eyes are fixed on Atlas now. He appears a little unsure for a moment but schools it, not wanting to show any vulnerability.

Both boys are on him then. "We meet again. I thought I told you to stay away from your daughter."

Twenty-Six

Killian

I wondered if this dick was Capri's father, and Atlas has just confirmed it for me.

I've got him pressed into an SUV using a hold he won't break free from. The old man thinks he's invincible, but he's weak.

He spits in my face after I ask him if he loves praying on those weaker than him.

"You know nothing. Capri is legally mine, and you can't do anything about that. She's coming home with me."

My brother has appeared and is speaking to Capri, but it's just background noise. My anger meter is through the roof and if this douche thinks he's taking her anywhere, he's insane.

I hear the click of a camera or two not far away,

knowing some strangers are filming, but I don't care. I'll use it to my advantage.

"I'm not sending her anywhere with you. You're nothing but a child abuser, you sick fuck. You're gonna have to get through me and my brother. Looks like you failed the first time."

I grin in his face, watching his skin go scarlet with rage. Oh yeah, this bastard has issues.

Atlas is at my side. "Did I not make myself clear last time? I think I need to release those emails to the cops and get you off the streets. Seems like you're too stupid to take good advice and let your daughter go. She's nothing to you. Nothing but an outlet for your anger. I'd say you'll get quite a few years locked up, don't you?"

Atlas runs his thumb over one of the moron's bruises on his cheek and pushes, causing the man to buck and fight. I'm high on adrenaline, so there's no way he's getting away.

"Purple suits you. Perhaps I need to paint all your skin the same color."

My face turns to Atlas. I've never heard him so dark. Where has my caring, compassionate brother gone? I mean, I've seen him pissed sure, but this is on a whole new level. He's like it because of *her*. He really cares for her.

In my own effed up way, I guess I don't want anything to happen to her either.

I push him further into the metal door. "Call the cops, brother. This trash needs to be taken off the street."

"You stupid prick. Let me go!" He turns to Capri, who is wide-eyed and as still as a statue. Ghostly pale. "Tell them! I do what any father does and give you the discipline you need. It's a cruel world, and I'm simply toughening you up."

Her gaze finds mine and then Atlas and I see the imperceptible nod, giving him permission to call.

Five minutes later, a squad car pulls up and two officers walk over.

"What's going on here?"

We tell them about how this debacle began. One female takes notes while the other assesses the situation.

We step back while they question Capri's father. It's not a surprise that he makes out like we accosted him.

I walk over to the girl at the center of it all. She stiffens when I approach, so I attempt to appear less intimidating by dropping my shoulders and offering a small smile.

"You okay to talk with the police and tell them everything? Show them your phone?"

"Yes. I'll do whatever it takes. I'll never be free until he's either dead or locked away."

I hold out my hands for the pizza's which she hands over and then walks to stand beside Atlas.

She seems smaller and even more timid right now, if that's possible. Something in me breaks. The iron bars breaking around my stubborn attempt at pushing her away. Watching her being taken away by the female to the back of the squad car where they can talk in private with her shoulders slumped, her steps cautious, I can't help but feel her pain. She didn't ask for any of this. She was born into a shitty situation, like some of us. Like me and my brother. It hits me like a lightning bolt. A feeling I don't give to many people. Compassion.

I was already amped up after my mom's phone call, begging us to go to our father's bedside because he doesn't have long left. I told her straight out, no. Now as I stand here though, I wonder if I should suck it up and say my goodbyes.

Perhaps he'll have a few nice words to say before he departs this world. To make up for his lack of parenting skills. If not, it will close the book once and for all, and we can both move on. A finality we desperately need. Just as Capri is getting hers, we too will get ours.

I need to talk to Atlas later. Once all this is resolved.

The female officer helps Capri out of the car. She's been crying. The humane side of me wants to go to her, snatch her away from the cop, and wrap her up in me. The side that has become cold and indifferent because of my upbringing keeps me cemented to the spot.

She joins me just as Atlas wanders over. He puts his hand on her shoulder, but she jerks back. I've noticed that with her. She hates being touched. It's obvious who made her like that and if there weren't police present, I'd beat the motherfucker unconscious.

"You, okay?" my brother asks.

"I guess. Just hard to relive everything." She's swiping at her eyes. The brave girl. I don't know exactly what she went through, but it must have been horrific. "They're, ah, getting a warrant to search the house." Her eyes flicker away. "They'll see the basement."

Jesus. The basement? It sounds like a horror film. Did he keep her there? My barely restrained anger is about to go nuclear as I picture her tied up, help prisoner in her own home.

We hear the Miranda Rights being read by the male officer who turns Capri's father around and places cuffs on his hands. All I see when I look at him is a waste of space. A person who should have never been given life.

The idiot turns to his daughter with a look of death in his eyes before he's offering a yellow-toothed snarl.

God, I hope they have enough evidence to keep him locked up. He'll come for her, of that I'm certain. None of us need this right now, which is why I didn't want Atlas to allow her to stay with us. I run a hand across my face and grit out, "Let's get the fuck out of here."

Twenty-Seven

Capri

My worst fears have come true. Seeing *him* again. I've been able to pretend he doesn't exist, mostly, since living with Atlas and Killian. I've felt a little… normal. It's been nice.

Seeing him approach me again. Hearing his voice. Watching the sick smirk play out on his face has brought back all kinds of horrible memories.

We're on the way home, yet I'm not seeing anything outside. I'm in my head. If Killian hadn't been in the car, I would have gotten dragged back home and, for sure, I never would have been able to leave again. I would have died there.

The boys are quiet. I don't know if it's for my benefit or not, but I'm grateful.

Kill is riding passenger in the front again, holding the

forgotten pizzas and remains staring straight ahead, but his muscles are taut the same way they were back in the parking lot.

My stomach is all kinds of knotted up, tangy bile resting in my esophagus. I'm trying to keep my hands from shaking by squeezing them between my thighs.

Finally, when we're almost home, Atlas speaks. "Jesus, Capri. I'm so sorry. They were busy. Normally I don't have to wait the full fifteen minutes. Did he hurt you?"

I glance between the seats to see Killian's fingers go white from squeezing the pizza boxes even tighter at the question.

"No. Not physically. He caught me by surprise and scared me. Seeing him felt like I've never left. When he touches me... it..." I don't get to finish.

"Well, he won't be hurting you anymore. Hopefully, he'll be locked away for a while."

I hear his words but can't believe them. All the police have is my statement and a bunch of threatening messages, plus whatever they find at the house. Is that enough to keep someone in prison? A basement with brackets attached to the wall and a bucket that probably still sits there where I've relieved myself. I'm not sure of anything anymore but the justice system better not fail me.

When I remain silent, I see Atlas look at me in the rearview mirror. His brows are slashed, forehead creased with worry.

"I swear to God, if he gets out and comes after you, I'll kill him myself."

Words. As nice as they are, they're just words. As I've already figured out, neither boy can always protect me.

I need to learn self-defense. It's the only way I'll ever be able to defeat him. I can't rely on others to do it for me. I must fight my own battles.

"Either of you boys know self-defense?" It's said lightly, without any expectations either will come to the party, even though they both know how to defend themselves.

That's when the dark, brooding twin, whose hair has fallen across one eye, pivots toward me.

Atlas replies, "Both of us know how to protect ourselves. I'll teach you."

While still glaring at me, his brother grinds out in an authoritative voice, "I'll do it."

Surprise has my mouth open to say something, but I'm too shocked to form words. Even Atlas spins to quickly shoot his brother an 'are you serious?' look.

I'm staring. My mind is picturing the training sessions. I can imagine how much he would push me. Cause me to push myself beyond my limits. But is that such a bad thing? Atlas will want to go easy on me, so he doesn't hurt me. I'd love him for doing that, but it's not what I need. I need to be able to react without thinking. To harden up and not be the timid mouse I've always been.

It's time. Today serves as a reminder to step into my power and take back everything I've lost. I don't want to be afraid anymore.

"You're not training her," Atlas counters.

"No! Killian is right. He can train me." I move to the

center of the back seat so I can garner both their reactions. Atlas is now glaring at me in the mirror.

"What the hell, Capri? Are you serious right now? You want my brother to train you? Am I hearing this right?"

Even Kill's eyes are perfectly round as he continues to observe me.

"I need to harden up and tough training is what I need. You'll go easy on me, Atlas. Kill won't"

"Damn straight I won't." Kill gives me a hint of a smile and it heats my blood.

We pull into their driveway and the engine gets turned off, but no one moves.

The brothers exchange a look before Atlas sighs. "You get one shot. If you hurt her physically, I take over. No arguments."

Kill nods, and it becomes official. I'm going to be spending more time with the brother I like the least, yet the one who makes my heart gallop.

* * *

The pizzas are good, and even though I don't feel like eating after the run-in with my father, I manage three pieces. I don't want to disappoint the guys after they bought them. They, however, have no problem demolishing them until nothing but empty boxes sit on the coffee table as we watch some fight movie Kill picked out. Perhaps he put it on for my benefit, seeing as I'll be working with him to improve my fitness and 'take down' skills.

I get up and stretch. On a yawn, I mumble, "I'm going to do some homework. Thanks for the pizzas."

The nice brother smiles and asks, "Are you sure you're okay?"

I nod and return his smile. "Yeah. Just knowing he's behind bars for a while helps." Then I turn my attention on Killian. "Thank you for sticking up for me today. If you hadn't been there…"

I lower my gaze to the floor.

"That scum deserved way worse."

My head lifts. "Yeah, he did. But thank you."

Brushing a hand through his already messy hair, he ignores my offer of gratitude and instead says, "Be ready in an hour. We're starting our training tonight." His eyes glide over me from top to toe. "Change into something else and meet me out in the shed."

With that order, he turns back around, effectively dismissing me. Atlas clears his throat and gives me an apologetic expression. As tired as I am from school and work and then being accosted in the parking lot, all I want to do is escape for the night and sleep when I'm done with homework, but I won't give Killian the satisfaction of calling me a quitter or someone who isn't keen to train.

I wearily say, "I'll be there."

Learning to fight is going to be a huge sacrifice of my free time, but I'm hoping it will be worthwhile.

I also hope Kill doesn't destroy me in the process.

TWENTY-EIGHT

Atlas

Once Capri is in her bedroom, Kill says to me, "We need to talk about Dad."

Picking up the empty pizza boxes and walking into the kitchen, I throw over my shoulder, "Let me clear this first. You want a beer?"

"Yep. I'm gonna need it."

We haven't showered or changed from our work clothes. We were both thrown for a loop while picking up dinner. To find my brother, Capri and her monster sperm donor in an altercation had me nearly drop the pizza and do something that would have had me arrested, too.

But Kill had it under control. He's better and stronger than me when it comes to facing off with someone, even though I can hold my own. While I don't want him training Capri, she's right. He is the best man for the job.

He'll push her hard whereas I would be too worried about her to give her the best chance at fighting off an attacker.

Once my brother is finished with her, she'll be able to kick anyone's ass.

I throw the boxes in the trash and grab two beers, settling on the sofa for whatever Kill wants to talk about.

"Mom called today."

He doesn't even have to say anymore for me to know what this is about.

I want to say no straight up, but I also want to hear what he wants to say so I pull the top off my beer, take a swig and wait for him to elaborate.

"She begged us to see Dad."

"She's at the begging stage now?" I cross my legs and watch my brother swig his beer to nearly half and throw his head back on the chair opposite me.

"It would appear so. What do you think? Should we bite the bullet and go say our goodbyes?"

After our mother's recent visit, we were both adamant we wanted nothing to do with him, so I'm a little surprised my brother is even asking me. Thinking about it though, the right thing to do would be to go, no matter what he's said or done in the past. He is still our father and seeing just what a narcissistic abuser Mr. Lennon is makes him seem less evil.

Dropping my arms to my knees, dangling the beer between them with one hand, I lift my head to look at Kill. "I guess we should. I don't want to. Not one bit. But if we don't, Mom will never forgive us. Sounds rich, considering she went along with the way he treated us."

He's nodding, but doesn't speak as he gulps down his beer.

"What did you tell her?" I ask, taking another pull from my can.

"I told her no way in hell would we be going."

"So why the change of heart?"

"Not change of heart, Brother. I'm just trying to do the right thing for once. Show our old man that I'm better than he thinks I am."

"Is that what this is about? You don't want him taking his last breath thinking less of you?"

Killian huffs and stands to pace, placing his beer down on the side table. "How did everything become so screwed up? I know I wasn't an easy child, but all I've ever wanted is his approval. To know I'm good enough, you know?"

He stops and turns to me, placing both his arms up, clasping his hands behind his neck.

"Yeah, man. I do know. I'm in the same boat, remember? The gay son who has disgusted his old man."

"Bro, if he can't accept you for who you are, then he's failed as a father." He walks over to me and sits, with about two inches between us. His large hand comes up to put his arm around my shoulders and draw me to him, ruffling my hair with his hand like he always has, since the time we were little when he consoled me after Dad roused on me. It's stuck ever since. He's the only one I'd allow to do it.

In a huff, he grumbles, "So are we doing this?"

"Yeah, I'll call Mom in the morning and tell her we'll go to the hospital tomorrow night. One night. That's it.

We give him nothing more. If she moans about that, well, tough. She's lucky we're even going."

We finish our beers, having not watched the rest of the movie after I muted it before our conversation.

"I'm going to go have a shower and change, ready to teach the little kitten how to grow some balls."

I cringe, hoping like hell she can handle whatever Kill throws at her.

TWENTY-NINE

Capri

Once I've done an hour of homework, I take a quick shower and change into a pair of long leggings and an exercise tank with a racer back. I throw a sweater over the top to avoid freezing until I warm up. After tying up my only pair of joggers, I head out the back to the shed with a high amount of trepidation. I'm regretting my decision to allow Kill to train me, knowing he's going to enjoy every second of pushing me to my limit tonight.

Atlas must have gone to his room because the kitchen and living room are empty as I walk through and step out the sliding door onto the deck.

The exterior light is on, enabling me to see where I'm going. Apart from the shed, the yard is kept tidy, with mowed grass and a garden bed full of plants. A timber fence surrounds the property, giving great privacy, which I like.

The shed is lit up, telling me Killian is already waiting for me inside. I know I'm running a few minutes late, but I wanted to get an assignment finished before we start so I don't have to worry about it after.

It's already eight o'clock and I'm dog tired. My legs barely carry me over to the open side door.

I'm not sure what to expect when I step inside, but an impressive gym at one end and a large mat in a cleared space is not it.

My insides hollow out when I see Killian walking with his back to me, carrying a box to the far end and placing it down gently. He's only wearing a pair of basketball shorts and Nike Airs.

Rising to his full height and turning, he stops when he sees me standing all shy, just in the doorway. I must appear like a tiny lost fawn, standing all wide-eyed, gawking at him.

His ripped body gleams as if he's already been working out. His dragon tattoo appears to come alive as he slowly strides closer, his gaze never leaving mine. The gold hoop nipple ring pulls my attention from his ink as he nears. I wonder how sensitive it would be if I pulled on it.

Stop Capri! You have no right ogling this guy's physique. He's mean and hurtful, remember? Get a grip.

"Thought you weren't coming." He moves to the center of the mat and inspects me all over, causing my arms to fold in front of my chest because of my insecurity.

"I had an assignment to finish. I didn't want to be up

too late tonight." My breathing is choppy. He's awfully intimidating. I want to back out and run to the house where I feel secure. Out here with him, I'm so far out of my comfort zone. I'm surprised I'm not hyperventilating.

"Come onto the mat. Remove the sweater," he commands. I comply immediately, used to doing so with any male authoritarian voice.

When I'm closer but far enough away, he tilts his head slightly, as if figuring something out about me.

He steps closer, causing my panic instincts to take flight. I take a step back.

"How are we going to do this if you don't like to be touched?" he asks, making me suck in a breath.

He's seen me pull away from Atlas. I was beginning to get comfortable with his touch. I welcomed it, even. But straight after my father's fingers had gripped my arm, I'd pulled away from Atlas again as if we were back to square one.

How will I cope with training? It's going to be something I need to overcome if this is to work.

"I'm fine." Bravado at its best, but certainly a false front.

His tongue comes out to lick his upper lip, distracting me for a second. His piercing stare is making me nervous. This was a silly idea, made in haste this afternoon.

He brings a hand up toward my face, and I flinch.

"Don't move," he orders. I breathe in through my nose and out through my mouth as I've learned to do to help calm me. And then. One. Two. Three. Four. Five….

He's not my father. He's here to help me. I'm safe. He won't hurt me when Atlas is not far away. I'll scream if I have to.

I'm deathly still as his hand closes the gap in tiny increments. His fingers are trembling as much as I am.

Gently, the calloused pads graze my jawline. Goosebumps erupt all over. This is the first time a guy has touched me like this. Ever. And I'm letting him. He's watching me closely for any reaction or for me to flinch away like I normally do.

It's taking everything in me not to pull back, and I think he knows it.

Breathe. Inhale. Exhale. Count.

"See, you can do it." His voice is softer than I've ever heard it. And is that pride I see in his heavy gaze?

But as quick as the moment happens, he takes a step back, his mask in place.

"Now that we have that out of the way, let's start." As if one touch is all it takes to allay my fears.

He motions for me to stand in front of him, my back to his front. "Now, I'm going to teach you what to do if you're grabbed from behind." A large arm comes around my neck from behind, causing me to freak out. It's not tight, but tight enough to keep me frozen to the spot.

He's touching me more than fingers down my jaw. His entire forearm is on my throat.

I draw in a harsh breath, willing my mind to calm, but it's no use. My hands come up to grip him, attempting to get the shackle off me, but he's way stronger.

"That's not going to work. You're going to have to use your right elbow to ram it into my stomach. Figuratively speaking, of course." All I hear after that is a buzzing in my ears.

I'm back in a horrible place and instead of Kill behind

me, it's my father. Sweat beads on my temples. I feel it drip down to my cheeks. It's like all the air in my lungs is gone, but I know it's not from the pressure on my throat column but because of my rising anxiety.

"You dare backchat me, oh daughter of mine? Who do you think you are? You're a nobody around here. I'm your boss. You do as I say. You will show some respect!"

He's behind me, growling in my ear. I can't breathe. He's choking me. I'm trying all I can to get his arm off my airway, but it's useless.

"Please. I won't talk back to you again. I promise."

"That's right. You won't, because you're going down to the basement for the weekend. You have no phone. No shower. And I'll only bring you food when I feel like it, got it?"

I'm nodding but it's not my father's voice, it's Kill's.

"Do it. If you think you're dead. You can't afford to wait even a second. We're going to practice this until your reaction time is instant."

Tears leak from my eyes at the memory in the forefront of my mind.

Hatred. Fear and pain. They grip me. I'm still attempting to pry Killian's arm from me, but he keeps going.

"Elbow me. Now!" It's a growl like the monsters. I'm feeling desperate. So, with more strength that I realize I have, I thrust my elbow back into his stomach, causing him to let go of me with a grunt. I fall to the floor, crying as I turn to see him bent over, clutching his abdomen.

"I'm sorry. I didn't mean to." My hand comes to my open mouth. I'm horrified. But sheer relief washes over me because I'm free.

Slowly he stands. I expect to see his face screwed up in anger, but he's smiling. "Good. Now let's go again. This time, ease up a bit."

Dear God. Why did I agree to this?

Thirty

Killian

I wasn't expecting her to elbow me forcefully. When provoked, the kitten's got a good right arm. Perfect. I just need her to act without thinking. She's not a big girl, which is a disadvantage. A male attacker is always going to be bigger and stronger than her, so she needs the element of surprise. She needs to be smart. There are ways to take someone down, regardless of how big they are if you know where to hit.

A gun is a different story. If someone holds one to her temple, of course she will freak out and take pause. I am confident enough to disarm a man, but she's different. Untrained. When I'm finished with her, though, she'll give any man a run for his money.

Using her natural fear of being touched to my advantage, we practice for an hour on the same move and when it appears her legs won't hold her up anymore, I call it an evening.

"We'll keep going tomorrow night." It's not up for debate. She needs some skills before or if her abuser gets released.

With a barely there nod, she sighs. "Thank you."

I watch her shuffle out and when she's nearly out the door, I call out, "You did good."

I hadn't meant to touch her face, but seeing her standing there peering at me with those devastating eyes cracked my hard shell even further than it already has with her.

Capri's skin felt like the softest velvet, and I'd be lying to myself if I said I didn't want to feel more. Jesus. This is exactly what I didn't want.

My mind is all over the place. I've got to keep my head in the game. I'm doing this for a reason. So she can protect herself.

Atlas and I have arranged to visit our father in the hospital tomorrow night, but we won't be staying long. We'll show our faces and be back here within an hour, so I can train Capri further.

The very idea of seeing my old man again has me antsy. It's been a while. Part of me is scared to find him frail and a shell of a man, but the other part of me couldn't care less. He deserves it.

I lock up the large shed and head inside to shower. My skin is sweaty from the small workout I did prior to Capri's training. I needed to warm up after spending most of the day lying under a vehicle.

Once I'm standing beneath the jumbo shower head, I

let the spray rain down on me, feeling my muscles relax. Ever since she showed up at work, I've been coiled tight like a bowstring. I lower my head, allowing the hot water to soak into my shoulders and neck, sighing in relief.

It's difficult bearing the weight of my brother's 'coming out' to our father and watching him get shunned by not only his life giver but by friends as well. It's certainly not easy having been raised with expectations that I didn't fulfill and then having to suffer the same ostracization he did.

And it certainly wasn't a walk in the park grieving a mutual friend who decided it was easier to end it all, rather than turn to us for help. Not to mention running a business and having to deal with that stress.

It's been a tough couple of years, but Atlas and I are doing okay. We're survivors. And it would appear our new houseguest is as well.

Perhaps that's why I'm slowly softening to her. Knowing what she's been through and then seeing her father attempt to take her from the parking lot brings a certain amount of guilt over how I have treated her.

I haven't been horrible as such, just not welcoming.

When I feel I've lowered my heart rate and used up enough hot water, I exit the shower and dry off, wrapping a towel around my waist.

Opening the door, I'm halfway to my room when Capri steps out of hers. As if on repeat, we both stop dead in our tracks when our eyes meet. Her's rove over my chest with its tattoo, landing back on my face.

She's still wearing her workout gear and is carrying a towel. My eyes flit to the side of her jaw that my fingers touched, and a funny sensation happens to my chest. Flutters. And my stomach. It's rolling.

She meekly lifts her hand in a half wave. "Hey."

"Hey." And why is my voice scratchy?

I want to think of a smart-ass remark, but it's as if my brain has taken pause. All I see is her. In this moment. Right here. Right now.

"I'm just about to have a shower." As if she needs to explain to me.

"I see that." Because I do, right? The towel gives it away.

Her feet shuffle forward, but I remain like a century old tree. Solid and unmoving.

She sucks in her top lip and lowers her gaze to the floor. "I'll just... um... go in the bathroom if you've finished."

I turn as she passes. I can tell I make her nervous. Good. She should be. I'm a lion to the little kitten.

I don't miss her sharp intake of breath as her arm grazes my bare chest and goosebumps pop up on all her visible flesh.

She's affected by me. I scare her but she's also intrigued. Little Miss Virgin must think about boys, even with her tragic past. Hormones won't allow otherwise. I see how her pupils dilate when I get too close.

"Enjoy your shower."

A small squeak comes from her pretty mouth, making me snicker before I wander to my room and shut the door, wondering if she takes her shower hot or if she'll need a cold one.

THIRTY-ONE

Capri

It's my second week in the house, early in the morning, when Atlas strolls in looking all sleepy and disheveled. It's 6 a.m. I literally fell into bed after my shower and slept like the dead until around half an hour ago when I couldn't fall back asleep. My mind wandered to my training session with Kill last night and how much progress I'm making.

His hot and cold vibes still leave me dizzy, though. When he's nice, I latch onto it with both hands and when he's back to being arrogant, I hate him all over again.

My reflexes are becoming sharper the more I train. I'm slowly getting used to Kill's hands on me because I understand that he's preparing me for moments when I might need to defend myself. He's remained professional, except for his faux pas of brushing the tips of his fingers down my cheek to make sure I could handle being touched on the first night. It had taken my breath away. To experience such gentleness when all I've known is rough and harsh. He hasn't done it again, much to my disappointment.

"You're up early," Atlas says, breaking me out of my daydream and walking to the coffee machine, which I turned on as soon as I got in here. "How did training go last night? I've heard you are making progress."

"It went fairly well. I'm getting the hang of how to fend off someone coming at me from behind. We've practiced different scenarios so much I think I could do it in my sleep."

He nods, pouring a cup of coffee and turning to lean against the counter. "That's good. That's the whole idea. Act, don't think."

Atlas frowns suddenly, as if a thought has come to him. He's not comfortable asking. "Ahh, how is the whole 'being touched' thing coming along? Especially by my brother."

Indeed. "I freaked at first. It brought back my anxiety, but I breathed through it and it wasn't as bad as I thought. I've winded him on many occasions now."

A smile comes to my face at the picture of him hunched over, sucking in air. Not just on the first night, but every night after it. The mouse can bring the big bad wolf to his knees.

A full-blown laugh drags me back to Atlas's face, which is way too happy about the fact that I hurt Kill.

"That's gold. You're the first girl ever to penetrate his armor." He scans me from head to toe. "And look at the size of you."

I chuckle along with him. "I'm quickly learning that size doesn't matter when it comes to escaping an attacker."

He moves to the other side of the table where I'm sitting and takes his own seat, glee still evident on his face.

When it fades, he clears his throat and asks, "Does he, you know, treat you okay?"

My mind wanders to the way my body responds to his when he gives me a command. As if it wants to obey. There's something different about a hot guy putting his authoritarian voice on as opposed to an abuser.

"Capri?"

"Huh?"

"I asked if he's treating you, okay? Does he hurt you?" He's scratching at the two-day stubble on his chin, watching me carefully.

"No. He doesn't." It's the truth. I'm surprised he hasn't tried to, given how much he's shown his disapproval at my arrival. "He's pushed me hard, but it's nothing I can't handle."

"Well, okay then."

It's six thirty when I leave to get dressed for school. There's no sign of Killian yet. I listen for any sign of life at his bedroom door, but all is silent.

I decide on a pair of jeans and a fluffy hoodie. It's not an outfit to impress, but the weather doesn't allow for anything else. It's overcast and threatening rain, giving the early morning a gloomy feel. I'm fine with it, though. I've always liked days like this.

I'm working at the shop again this afternoon which I'm excited about. I can get stuck in tidying and sorting, zoning out for a while. It's nice not to have to think about anything other than work for the hour and a half I'm there. For so long, I've been in my own head because I've never had an outlet to distract me. I'm grateful to have that now.

Back in the kitchen, I grab a bottle of water and put it in my bag, noting Killian has now risen. He's dressed for work, his hair still a mess but otherwise looking more than decent. My eyes flit to his, to the floor, and back again. He's still staring.

Atlas moves his head between us before rising. "You good to go?"

I nod, tearing my gaze away from Kill. My insides heat at the odd exchange. He hasn't spoken a word and neither have I. That seems to be our thing. Speak with our eyes and not so much our mouths. He speaks when we train, but it's only to tell me what he needs me to do.

As we're leaving, Atlas looks to his brother and back at me. "Oh, I almost forgot. Killian will pick you up after school and take you to work. I've got to go look at Coby's SUV. It wouldn't start this morning. He took an Uber to work and won't be home until two thirty, so I said I'd head over and look."

Kill appears less than impressed judging by his narrowed eyes, but he doesn't reply.

My head spins to Atlas. "On his bike?"

"You good with that?" he offers kindly, obviously sensing my mood change.

"Yeah. I've just never been on one. They um…" How

do I explain it so they don't think I'm a baby? "They kind of scare me."

Killian laughs fully, dragging my attention away from Atlas. His laugh takes me by surprise at first and then I'm frowning at his reaction. He does think I'm a baby. I feel my neck and cheeks flame while I watch his shoulders shake and his eyes close with his laughter. His whole face lights up and if it wasn't mocking me, I'd think him the most handsome man alive.

When Atlas laughs, his voice is slightly higher, and he has a definite snort at the end. Killian's is rough like gravel and his throat bobs with the effort.

I'm momentarily stuck staring and get caught when he calms down.

"Brother!" Atlas offers in warning. "You got something to say?"

Still with a grin, Kill says, "Nope. Not a thing. I'll see you after school, little kitten."

Oh God. What will I be in for? I hope he's a safe driver. Will he purposely go fast to scare me?

I swallow the ball of anxiety lodged in my throat and follow Atlas out.

* * *

Each hour of the day feels like ten. School, work and training yesterday has me lagging behind Carly and Steph as we walk the hallway to the gym for PE. Volleyball is the last thing I feel like doing but it's the end of the day, so it'll be over in an hour. We've changed into our sports gear and leave straight after. I'll have to change back into my jeans at the repair shop.

"What's up with you?" Carly asks. "You've been out of it all day." She opens the gym doors, and we walk through to students milling around.

"Just tired. Catching up on my time away has me pulling longer hours at home. I'm still attempting to finish the assignment for history." I lie. I don't want to mention my training with Kill. They'll never let me hear the end of it. So, I add, "I got my period in class."

Steph gives me a knowing frown. "That sucks. Happened to me once, right here in the gym. I was so embarrassed. Blood leaked throughout my shorts. I keep a change of clothes in my locker, just in case."

They both seem appeased by my explanation, so we drop our bags in the corner where everyone else's are and line up into teams when our names are called not five minutes later by our gym coach.

As the class ends and we're all sweating and exhausted. Well, me anyway, my nerves ratchet up about getting on a motorbike. The idea of not having metal surrounding me if we crash worries me. And bikes always seem to go super-fast out on the roads. I'm not exactly dressed for riding. Shouldn't I be in leather or something a little more appropriate?

And being up so close and personal with Kill brings about a different kind of nervousness. Having to put my arms around him tightly. Press my body into his. I feel sick.

Steph and Carly walk me out and as soon as we're at the gate, I spot him. My feet stop, my brain short-circuiting. When my friends see me not moving, they walk back to me.

"Capri?" Carly asks, worry in her voice.

Carly and Steph turn to see where my attention is and we all star at Kill. He's dressed in his work clothes and stands against his bike, one leg crossed in front of the other, dark helmet on. I can't see his face, but I don't need to. I know he's already locked onto me. I can feel it.

"Oh, sweet Jesus. Who is that, and why are you looking so afraid?" Carly asks, fanning herself. "Damn, he's hot."

"I… uh… I live with him. It's Atlas' twin brother. I'm meant to be getting a ride with him."

Both my friends are gawking. The three of us are openly ogling. He's turning heads, with most of the female population exiting the gate.

"Girl, I'll switch with you. Just give me the word," gushes Steph. "You can catch the bus and I'll ride off with Mr. Sexy and Dangerous."

I stare at her, wondering where my friend has gone. She never reacts to guys like this. Ever. But then, Killian is a different kettle of fish, altogether.

I glance back to the dark angel, who is now stalking forward to me. My breath falters. Officially, my two worlds are colliding, and I don't know how I feel about my friends fawning all over him. He appears tense in the way his hands are balled at his sides, his stride mechanical.

"Oh, here he comes." Steph has a grin on her face I want to wipe off.

When he reaches us, he focuses only on me. "You

coming? We don't have all day. You're on the clock now. There's work to do."

Just as I thought. The girls are quiet beside me, so I move forward. "I'll see you both tomorrow."

"Have fun at work." Steph is still smiling and wiggles her eyebrows. Carly is wide-eyed, staring at Kill as if unable to look away. A couple more girls nearby are whispering as they watch me walk off with him.

"Bye." I give a short wave before turning my back on them. There will be time for talk tomorrow but Kill is right. I shouldn't be stalling. It's just the very idea of getting on that bike, which seems bigger the closer we get, is all kinds of stressful. It's intimidating, like the owner.

He hands me a helmet which I have no idea how to tie up or tighten. When he sees me faltering, he asks, "What are you doing? Put the damn helmet on. And place your backpack on so you don't lose it."

I secure my backpack over my shoulders and pause, hoping he won't yell at me. "I'm not sure how to tighten the straps." It's quite heavy and like Kills. Black with a visor. I lift it to put it over my hair, which is in a ponytail. It's not comfortable at all.

I really don't want to do this. My head swings around to the bus, which is pulling out of the lot, taking away my only other vehicle option.

Kill is scrutinizing me, waiting. My shaking hands falter as I attempt to flatten the helmet on my head. How am I meant to do this?

In another heartbeat, he's towering over me, lifting the helmet off. Without asking, he grabs my hair, pulling the tie from it so the brown strands spill around my shoulders.

He's touching me. Again. Only this time, I'm taken aback by the gesture. Is he trying to make me more comfortable or is he getting annoyed because I'm stopping him from getting back to work? Either way, I drag in a long breath at the realization, his touch isn't bothering me. Just the opposite.

I watch on wordlessly as he stuffs the hair tie in his shirt pocket and replaces the helmet, which slides on easier. It grips the side of my face, pushing my cheeks in slightly, but I'm guessing they're meant to be tight.

When fingers gently pull my hair away from my ears and around to the back and then knuckles graze the skin on my neck, I whimper quietly, not sure if he can hear me.

It's just me and him again, the surroundings lost to whatever spell he continues to cast over me. I'm fully in his orbit. This Kill, the one who touches me as if I might break, is doing things to my insides.

"That okay?" he asks, sounding a little drugged.

"Mm hmmm." I can't give him anything more.

He stands in front of me for moments longer and then clasps the buckle underneath, pulling on the straps so they rest snugly under my chin. The entire time, I can feel my heartbeat in my ears, louder than any drum.

Twisting around, he pulls a leather jacket from a bag tied to the side of the bike and throws it at me.

With a gruff mumble, he says, "Wear this, climb on and hang on tight."

I watch as he swings his leg over and straddles the large machine, hoping I do it gracefully.

Thankfully, I have my gym shorts on and won't flash anyone. I pull the oversized jacket on, inhaling his scent, which stimulates every nerve ending I have, bringing about a shiver. Luckily, it's big enough to go around me with my backpack on, even though I don't think I'll be able to zip it up.

It takes me two goes to get seated. I feel like I'm out of my body as I scoot forward and wrap my hands around his waist. He smells of grease, with a hint of the spicy aftershave he wears. My chest is pressed against his back, the jacket hanging at my sides, but it will keep me warmer once we're moving. While I'm still a tad sweaty from gym, the cold air is quickly changing my body temperature. By the time we get to work, I imagine I'll be one giant icicle.

When the engine roars to life and he kicks up the stand, I know this is really happening.

He must feel my death grip on him, because he chuckles and turns his head. "Ready?"

No. I'm not. I'm so afraid. My eyes are squeezed shut but I call out, "Yeah," anyway.

And then we're off. Backing out of the parking lot and picking up speed. My squeal is lost to the sound of the bike and the rush of air that hits us.

The position of my body feels very intimate against Kills as I adjust to the sensation of the vibration underneath.

Somehow, with me wound around Kill's large frame, I feel protected. As if he won't let anything happen to me. As if he's got the power to keep me safe, no matter what. It's both comforting and confusing. To have the idea that this hulk of a guy will protect me from harm. Even though he won't admit it. But I guess I've already seen it once in the parking lot while getting pizza.

After a minute or two of not having crashed, I slowly open my eyes.

We're cruising behind other cars doing the speed limit. He's not racing off, weaving in and out of traffic like I see a lot of bikes doing. Maybe he's being careful. For me.

"You, okay?" he yells, his head angled back to me as we slow down for a red light.

I am. And as much as I hate to admit it, I'm calming down and finding it not as scary as I thought. In fact, there's a sense of freedom about it. The wind in our hair, me wrapped around Kill. He's asking if I'm okay? Is he beginning to care?

I'm slowly learning there are many layers to Killian MacKenzie and I'm only just getting a glimpse of what's inside.

"I'm good. It's quite fun."

With a nod, he takes off, another squeal letting loose as I grip him tighter. A giggle bubbles out of me. I can't help it. I've never experienced anything like it. The initial fear morphs into exhilaration. The total trust I'm putting in the driver. Feeling him solid beneath my fingers. I allow myself to bask in the experience, another first to add to my growing list.

I know he's being extra careful with me and I'm grateful. He's getting me used to it, obviously knowing I never would have been on one before with my sheltered life.

I'm almost disappointed when we turn into the repair shop and slow down.

Thirty-Two

Killian

I climb off my bike, eyeing the little kitten as she gets off, albeit a little clumsily. She's never been on a bike before. The way she clutched me like I was her lifeline proved it.

To have her pressed up against me was surprisingly good. My body responded accordingly and now, as I turn away to adjust myself, I wonder how the hell I'm going to be able to focus on work. She's the first girl to ever be on the back of my bike. I've always preferred to ride solo, so it was a first for me too. Her thighs clamped around me the way they were, will be a memory I'll go back to again and again.

The sight of her swimming in my jacket has me swallowing hard. She suits leather. Just not one that drapes over her like a blanket. She's bathing in my scent as if being marked, causing me to mentally pound on my chest like a caveman.

When I turn to face her again and remove her helmet, she's beaming. Her eyes are alight for the first time since I've met her. It changes her whole appearance. She's stunning. I feel a sense of pride at her happiness, knowing I put it there.

"That was crazy! I'm not sure why I was scared, but I want to do it again!"

She's like a five-year-old and I smile before I can think too much. Her lyrical laughter that follows almost brings me to my knees. How can I stay mad at her?

"Well, if Atlas doesn't make it back in time, you'll be coming home with me."

Her clapping hands let me know she likes the idea. Hell, I might even ask her to come for a longer ride, even if Atlas shows.

I don't get out on my bike enough for long rides. There are some nice roads out of town that have been begging me to discover them, but work has been taking up all my time.

We can't go too far though as tonight is the hospital visit and then training and I'm sure she'll have homework. Just the thought of seeing our old man helps to dampen my mood. A dark cloud looming.

After tying the helmets to the bike, we walk into the shop, Capri going into the office and me returning to what I was doing prior to the school pickup. She's still wearing my jacket and I can't bring myself to ask for it back.

She seems to know what to do, so I leave her and for the next ninety minutes, we work unhindered.

My mind wanders as I try to focus on the job at hand, but all I see in my head are two striking mocha eyes that don't look sad. She's like a budding flower, opening. With enough sunlight and water, she's going to bloom.

More of my ice melts into puddles. I want to hate her. But I can't. She's getting under my skin and there's nothing I can do about it. I can continue to force myself to be a dick, or I can be genuine and accept her the way my brother has. It's tiring being a jerk. It's not who I normally am. Perhaps it's time I accepted the fact that she's not going anywhere for a while.

Atlas doesn't return, but upon checking my phone, he's left a message to say he's been held up and will just head home afterwards. Yeah, I bet he's been held up. Maybe tied up too. I shake my head with a smirk and go wash my hands with degreaser.

When I reach the office, I find it clean and tidy, files all away, the desk cleared, apart from our computer and a couple of notepads. She's vacuumed too.

It looks… amazing.

"Wow. You've really straightened the place up."

She spins to me after closing the bottom filing draw and standing.

"Thanks. I guess it just needed some TLC." Her eyes are still bright from the ride, her hair unkempt from the helmet. But she's changed from her gym gear back into the clothes she wore this morning, multiple creases letting me know she had them stuffed into her bag.

I still have her hair tie in my pocket, but if she's going to be on my bike again, she won't be needing it. Who knows, I may keep it. And then I'm internally scolding myself for thinking like a wuss. I need to get a grip.

This girl is derailing me fast and I'm worried I'll crash and burn.

"You finished up? Atlas will meet us at home. Thought we could take a ride before we head back."

She's closing the gap. I can feel her excitement leaching from her. And then the unthinkable happens. She's gripping both my arms in her flurry. "We're going for a proper ride?"

We both freeze. She realizes what she's done and draws her hands back like I've burned her. A gasp leaves her.

She touched me. On her own. Without thinking. She's never done that.

She touched me.

The shock on her face must mirror my own. Her attention is on her hands and then it's lifting to me.

"I... I'm sorry." She steps back as if I'm going to be angry. She touched me without my approval. Is that the way her old man trained her? He could put his hands on her but not the other way around? Or perhaps she hated him so much she didn't want to touch him. Understandable.

I take a step forward into her space. "What are you sorry for, kitten?"

"I've never done that before. Not with you. Only with Atlas. I mean, aside from our training. Not like that..." She's rambling. Her mouth is wide, eyes wider.

"You've never touched someone besides my brother? Willingly? Just for the sake of it?" My voice is off. Like I've swallowed sand.

My hands itch to lift to her delicate face. My fingers twitch at my sides.

She smells of purity, even though she's been manhandled by the devil himself. I imagine no high school guy has ever laid a finger on her. She wouldn't have let them. Look how she reacts to Atlas and me.

A subtle shake of her head. I can't hold back. My fingers come up and grip her hand. She flinches, but remains where she is. When I lift our hands and touch my face with her delicate fingers, she goes to pull back, but I hold them there.

"Like this?"

My breathing has changed to mimic hers. Loud and heavy. There's no other noise in the office.

When I'm sure she won't pull away, I slowly lower my hand, leaving hers on my cheek.

She's so out of her element.

I'm not sure she's going to move, but I let her get used to it. Then my face is being traced. Across my nose. My eyes. Forehead and down to the stubble on my chin. Her fingers shudder and if I'm not mistaken, she's failed to take a breath in the last five seconds.

Her touch ignites my skin, firing at every nerve ending. The sheer innocence of her steals my breath.

Normally girls attack me and I attack them and it's all over in a short while. I've never had a girl study me like this. It's like she's feeling the features of another for the first time. And perhaps that's the case.

She confounds me.

When I feel she's had enough and I feel myself losing control with this girl, I move back.

"Come on. Let's lock up and hit the road."

THIRTY-THREE

Capri

Riding on the back of Killian's bike may be my new love. We've left town and are winding up a narrow road into the hills. He warned me before we took off to lean into the corners so I'm trying, using his body language as a guide. I'm wearing his jacket again.

I'm not sure what passed between us at work, but he's thawed, even letting me touch him. Wanting me to touch him. What has changed? And is it going to remain? He's fooled me too many times now to know for sure, but the moment spent in his office leads me to believe he doesn't totally hate me.

What's most surprising, though, is *I* wanted to touch *him*. If he had not pulled back when he did, I'd still be touching him. Feeling his warm skin under my fingers. Watching the way his eyes closed when I delicately feathered over his eyelids. Hearing his breath quicken. It's all new to me, but I felt powerful the way he reacted to me. He wasn't disgusted. Something's changing and I like it. I like it a lot.

The bike slows at a lookout over the town. Not the same one Atlas took me to. This one provides a slightly different bird's-eye view from a higher elevation. The sun is lower in the sky, so we squint when we raise our visors. I pull mine back down to avoid the glare.

The view is gorgeous. Our town. Still relatively untouched from the progress of the big cities. Yet, it is modern enough to provide great infrastructure. We have everything we need without having to travel.

The fall colors have all but dropped and withered, leaving behind naked trees which will be covered in snow soon. We've been forecast for light snow into next week and heavier after that. You can feel it in the air.

This is what living feels like. To embrace the beauty of nature and become a part of it. I wish I had a proper camera. Maybe now that I'm working, I can save up for one. Instead, I pull my cell from my back pocket and go to get off the bike.

Only my foot catches on the seat, and I stumble, falling flat on my backside.

Kill is off the bike in a heartbeat and leaning down to me. "Are you okay?"

But I can't answer because I'm laughing. I undo my helmet and wrench it off, throwing my head back.

"I guess so," he mutters, removing his own helmet and placing it on the bike with mine.

My butt hurts but it's okay because the way I fell had me looking like an uncouth ballerina.

I managed to keep my phone in my hands without dropping it, so I stand up and wipe the gravel off my jeans, happy tears forming.

Killian is watching me as if I'm crazy.

"I'm all good. Just wanted to get a photo." I lift my phone up to show him and take a few steps forward, feeling slightly embarrassed at his perusal but still letting laughter bubble out of me.

I click away, wanting to keep a photographic reminder of this ride. Of this experience. Knowing it's been with Kill. A special memory just between us. When we appear to be at a truce of sorts.

"It's beautiful." Lowering my phone, I stand in wonder and raise my arms above my head, closing my eyes and breathing in the chilly air. My lungs almost burn, but I feel alive. For the first time ever, I realize everything is going to be okay. I'm going to be okay.

"It is." I turn to Killian to find him staring at me and not at the view. The sun catches his dark eyes, lightening them ever so slightly from a dark mahogany into chestnut. His curled lashes flutter and his mouth pulls in as if he's biting his bottom lip.

My face heats. Is he saying I'm beautiful or did I catch him looking at me because I turned to him? Surely it couldn't be me he's referring to. But what if it is?

He runs a hand through his helmet hair, causing it to stick up everywhere, drawing my attention higher.

If I were confident and prettier like the popular girls at school, I'd have a chance with a guy like Kill. I don't have the experience like I imagine the girls he's been with do. I've never been kissed. Never had a guy worship my body like I read about in romance books.

My neck and face flame at the images of Killian covering my body with his, adoring me with his hands and mouth. Whispering how much he wants me…

"Ah, we better leave. Atlas and I have to go to the hospital to visit Dad, and then we've got training."

My visions cutting short, I quickly nod to his retreating back.

I want to ask about their father, but I get the impression he'll close off again. I know their relationship is strained and totally understand why he wouldn't want to talk to me about it, so I simply follow him, pocket my cell and don the helmet.

It's a little disappointing to be going home. We didn't stay long enough but fingers crossed we can come back here.

Atlas is already home when we return. Upon entering, he's up off the sofa. "Hey. I was wondering where you guys were. I've messaged both of you and didn't get a reply. I called the shop, and the phone went to message bank. I was getting worried."

"Sorry. We took a detour home," Kill responds, glancing to me and then back to Atlas, who has his right brow quirked.

"Oh?" His head's pivoting between me and Killian.

I jump in with, "We went up the hill to the lookout on the other side of town. I got a couple of photos."

He still seems perplexed. "Really?" And then a slow smile drifts his lips up.

He's clearly wondering why the two of us would do something reserved for friends and, to be honest, I can't answer him. It doesn't make any sense. Instead of a reply, I remove Kill's jacket and hand it to him. "I'm going to get changed and start on my homework."

When I'm halfway down the hallway, I hear Atlas say, "Start talking, Bro."

Thirty-Four

Atlas

"So let me get this straight." We're in my pickup on the way to the hospital. My brother didn't want to talk at home, so we've waited until we're on the road. "You took Capri up to the lookout on the way home? Why? Is this the same brother who made it abundantly clear he wanted nothing to do with her? The same brother who offered to train her to defend herself every night? Who are you?"

I turn and watch him fidget. His leg is twitching. I know it's hard for him to admit to his feelings, but something has clearly changed his mind to have him soften like this.

He glances out the window before giving me all of two seconds acknowledgment and then staring ahead. Then he blows out a forceful breath and throws his head back into the seat. "I don't know, man. I guess when I saw her old man try to grab her, it made her circumstances real. When you first brought her home, I didn't fully comprehend just how fucked up her home life was."

There's a moment of silence. I don't push, just let him gather his words as I turn a corner, letting a guy in the left lane merge in front of me.

"She's not as bad as I thought."

A chuckle bubbles up out of me. "I hate to say it, but I told you so."

"Yeah, yeah. I was merely being cautious, okay?"

"Well, it's nice to see you both getting along. It'll cut all the tension out of the house."

His legs are still jiggling, so I'm assuming it's not from Capri but about our impending hospital visit. We're almost there and with each mile closer, his body language tells me he's getting more agitated.

"You sure you want to do this?" I sure as hell don't. It's not too late to turn around.

"No, but I don't want to regret it later. Remember, we're doing this for us, not him."

It doesn't feel as if we're doing it for us. Unless we walk away from there with some closure, then it hasn't been for us.

This isn't the way things were meant to go. Us begrudgingly showing up to bid farewell to our dying father, not because we want to but because we feel we must. There's so much regret, disappointment, and anger. I've always been good at burying it but as of late, the dam walls are struggling. My emotions are barely holding together.

Another couple of minutes and we're parking in the

large lot, toward the back. Busy night with visitors. The transition from my warm truck into the frigid evening temperature has me zipping up my hooded black jacket. There's a chance of early snow tonight and it feels like it. Add to it the bitter wind and I'm making short work of the pavement to get inside. Kill is on my tail.

He's wearing the leather jacket Capri took off earlier. Another thing I didn't bring up with him. My brother acts all tough on the outside, but he's really got a good heart to those he deems worthy. Many people just don't get to see it. Without him knowing it, I see her changing him. Little by little, he's letting her in, and it warms my heart. She's good for him. Good for us both.

Mom left us instructions to get to Dad's room, so we follow them onto the elevator and then down a long corridor.

Room 205. Fourth floor. My breathing has picked up. Kills hands are fisted tightly, veins popping in his neck. This isn't easy for either of us. We don't know what state we'll find him in. A nurse walks past and gives us a friendly smile, one reserved for families who grieve in times like this. If only she knew.

The door to his room is open, but we pause before we reach it. I listen for any chatter, wondering if Mom is here, but all is quiet. I'm kind of glad if she's not here. I don't want to deal with her if things go south. Which I know they will. When have they ever not?

I look to my brother whose expression is fierce. I hold my knuckles up in solidarity and receive a fist bump in return.

No matter what happens, we'll still have each other's backs. Twins by genetics. Brothers by heart.

I'm shocked to see Kill walk in first. His gait is determined to do this and then leave, so I pad in after him, using his presence as support.

It's a funny thing when you haven't seen someone in a long time. Especially when they're laid up in a hospital bed.

He appears much older and frail. Skin and bone. His eyes are closed, giving us a moment to assess the scene and adjust.

There's a chair near his bedside and one in the corner, so I motion for Kill to take the closest one while I retrieve the other.

A constant beep is the only sound. The atmosphere is sterile and cold. A great representation of the man in the bed. Gone is the dominant, intimidating persona we know. He's been replaced by this shadow of a thing whose hair is thinned to the point of balding. Skin sallow and droopy. It's hard to gel the two into the same person.

When our dad hears us shuffling about, his eyes open. It takes a moment for him to register that it's his two sons visiting. For a split second, his eyes widen and then his mouth opens. "Took you long enough."

Great. The first thing out of his mouth is that. This really isn't going to plan. Deep down I knew that, but there's always a flicker of hope that has failed me so often. Maybe this time, he'll offer a crumb of love. A few kind words. Wishful thinking is so destructive. "Nice to see you too, *Dad.*" Kill turns the chair so the back of it is facing our father, leaning his arms on it.

I pull mine up beside him and sit, deciding to ignore his greeting and ask, "How are you feeling?"

He never fails to disappoint. "How the heck do you think I'm feeling, laid up here?" Kill's hands tighten on the back of the chair, so I nudge my knee into his leg to stop him from erupting.

We can do this. In and out. Just a few more minutes. Don't let him get to you. Switch off.

"They are taking good care of you, though?" I ask, ignoring the need to run.

A grunt, followed by, "I'll be better when I get home."

Kill's gaze clashes with mine at the same moment. Our mom has said he won't be returning home, but apparently, he thinks he will. Who are we to burst his bubble?

There's an awkward silence. Kill is remaining mute, letting me deal with the conversation. Or lack of.

"You found yourself a nice girl yet?" he asks, licking his dry lips and turning his head back to me.

Here we go. He's on the starting block. Ready to do this right now. Straight into it, as if my situation is always in the forefront of his mind. As if he's been waiting for me to show up so he can beat me back down again. We shouldn't have come. No matter what Kill said. Stupid. Stupid. My chest is splintering as I watch his labored breath. While he still can speak, he's going to keep hounding me.

I clear my throat, my hand coming up to run through my hair. "You know my situation."

He's staring into me, waiting for something. What? A moment of clarity on his behalf whereby I say, 'Oh, you're right. What was I thinking being into guys? I'll find me a nice girl, just to make you feel better, Dad.'

No. I'm not doing it. I won't appease him. "I'm gay. I won't ever have a girlfriend. You know that. It's time you accepted it."

Kill syphons in a harsh breath and when I look over, he gives me a nod, knowing what's coming. His silent approval of me speaking my truth.

"You not over that phase yet? What's wrong with you? Any boy who is into other boys has something wrong inside. That's not how I raised you!"

He's trying to yell and push himself up onto his elbows, but he's too weak. Still, even in such a state, he's frightening. The sound of his pulse through the machine spikes. It'll only be a short while until a nurse comes in and kicks us out.

You know what? I'm done. I'm done with this man. Done with this conversation and done with caring what he thinks of me. We've come. We've seen him and now we're leaving. By choice. He doesn't get to do this anymore.

I stand, pushing the chair back, tears close to bursting free as my heart finally cracks in two. He couldn't do it. He couldn't make his last words to me matter.

I hate him. If I wasn't a good man, I'd pull his pillow out from under him and press it into his face until he took his final, gasping breath.

Kill joins me, standing by my side as he always has. His voice is deep and menacing.

"You know what? Fuck you, old man. We came here to

say our goodbyes because we thought we were doing the right thing, even though we knew it would turn out this way. You don't get to judge your son. It's not a fad, he's going to grow tired of. It's who he is and if you can't see what an amazing man he's become, then you're too blinded by your own prejudice and bias. You've disowned both of us, and for what? Because we didn't fit the mold you had for us? You're pathetic. Even on your deathbed you've failed us both, but you know what? Your time on this earth is ending and so is your judgment and criticism."

Our father is blinking at us both, surprise registering on his emaciated face. But he doesn't get to speak. Not yet, because Kill isn't finished.

"Thanks for asking, but the repair shop is going brilliantly. We're busier than we've ever been, so much so that we work on Saturdays. We're happy. Does that mean anything to you? We. Are. Happy."

"I..." he goes to speak.

"Stop! We don't care what you have to say. It's too late. You were meant to be there for us, cheering us on. Patting us on the back, saying 'good job'. That's all we've ever wanted. Even with only days left, you can't bring yourself to say it. So, we're done here. There's nothing for us to say except goodbye."

He's moving to walk out the door and I take a moment to linger, a stare down happening. I'm giving him one last chance to say he's proud of us. To apologize.

I wait. He's either too stubborn or he genuinely doesn't feel it.

After a beat, I turn, calling out before I reach the door. "Goodbye, Dad."

It's not until I join my brother in the hallway that I fall apart.

Thirty-Five

Killian

Atlas is a mess. I haven't seen him shed a tear over our father in forever. We've both steeled ourselves against him over time to a point where nothing he says really bothers us, but I guess in hindsight, my brother has just become better at hiding it.

I lead him into the elevator and watch him break apart.

With a hand on his shoulder, I don't need to say much. "You're a far better man than he ever was. I'm so proud of you."

He's sobbing and attempting to keep the pain inside, causing him to gasp. I hate seeing him so distraught over words that shouldn't even matter.

We hit the ground floor, and he's out, rushing to the truck so people don't stare. A few do, but they probably just assume we've suffered a loss. It's a hospital and to be expected. In many ways, we suffered the loss years ago and today we simply get to re-live it. I hope he's up in his bed thinking about my words. But I doubt it. Men like him don't think there is anything wrong with them or their views. It's sad. To be so unaccepting.

As I'm thinking this, a jolt hits me. Not physical, but mental. Haven't I been treating Capri the same way? Not accepting her because she is a stranger to our house? Scared of the extra baggage she brings when I should have been more compassionate about her circumstances. The way I've wanted my father to be with us?

I've treated her like he treated us, and it fills me with shame. I'm no better. I've become the person I didn't want to become.

My feet have stopped. Atlas turns, his face red, his eyes watery. "What's up?"

An ache forms in my chest. "Nothing. Don't worry about it. Just digesting everything."

I'm not ready to admit I was wrong about Capri. Not yet. Fuck!

He waits at the truck for me, but instead of taking the passenger seat, I hold my hand out. "Give me your keys. You're in no state to drive."

Atlas digs into his pocket and throws me the keys, which I catch one-handed.

Once we're in the safety of the vehicle, Atlas speaks. "I'm sorry. I didn't mean to get so emotional. I guess it's been building for a while."

"You don't need to apologize to me, Bro. He was being

a dick, as usual. I'm sorry we came. I shouldn't have mentioned it to you."

He's shaking his head as I pull out of the lot.

"I came for you. Not him. Some part of me hoped he'd changed. The part of me that has always hoped."

There's an edge to his voice, which scares me. A tone I haven't witnessed. His fist hitting the side of his door has me startle. Once. Twice. Three times.

"Ahhh. Fuck! Fuck him!" He's screaming, voice breaking again. More tears flow and I'm not sure how to handle my brother splintering apart. He's always the composed one. The one I lean on. Sure, he's raged at our dad after confrontations, but this feels different. Darker.

Males are always taught to toughen up. Be strong. Don't show emotion. It's weak. We push it all down until there's no space left. Until there's nowhere for the sadness and pain to go, except outwards. He's unraveling in front of me.

The light changes to red, so I pull the handbrake on. "Hey. Dude. It's okay, man. They're just words. They don't have power over you. Don't let him win. Don't let him destroy the man you are. You're amazing. The best. Those who know you agree with me. I'm all that matters. I'm your family. I love you so hard."

My voice cracks too as I swallow my need to roar into the night and go hit something. "It's over." I place a hand on his shoulder and squeeze it. "It's over."

We sit in silence as I let him process my words. There's nothing more I can say. Eventually, when the light turns green, I put the truck in drive and head home.

"You up for a beer? I can call into a drive-through and get us some."

With a harsh exhale, he glances at me and nods, eyes the color of blood. "Don't you have training with Capri soon?"

I do. But with the way I'm feeling, I need to settle so I don't take my anger out on her.

"Yeah, but a couple won't hurt."

When we get home, as soon as we step through the door, an aroma greets us. It's coming from the kitchen and smells divine.

Hoping whatever it is, there are leftovers for us. I'm shocked to find there are two plates on the table, covered in foil with cutlery and a glass of water each.

What the hell?

My brother and I exchange a look and I have officially decided that, beginning from tonight, I'm going to make it up to this girl. She's gone above and beyond to show that she cares. For both of us. Even though I've treated her badly. It's as if somehow she read our minds and knew we'd be needing this.

I'm not sure about Atlas, but I need food.

He appears to have settled and schooled his meltdown. His eyes still look like he's on crack, but apart from that, I think he's okay.

Atlas opens both beers and hands me mine, so we take a seat and peel the foil off our plates.

Before us sit two large steaks with a brown sauce over the top, mashed potatoes and steamed vegetables. She's outdone herself.

"This looks amazing," I offer, cutting a large chunk of steak off and shoveling it into my watering mouth. "Holy shit. It's cooked to perfection. And that Dianne sauce is perfect. The girl has skill."

Atlas lifts his head up to show me the smirk he's throwing my way, even if it is fake. He's trying. "You accepted her yet?"

Time for a little truth. "Ahh, look. I know I've been a dick to her but after seeing our father today, I recognized similarities between the way he treats us and how I've treated Capri. I'm ready to call a truce."

My brother frowns after cutting his meat. "You're nothing like that maggot. Sure, you're wary about new people, especially a girl we knew nothing about when I brought her here."

He lifts his fork to his mouth, filling his cheeks out with the tender meat, a swig of beer to wash it down with. "But, yeah, you need to apologize. You were an ass."

I can't help but grin. He's dead right.

After a pause, I ask, "You, okay?"

Without glancing up, he shrugs. "Better now that I'm out of that place."

I don't push. He'll deal. He always does. He knows I'll be here for him, no matter what. And so will Capri.

Speaking of said girl, a door opens, and she pads down the hallway, already wearing her workout gear.

When she pauses just inside the kitchen, I can't help

but take her all in. Her eyes find mine and there isn't a hint of malice there, making me feel even smaller.

"How'd the visit go?"

My brother and I stiffen, not thinking she'd ask, but here we are.

I look to Atlas, who is suddenly finding his beer extremely interesting. Head bowed, shoulders forward.

"Let's just say it went how we thought it would." She's wide-eyed, waiting for more, but I don't give it to her. Not tonight. Instead, I offer, "Thanks for cooking us dinner. You didn't have to. We could have taken out a frozen meal."

Capri walks over to the fridge and takes out a bottle of water. Probably for our session that'll happen once my food has digested.

"It's no drama. I was cooking anyway. I just made a little more."

Knowing I need to add something, I chew and swallow before saying, "This steak is perfect. Just the way I like it."

She flicks her head to me super-fast, eyes perfectly round. God, she's stunning. My chest stutters inside my ribs and speeds up when she holds my stare.

"Uh, that's good. I'm glad." The smile that follows nearly unmans me. It's so genuine and lights up her entire face. I find myself breathless.

Atlas coughs and then stands. "I'm going to head to my room for a bit. It's been quite an evening."

Capri watches him with concern, a frown forming. A quick glance at me whereby I shake my head, she lets him go.

"I'll finish up here and meet you out in the shed in..." A quick glance at the clock on the wall tells me it's almost seven-thirty. "Twenty minutes?"

"Sure. I'll go finish up my homework and meet you there."

Thirty-Six

Capri

What in the ever loving? There's been a further shift in Kill's attitude toward me since they've returned from the hospital. Did their dad say anything? Does he even know about me?

Either way, I'm not complaining. He was nice. Perhaps we got off on the wrong foot. That's all. After our ride, I feel as if things are changing for the better. Much has happened in such a short span of time.

The way he perused me from head to toe left me tingling. His stare makes me feel everything, everywhere. It shouldn't and I don't want to cause new friction in the house, but holy hell, the guy is painfully hot. In such a way, that even when he was being nasty to me, I still felt a pull to him. Is that weird?

I guess deep down you just know.

When I reach the shed, the lights are on. I'm yet to get here first. Tonight, I'm nervous for a whole other reason. That we're possibly moving past our animosity and becoming amicable has me wondering just how I'll react if he gets all up in my space again. My body acts of its own accord when he's around, and I can't stop it. Only him. Perhaps because he didn't come onto me from the get-go, I know he's not like the boys at school with only one thing on their minds.

He's leaning up against a workbench on the far side, checking his phone when I walk in. His head snaps up when I enter, making me the sole focus of his attention. Under the fluorescent lights, he presents like a God. Eyes almost onyx in color from where I stand, dissecting me from my head to my toes and back again.

It's hard not to react to the way he sizes me up. Is it as a sparring partner or something more?

Either way, goosebumps dot my flesh, a low ache forming in my belly.

I can feel my face heat.

"Let's get started," he offers, clearing his throat and rubbing the back of his neck, gaze dropping to the floor. Is he nervous?

"Okay." I place my water bottle near the mat on the floor and wait for his direction.

I'm suddenly feeling all sorts of things I shouldn't be as I watch him move closer.

When he's not being an ass, I can imagine what it would be like to have him as a boyfriend. His intensity rolls off him. All-encompassing. To be consumed by him in such a way might just be my undoing. Could I ever be with someone like that? And why am I even thinking about it?

Suddenly, the room feels half its size.

"Tonight, I'm going to show you some fighting techniques if your attacker is in front of you."

Kill explains and shows me and then we're practicing. There is no hostility at all. The air is much lighter around us and I'm able to fully immerse myself in the hour we spend.

"Good work!" He praises me after I fake jab him in the eyes with my fingers. I soak it up like a small child, never having received it before. I want to please him to hear it more.

Sweat rolls off both of us.

He comes at me with both hands around my neck. On instinct and because it's fresh in my head, I bend his fingers right back until he loosens his hold and then I pretend to kick him in the groin. I'm not meant to make contact, but my bare foot gently touches him, causing him to hiss and move back. My own surprise at how hard he was *there* has me sucking in a breath.

"Oh, God! I'm so sorry. I didn't mean to hurt you. Are you okay?"

I'm on him, my hand on his arm, worry frowning my face. It's not a look of pain that shines back at me, though. No. It's something far more dangerous. His glazed eyes let me know I've affected him in totally the opposite way.

He glances down at my arm, so I draw it back quickly. Once again, I touched him. Of my own volition. As easy and breathing. Without faltering.

A large hand comes up and a thumb rubs across my

bottom lip, his eyes following the movement. I'm not sure what he's doing.

"Are you angry?" The words come out as if I'm drunk because he's still touching me.

A shake of his head and a quick step further into me until we're touching everywhere.

"Not. Angry," he grits out.

What then?

Oh.

Gentle, calloused fingers trace my mouth. Then my cheeks. Up to my eyes, which I close on instinct and then down my nose before he drops his hand.

Don't stop. Please!

His breathing is loud. I risk a peek and find him chewing on the corner of his bottom lip.

"Have you ever been kissed?" It's nothing more than a gravelly rumble.

This time, I have no words, so I simply shake my head the same way he did.

My eyes widen as his head closes the small gap, causing me to go cross-eyed. He's still holding eye contact until right at the last moment he closes them, and his lips touch mine. Feather light. A brush as if to test my reaction.

I'm tingling all over. My chest feels like it's too narrow to contain my heart, which thunders below my ribs.

How can this man be so gentle?

He pulls back slightly as if asking if I'm alright, which further confounds me, so I just stare.

And then he's cradling my face in his hands, our mouths fused in a delicate dance. I'm not sure what to do, so I copy him, opening slightly, hoping like hell I'm giving something back. My mind is chaotic, but in a good way. It's soaking the moment in. Every nerve-ending I possess is buzzing as he opens slightly more, his tongue coming out in search of mine. I never, ever thought my first kiss would happen, let alone with a guy like Killian.

I'm suspended in this moment, each sense coming alive. Taste. Touch. Feel. Sound.

A noise he makes from his throat into my mouth has me falling off a ledge with no safety net. I'm dizzy. Swooning.

It's over all too soon, just when I feel like I'm getting the hang of it.

My hands are still at my sides. I should have placed them on his shoulders, but he took me by surprise. It's a miracle he even wanted to kiss me.

Me. Mouse. Or as Kill refers to me, little kitten.

When I raise my face, he glances away and then turns his back to me. "I'm sorry. I shouldn't have done that."

"No. It's okay."

It truly is. It's more than okay. In fact, I'm smiling. Not only on the outside, but on the inside too. A boy kissed me. Not just any boy. Killian MacKenzie.

THIRTY-SEVEN

Killian

What the hell have I done? I kissed her. And I'd be lying to myself if I said I didn't enjoy it. I did. Now I can't look at her. I shouldn't have done it. She's so pure and innocent. I doubt she's ever been touched by a guy. I couldn't help myself. The way she'd stood and looked at me so innocently. Her purity calls to me. That mouth. It tasted better than I could have imagined.

I'm floundering. She's behind me waiting on… something. And all I want to do is dive in headfirst and lose myself in her. Possess her.

"I'll just, ah, go and shower." Her voice is breathless as she moves past me while I stand stock still, not knowing what to say or do. It's when she's out the door that I mumble, 'Okay.'

With my face to the roof, I attempt to sort through my

feelings. I'm a mess inside. My stomach is upturned, my pulse still in upbeat tempo, but it's the beating organ in my chest that must have a direct pathway to my brain. They're both sparring with each other. Logic says I'm not good for her, but my heart is already wanting to see her face again. That upturned nose. Kissable lips and mesmerizing eyes. She has an allure. It's not one singular thing. I've tried to hate her, and I did to begin with, but there's a fine line between hate and love. No, not love. I don't love her. I don't love anyone except my brother.

Needing a breather, I walk out into the biting air, letting it cool my blood.

Before we started our training, I was angry from the hospital visit with Dad. As soon as I'd seen her walk in wearing her gym clothes and an unsure expression, my rage dissipated. I don't want to be like him. I need to prove to myself that I'm not. And it starts with how I treat others, namely Capri.

Only I didn't expect things to turn in the direction they have. A short while ago, I didn't know she existed. And now? Now I wonder how I never knew she existed.

Inside, I grab another beer and find Atlas in the living room, playing COD. I'm glad he's out of his bedroom and doing something to take his mind off things. He worried me tonight. I'll continue to worry. I'm going to need to keep an eye on him to make sure he's coping.

"Can I join in?" I ask, taking a seat on the sofa.

He waits a moment as he takes a shot on the screen and then turns to me. "Sure, grab the other controller." He's got his own beer beside him, so I sit on the floor and wait for him to finish his game.

"How did training go?"

The ache in my chest forms again. I'm not going to tell him about the kiss. He doesn't need anything else added to his plate.

"It went well. She's a quick learner." I take a swig, watching him drop to the ground after getting shot in his game.

He pauses it. "You think she'll be able to handle herself if her loser of a father shows up again?"

"It's hard to say. She may freeze up like I saw her do in the parking lot. But she needs to act without thinking. She can't question it or let him intimidate her. That takes practice. We'll keep working on it. Her reaction time is better, a lot better with me, but who knows with her father? He's another story altogether."

He watches me funny. "Thanks, Bro."

I pause my beer as it nears my lips. "For what?"

"For getting along with her. For helping her. For helping me." He swallows hard, facing the television.

"I'll always be here for you. Always. As for Capri... I don't want to be like him." My words taper off into a whisper as they shoot me straight in the chest.

Atlas places the controller down and turns his head. He appears haunted, but still he calms me with his words. He always has.

"I've told you, you're nothing like him. You've just had to deal with the same shit I have. You're a good person."

I shrug. "Maybe. But I'm going to do better." For all of us.

THIRTY-EIGHT

Capri

School the next day gets off to a bang with an impromptu fire drill. They let us know it's practice even so, it's an inconvenience to teachers and students.

We file onto the sports field and wait until teachers mark the roll, some stragglers not caring to hurry, knowing it's not real, so we're left outside for almost forty-five minutes before we're allowed back into class.

I'm sure some couples use it as time to make out before ambling over to the rest of us. "This totally sucks. It's freezing out," moans Steph, folding her arms across her black sweater. Her dark eyeliner is winged today, giving her a witch vibe. The only part of her that isn't black is her green eyes and pale skin.

Carly shrugs as we walk side by side. "I love getting out of class. I wish it would last longer."

Steph glares at her. "That's probably because you've got seven layers on."

"It's not my problem that you don't dress for our conditions." She has a huge puffy jacket on with fur around the edges that reaches her knees.

"I prefer to dress somewhat decently," Steph replies. Not that she's the trendiest person in school with her goth appearance, but if she feels she is, then who are we to tell her otherwise?

"Later, losers." She gives us both a smirk, then heads to her class.

Carly is looking down at what she's wearing. "Do I look like a loser?"

"No. Of course not." Even though her green jacket clashes with her red hair, I keep my opinion to myself. If I didn't have Steph and Carly, I'd be the loser with no one.

We head to math class together. Steph is in the lower group because she's not as good with numbers. Carly and I are in the advanced class. Like me, she breezes through the subject.

Inside, we sit at our regular seats and wait for the teacher. "There's a party this weekend. You should come."

Since when does she party? I've never heard her talk about them before. Lately, everything seems to be changing. And who even asked her? We don't mix with the regular crowd who indulge every weekend. "What do you mean, party?" The class is filling up, so I lower my voice to avoid stares and whispers about me even talking about parties.

"You know. A night out with other students?" She

places her backpack on the ground after pulling out her laptop.

"I know what a party is. What I want to know is why are you suddenly wanting to go? And who invited you?"

With an indifferent shrug, she replies, "A guy in my economics class mentioned it. We had to sit together after I got to class late and the seat beside him was the only one left."

She makes it sound like it's no big deal, but it is.

"A guy asked you to a party?"

A quick hurt expression covers her face, so I quickly add, "I mean. Not that one wouldn't. It's just, well, we don't get invites, that's all."

"Yeah, well, maybe we should go check it out and see what all the fuss is about. I mean, if you want to. Steph wants to go. I've already mentioned it to her."

Mr. McIntosh enters the room, so I quickly say, "I'll think about it."

Shock registers on her face. "You will? You never do anything with us."

I smile at her, genuinely contemplating going to my first party. "Mm, hmm. I'm not at home, remember?"

"Yes! That's awesome! We'll have so much fun. It's Saturday night at 8 p.m. at Cheryl Turner's house. She's turning eighteen. Her parents are rich. She has a huge mansion. I can pick you up."

I haven't said yes yet, but Carly isn't bothered by that fact. As far as she's concerned, I'm going. The very idea of it is scary and exciting. Will it finally be a case of us being accepted by our peers if I say yes? To fit in. What will I wear? Just the thought of attending and being a regular girl for one-night sways my decision.

Before the class has ended, I know what my answer will be.

* * *

"You look happier this afternoon." Atlas notices as I place my bag on the floor of the passenger seat and climb in.

"It's been a good day. I got invited to my first party."

"Oooh, Miss Popular! I got so trashed at my first party, I don't even remember it."

I laugh. "Well, you don't have to worry about that with me. I don't drink."

We're crawling out of the parking lot in a line of cars. He glances across at me, a frown taking over. "Just make sure if you do decide to have a drink, you don't let anyone else get it for you or pour it. Spiking drinks is rife at high school parties."

"I promise, Dad."

His mood is chipper compared to last night. Perhaps a good night's sleep has worked wonders. I hope it stays that way. Then again, I know better than anyone that a smile doesn't mean a person is happy. Just the opposite can be true. Everyone deals with sadness differently.

It's a nice change to have someone who actually cares about my well-being. Atlas is fast becoming the big brother I never had.

He grins at me as we finally leave the school grounds.

"Oh, before I forget. When you get a spare moment, can you teach me how to drive?"

"You want me to teach you? Why, I'd be honored. To be honest, when Kill offered to teach you how to fight, I was a little jealous."

My mouth opens in shock. "You were? Why?"

He pulls a sheepish face. "Because he'd be getting to spend more time with you. And I kind of found you first." His glance my way is filled with other emotions. It's so quick I almost miss it when he covers it up with a fake pout.

I humor him. "I'm not a toy you can share. And besides, you're batting for the other team, remember? Even though when I first saw you that night, I thought you were handsome."

I don't know why I'm suddenly sharing my secrets with him. He just makes it so easy.

A bark of laughter rings in my ears. "You thought I was cute?"

We stop at a red light, and I turn to him. "Well, yeah. Have you seen yourself in the mirror?"

His full lashes flutter, his lips quirking up. "Hmmm. Interesting."

We take off again and I wonder what he's thinking. Normally I wouldn't ask, but my newfound confidence has me doing just that.

"Interesting, how?"

"You realize I look exactly like my twin brother, right? So does that mean you find him cute?"

There's no way I can tell him the truth. I'm not sure how he'd take the fact that I had my lips on his brother or that I loved it way too much. Even now, on the way to see him at work, my stomach is twisting with nerves.

"He's different to you."

"Not in the looks department."

No, not in the looks department. It's not so much their striking similarities there, it's more the aura they project. Killian has a presence that commands attention. Atlas is like a balm that soothes. So even though they may be identical, I don't see them as such.

He's waiting for my answer, so I appease him a little.

"I imagine other girls find him attractive."

I peek over at him to find he's holding in a chuckle, but we don't get time to pursue the conversation, thankfully, as we pull into work.

The butterflies in my stomach go berserk when we step through the doorway into the heated office.

Kill is leaning against the far wall of the office, watching us walk in as if he's been doing so since we stopped outside. He's got a mug of coffee in his hand, head angled, while he watches us.

As soon as our gazes clash, I'm back in my head, thinking about last night. The kiss. How he'd treated me so gently, like I'd break if he touched me firmer. His soft lips caught me by surprise. Every other part of him is hard. Including what lies between his legs. I'd felt it. And some strange part of me felt powerful at having that effect on him. Now I know what all the girls gush over at the lockers or in the cafeteria. I hear them talk.

I'm curious about sex and what the big deal is. Girls squeal and rave on and on about how good it is. Some I'd even call obsessed. Just like all the guys. I've never yearned for it like they do but maybe that's because I've been in survival mode most of my life.

Killian's inspecting me with the same intensity I'm giving him, even as my mind briefly wanders. Is he picturing the kiss, too? Or does he regret it? Afterwards, when he turned his back on me, it was as if he had.

"Hey," I say to him, cautiously, hoping today he's not in a mood.

His focus shifts to my mouth, causing me to inhale sharply. Yep. He's thinking of it. When he takes a swig from his mug, eyes still connected to mine, some of the brown liquid beads on his bottom lip. As if in slow motion, his tongue comes out to swipe across it, causing everything south of my navel to contract. Holy hell, that is hot.

Atlas seems oblivious while he shuffles files around on the desk.

"Hey yourself, little kitten."

That grabs Atlas' attention. "Why do you call her that?"

A shrug and then, "She's timid like one."

He's never removed his eyes from mine, and it's a little too unnerving. I need to move. So, I shuffle over to the desk, clearing my throat, hoping he'll leave so I can relax.

Atlas saves the moment. "Here, I'll show you how to book cars in."

Thank goodness.

In my peripheral vision, I see Kill walk back into the shop and I finally let out a full breath, focusing on the task at hand. My stomach never goes back to normal, though, knowing he's still in the same building.

For the next little while, we're going over bookings and taking cash off customers along with card transactions.

It's easy and I pick it up fast.

When Atlas makes his way out to work on a vehicle, I'm left to it, happy with how the place looks now, compared to when I first started.

Thirty-Nine

Killian

I've dropped the wrench four times.

"Someone's clumsy today. You okay, Bro?" My brother asks, poking his head out from under the hood of a blue Buick.

"Yep. Just got oily hands." I'm lying, of course, and only have a couple of spots of grease on them because I washed them ten minutes ago.

Damn her. The girl in the office. The one I haven't been able to stop thinking of. The one whose lips I still feel on my own. I'm not this guy. The one who obsesses over a girl. But this one? She's like a sickness. You don't know it's coming on. It's mild at first and then, bam. It takes a hold of your entire body.

I can't focus.

A hand lands on my shoulder. "Hey. You're miles away. Want to talk about it?"

No. I don't. Not with him. Least of all with him. He'll only tell me to leave her alone. That she's been through too much to deal with my crap. And it's all true but after last night, I need another taste. While he's happy we're getting along better, he has no idea what's been going on between us.

"Nah. I'm good. Just didn't sleep well last night. Nothing some more caffeine won't fix."

I leave him staring after me as I stride into the office, determined not to let Capri affect me. It's impossible though because when I wander through the door, she's bent over picking up something off the floor. Upon hearing me, she stands upright and spins, but it's too late. I've already had an eyeful of her long, slender legs and almost her panties.

My teeth grind and my hands fist as I steady myself. Her innocent eyes spark at my arrival.

"Oh, sorry. I just dropped this." She holds up a pen as if she needs to explain herself to me.

Because me being me, I like to see her reaction. I step forward into her space until we're toe to toe.

Surprisingly, she doesn't back away. Instead, her head lifts to mine, lips parted, a nice flush to her neck and cheeks.

My pulse is haywire, gut wrenching as if I'm about to jump off a plane with no parachute. Today she smells like flowers in spring. Like the sun after the rain has cleared. Like all the good things I've never had.

So slowly, I lean down until we're at eye level, making

sure I have her full attention. I'm breathing in her air. Her scent. It's intoxicating.

"Do I make you nervous?" All it will take is for me to lean in one inch and we'll be kissing again. The temptation is so great, but I restrain myself.

"No."

Liar. Her heavy breath and wide eyes give it away.

"Tell me, little kitten. Did you think about the kiss when you went to bed last night?"

She takes a step back and I match her.

"Of course not. Why would I?"

Indeed.

My hand comes up to pull her bottom lip out of her teeth. "Because I see the way you look at me. I was there last night. I felt how you responded to me. You can deny it all you want, but you've thought about doing it again. Just like I have."

"You have?"

"Mmmm. And if my brother wasn't close by, I'd kiss the hell out of you. I'd show you what it's like to not be afraid."

Just to prove my point, my knuckles graze down her cheek, bringing about goosebumps all over her.

"I don't want to want you. I've tried hard to keep my distance. But there's just something about you that draws me in."

I glance over to see my brother leaning over an engine, wrench in hand, elbow deep.

My head moves so my lips ghost over hers. "Would you like me to kiss you again?"

A subtle nod. "Yes."

The phone rings. Capri jolts, so I back off. She almost runs to answer it, causing me to chuckle. She answers the call, breathless and I silently high five myself for doing that to her.

While she's taking the call, I pour another coffee and head back out to continue work, my brother none-the-wiser.

If he were to turn around though, he'd see I'm sporting a massive erection and know for sure who has given it to me. With only her closeness.

What the hell is happening?

FORTY

Capri

Saturday night comes around quicker than I thought it would. After the almost kiss with Kill in the office earlier in the week, he's been distant. More like when I first moved in. We haven't practiced our self-defense either, which concerns me. I'm nowhere near ready to fend off my father, although I am more knowledgeable about various methods of attack to escape his clutches. It's a gamble, though. My father is tough.

Am I strong enough to overpower him?

Will he chase me if I run?

Perhaps I need to start gym training to improve my strength. Tomorrow I'm going to use the gym to do some weight training. If I'm going to survive an attack, I need to make it worthwhile and take him down fully.

At 7:45p.m., I'm dressed in a pair of skinny jeans, some ankle boots, and a tight fluffy sweater.

My makeup is understated yet classy, with just the right amount of eyeliner and mascara. I've opted for clear lip gloss instead of lipstick, which I rarely wear. My hair is curled slightly instead of its usual straight style, making me look like a new person.

I feel it too. This night will be good for me. I want to have fun and enjoy the party like a regular teen. Sans the alcohol.

Just as I'm about to make my way to the living room, my cell peals out. I'm hoping it's not Steph or Carly to say they can't make it.

When I see the number on the screen, I don't recognize it. For an instant, I pray it's not my dad using another cell. My fingers hover over the button to answer it. Part of me wants to ignore it but the other part of me wants to find out who it is. If it is my life-giver, I can always disconnect, right?

No more fear. Take back control.

"Hello?"

"Hi Capri. It's Officer Gina Sherwater. I took your statement the other day outside Pizza's R Us."

"Oh, yes. Hi."

Please don't say my father has been released. Please don't say it.

I walk back to my bed and sit on it, legs heavier than they were a moment ago, heart in my throat.

"I just wanted to update you on your dad. We've got a search warrant and found evidence in your home to build a good case against him for child abuse, child endangerment and neglect. There were diaries he kept in his office."

The words hang like bullets in the air.

"Diaries?"

"Yes. Ah, without going into too much detail as they've been kept as evidence, he kept records of the things he did to you."

"Oh God!" He wrote everything down. They'll know what he did to me. My hand flies to my throat in horror.

"Hey. Are you okay?"

"Yes. No. I'm not sure. It's just, my life is going to be exposed in front of a courtroom. It's humiliating enough without others knowing."

"I understand., And we'll keep it to a minimum who sees the evidence. I can guarantee you though, we won't put you on the stand if we can help it. What the other officers found is proof enough. He's sick and needs to be locked away."

My brain is all over the place. Will this mean I'm finally free of him?

"How long do you think he'll get in prison?"

"I know the judge we'll attempt to get assigned to this case. She's harsh when it comes to crimes against minors. Sentences can range from two to ten years. We'll push for the latter."

Only that amount? I want him locked away for life for what he's done to me. Gina picks up on my extended silence.

"Capri?"

"Yeah."

"Talk to me. What are you thinking?"

"It's just… even ten years doesn't seem long enough. When he gets out, he'll come for me."

"We will do everything to ensure he doesn't. He'll be on parole when he's released, meaning he won't be able to do anything without us knowing. You don't have to worry anymore."

"Will you keep me updated about everything, including whenever he's due to be released?"

"Promise."

"Okay. Thank you for everything."

"You're welcome, Capri. Take care."

After I end the call, I sit and process it. He's going to prison. That's good, right? I don't have to worry about the foreseeable future. I won't be looking over my shoulder all the time. If Gina is correct, the judge will give him longer than two years. That's enough time for me to get my life together. Who's to say I'll still be living in Maine by the time he's released? I can move away. Somewhere he'll never find me.

That idea has me blowing out a long breath. Things are going to be fine. This is what I wanted. Don't overthink it. Accept the fact you are now free.

A car horn sounds out, so I quickly grab my purse and head down the hallway, calling out to Atlas, who is in the kitchen.

"I'm going to the party. I'll catch you tomorrow." I'm not going to tell him about the phone call right now. I'm going to go to this party and celebrate with my friends. Celebrate the good news.

He shows himself and calls out, "Remember what I said about the drinks?"

With a salute and a tentative smile, I'm out the door, running to Carly's Volkswagen.

Time to be seventeen for once. We had light snow earlier, but it's now dissipated. Fingers crossed my fluffy sweater will keep me warm. Surely the mansion I'm headed to will have heating.

"Hey girl. You look good! You ready to let your hair down?" My friend practically sings as I open the door and sit inside.

She's wearing a woolen coat with leggings and black boots like mine. What has me doing a double take is her makeup. I've never seen her dolled up, and the result is striking. Gone are her freckles with a natural foundation and concealer, giving her skin a shiny glow. Her hair is blow-dried off her face, which highlights her lined blue eyes and mascara, which is on point. She's pretty.

Her energy is infectious, which helps me to relax, a spark of excitement taking hold. "Yes! Let's go see what all the fuss is about."

She lets out a whoop in response, turning the stereo up and easing out onto the road. Maybe in time, I'll let her know about my dad going to prison, but for now, I'm going to revel in the fact that he can't hurt me anymore. When and if I have to attend court, I'll let my friends know but until then, they'll remain oblivious.

My friend's not too bad of a driver, sticking to the speed limit, but she gets distracted sometimes while glancing over at me and yelling over the music, instead of turning it down. I'd rather she keep her eyes fully focused on the road.

At times, I'm holding my breath, but we manage to

make it to Cheryl's in one piece, rolling through a set of large gates and up a circular driveway.

The house is a massive two-story red brick home with white trim and two big columns jutting out from an overhead portico. There are at least thirty cars already parked, so we find a spot on the grass beside a red Audi. Luckily, the property is sprawling, allowing enough room for everyone.

Music is thumping, and the house is lit up like Christmas.

Nerves settle low in my belly. I'm not sure what to expect, but this is what I wanted, wasn't it? To be a normal teenager. Not stuck at home while everyone else was out having fun.

Carly must see apprehension in my expression because she's almost outside the door before she bends down to look at me. "Come on. Don't overthink it. Just relax."

And so, before I can talk myself out of it, I'm following her onto the front porch and through the open door.

We're greeted by a few students drinking, chatting, and loitering in the foyer, but I'm guessing the heart of the party is out back or in another room.

"Come on. Let's grab a drink." Carly shouts over the deep bass.

Hopefully, there is soda as well for those of us who aren't into alcohol.

When we wind through the house, we find a large kitchen and outdoor area with hordes of people.

There's an oversized keg to one side with students

lined up, all of which are no doubt underage. Where are Cheryl's parents? Is no one supervising?

Obviously not.

"Do you want a drink?" Cheryl asks, heading over to a guy handing out solo cups of wine.

"I don't drink. Is there any soda?" I scan the room, searching for anything that isn't alcoholic. Bottle are lined up across a bench, making the space appear like a professional bar.

"I'm not sure. Why don't you just have one? Try it and see. If there's no soda, you can sip on the one drink all night."

"I don't know. I don't think I'll like it." Plus, my father became more violent after drinking. I don't want to end up like him.

"Just one." We're now at the front of the line. A tall jock with a man bun greets us.

"Sup, ladies." His teeth practically glow. They're so white.

Carly takes a cup and hands it to me, ignoring the fact I told her I don't drink. I don't want it, but I don't want to seem like a total prude either. Maybe I can tip it into a garden bed.

"Do you have Coke or 7up?" It sounds juvenile, but I don't care.

He smiles at me. "What's the matter? You come to a party like this, and you don't drink?"

Is he really going to put me on the spot?

"Not really. And my friend shouldn't be either. She's driving." I look to Carly, who has already downed half her plastic cup full.

"No soda at this party. It's wine, beer, or spirits in a can. Sorry."

Well, that sucks. Who doesn't have Coke at a party? Not wanting to cause a scene, I nod and turn to Carly with a questioning look, my eyes pivoting to her cup and back up to her eyes. She is my ride home. She shouldn't be drinking. I thought she was more responsible.

"I'm fine. I'll only have a couple. Promise. Let's go find Steph."

She's dragging me away before I can protest. I guess I'm going to be holding the same drink all night and making sure Carly keeps her word.

Outside, the cold air hits us, but there are a couple of fire pits staggered in the yard with people huddling around.

"She said she'd meet us out back somewhere. Let's look for her."

There are floodlights streaming over the sprawling property which has a pool to one side and landscape gardens dotted around. Tall trees sit just over the back fence in the distance, making the space nice and private. Apparently, the pool is heated, which is why a few people are battling the cold to jump in and stay there. Not if you paid me. Would I get into a swimsuit at almost zero degrees, but each to their own.

A couple of people are already making out, others dancing.

I take a sip of my drink, thinking I'll hate it, but I'm surprised it's fruity and not bitter. Carly has finished hers and throws the cup into a large bin as we near a fire.

Drunken revelry attempts to drown out the pumping

music, which must be wired to outdoor speakers it's so loud. Squeals and hollers from boys draw my attention as a guy and girl get pushed into the pool fully clothed.

I grip onto Carly's coat as we weave through bodies.

"Hey, mouse," a deep voice rumbles out from behind me, causing me to jump and spill some of my drink.

Chase stands with a guy he hangs around at school, an enormous grin on his face. "Never thought I'd see you at a party."

Ugh. He's the last person I want to run into. After the close encounter at school, I don't want him flirting, touching, or following me.

Carly, however, is rooted to the spot, mouth open, eyes the size of dinner plates, watching him move closer to me, as if she's shocked a guy like him would be talking to me. He's never acknowledged either of us until recently.

"There's always a first time." I just want to find Steph and leave Chase to his own devices.

"Glad to see you outside of school." He eyes my drink. "Girl! You're liquored up too? Maybe you aren't the little mouse I think you are." He's in my space, causing me to back up.

"Ahh, I've got to go. We're looking for a friend." I give my attention to Carly, who is still staring like a stunned mullet. He hasn't bothered to even acknowledge her.

He leans down close, and I'm worried he's about to touch me. Or worse—kiss me.

"Make sure you come back and have a dance with me." His breath reeks of alcohol, so that will be a huge no.

I smile sharply and inch out around him, leaving him

chuckling. There's no way I'm going to dance with him. In fact, if he keeps drinking the way he is, he'll be passed out in another hour, and I won't have to worry about him seeking me out.

"What was that?" Carly asks, moving with me away from Chase.

"Ah. Nothing. We have a class together and he kind of tried to hit on me, I think."

"What?" she's yelling in a high voice. "Chase, the football quarterback likes you? I mean, why would he not but he's always got hordes of cheerleaders around."

She's right. I don't know why he's taken an interest in me, but it has to be some kind of joke. A dare. And speaking of cheerleaders, I wonder where Michaela is. So far, we haven't bumped into her. Who knows what she'd say to me if she saw Chase talking to me again?

"Whatever the reason, he's wasting his time. I'm not interested."

My mind goes to a tall, dark, and handsome guy who has been avoiding me. It's obvious he regretted kissing me, which shouldn't bother me, but it does. I want him to like me. Normally, I couldn't care less what anyone thinks of me. I also don't go around letting any guy kiss me or touch me. But I don't get too much time to overthink it because Steph bounds over to us from a girl I recognize at school. Maybe they share a class together.

"Hey! There you both are. I've been looking for you." Her words slur and I know she's had way too much to drink. I didn't know she drank, but then tonight is full of firsts.

Her outfit is typical Steph. All black. A dress that hugs

her curves with a large turn of the century looking pendant hanging down her chest. Her hair is in a slick bun with a scarf holding everything in place at the edge of her forehead. She's got long knee-high socks on with flats. Somehow, she pulls it all off effortlessly and rocks the look.

"We were looking for you," Carly replies. "Come on, let's go inside and dance."

All the furniture in the massive lounge room has been pushed to the sides and bodies are writhing as Green Day's "American Idiot" threatens to lift the roof and everyone goes berserk jumping in time to the upbeat.

I've never really been into dancing, but with everyone else doing it, the vibe is electric as a group of girls sing at the top of their lungs. I finish my drink and place the cup on a table.

We join in the chaos, and I laugh as we raise our hands, jumping up and down while banging into people.

This is what I've been missing out on. Letting go and not having a care in the world. After Chase's attempting to flirt with me, I need to forget everything, including him, my father, and Killian. What better way to do that than by losing myself in music?

I've always loved listening to it and have an extensive playlist on my phone. It's helped me through many nights of sadness when nothing else could.

We stay on the floor for a few more songs until we're all sweating.

"Let's go get another drink," Steph shouts.

My mouth is dry and I'm super thirsty, so I agree as the three of us leave the living room for the kitchen.

Cheryl is floating around the place but she's not really in our circle, even though half our grade is here. Word gets around when there is a party, and everyone turns up. It's to be expected in high school.

"There's a games room on the other side of the house. Let's go and check it out." Carly offers after we each grab a cup of wine. Because I don't normally drink, I can feel the effect after only one, my inhibitions lowering. This is the best I've felt and I'm not about to have it end. It's all about new beginnings and letting go. I can go back to being a prude tomorrow. This is me finding my purpose and enjoying myself, not following in the footsteps of my father.

We follow the long hallway to the end, where a set of double doors greet us. They're shut, so we push our way through to find a large space with a pool table, ping-pong table, two large flat screen televisions where people are playing COD and other video games. There are large sofas placed around and beanbag chairs, making the atmosphere a casual one. Quieter.

There's also a beer pong table set up. "Come on. Let's play." Steph grabs my arm and drags me over. I don't have any idea what to do, so we stand and watch four people play while we sip our drinks.

If you miss getting the ball into the cup, you have to take a drink. Seems simple enough, considering I've played netball at school and have a good aim when shooting goals.

There's a fifteen-minute wait for the table to be free. In that time, we've finished our wine and had a refill, compliments of Carly. I push the guilt down at how easily

I've been swayed into drinking, but push it away as quickly, determined to ignore my brain telling me other-wise. I'm finally fitting in.

"Okay, let's do this," squeals Steph, going to the end of the table and picking up the small white ball. She takes aim. The ball looks like it's going to hit its target, but lands on the cup rim and falls off. "Aww, I was so close." She takes a swig of her wine.

"Your turn." She points to me.

Confident I can avoid taking a sip, I move to where Steph was and take aim.

"Go, Capri!" Cheers Carly.

I smile and toss the ball in what I hope will be the closest cup, but it veers off and lands on the table. Wow! This is harder than it looks.

"Drink, drink." A couple of guys have gathered to watch. I don't recognize them. One is tall with blond hair and a goatee. Not my cup of tea, but Steph grins at him and checks him out. The other guy is a redhead. Shorter and stocky. Not unattractive, but again, not my type.

I take an extra-large swig from my drink and pout when I see I've almost finished it.

"I'll need a top up if I'm going to play again."

Tall, blond dude says, "I'll grab you one."

Remembering Atlas' final words to me before I left the house, I stop him as he's turning. "No. I'll go grab it."

He looks at me weirdly but nods, so I face the girls and say, "I'll grab three while I'm there."

Carly is lined up to take her shot as Steph sidles up to the dude I just spoke to. She sways a little, but he places a hand on her back to help steady her. As I turn around, I hear her giggle.

Oh boy. She's going to be unwell tomorrow. And Carly is way over the legal limit to drive. Looks like we'll have to call Uber.

In the kitchen, I fill up from the keg, which is now unmanned, noticing how evenly people are distributed. Music still blares from the impressive speakers in the living room and there are loads of people outside.

I realize in this moment, I'm officially part of the crowd. No one has told me I'm a freak and to leave, even though I've only spoken to three guys in total. There have been no weird looks or whispers. Everyone who came simply wants to have fun.

When I return to the game room, the blond guy has his arm around Steph's shoulders, the pair laughing at something no one else is privy to.

I've never seen her with a guy before, so it's odd to find her in an intimate conversation with one.

"You're up," cries Carly, holding out her hand for the wine when I get closer. I place Steph's at the side of the table.

This time when I aim, by some miracle, the ball goes in the cup. My head is light, and I feel the best I ever have, so when I cheer loudly and do a happy dance, my friends laugh along with me.

Carly moves in beside me. "You having fun?"

"I am. Thank you. This is the best night ever."

It's true. Not just because I've had some alcohol, but because I'm a part of something. With my peers. Outside of school. Something I never thought I'd get to do.

"I need to pee. You have your go and I'll be back soon." My bladder is so full it's almost bursting.

"You need me to come with you?" she asks.

"No, I saw a bathroom on our way down here. I'll be fine." I appreciate her offer, but I need to start doing things on my own. "You hold the table for us."

With a nod and a thumbs up, I leave her to it, exiting the game room and making the trek down the long hallway. A couple are making out halfway down and a girl exits the bathroom I'm heading to, so before anyone else comes, I quickly enter and lock the door. The space is what I'd expect it to be for such a large house. It's huge, with a large corner tub, double shower, and vanity basins. The toilet has a wall across one side, but otherwise isn't totally closed off. I go about my business, relieved to have an empty bladder.

I wash my hands and check my reflection in the mirror. I look… different. Maybe it's the booze, or maybe it's the fact that I'm not focused on being a victim. The monster is locked away and can't hurt me. I'm living with two great guys and have a new job. It's incredible to imagine, and yet, here I am. Still alive. Taking day by day.

The frown line that is often present on my forehead has gone, my cheeks flushed, and my eyes are unafraid. They've always had a sadness about them, but tonight they tell a new story. One I hope remains.

Straightening my shoulders, I unlock the door and come face to face with Chase, who leans against the opposite wall.

He's wearing a sloppy, drunk smile, which automatically has me on alert.

"Hey gorgeous. We didn't have that dance I asked for. I thought you'd gone home, but as I turned the corner into the hallway, there you were, sneaking into the bathroom."

He moves forward, so I shuffle back into the open doorway I just came out of, hoping to get inside and lock the door. He stinks of alcohol, a smell I'm too familiar with. It's all hard liquor. As much as I'm already on my third, it's nothing compared to him. The stale scent is all over him, as well as cigarette smoke.

A flicker of a memory has my pulse quickening. Before I can get the door properly closed, his footsteps inside, thwarting my attempt.

"Aww, don't be like that. I just want to chat. We don't get to talk at school."

His eyes are bloodshot as he shuts the door and locks it behind him. A new panic takes hold.

"I need to get back out to my friends. We can dance later. I haven't forgotten," I lie, hoping he's appeased.

His head angles slightly as he grins, moving closer to me with each step I take back, until my back is against the vanity, and I have nowhere else to go.

"I think you've been trying to avoid me all night." His hand comes up to my face, causing me to flinch. "Are you the frigid little mouse we all think you are?"

"Don't touch me," I grind out, pushing his hand away.

He tsks. I almost gag at his vile breath on me. My mind spirals back to not so long ago, when my father was in this very position. Over me. Using his size to intimidate me.

"Or what? Hmm? Come on. I've never been with a virgin before. You are a virgin, right?"

"Please, Chase. Don't do this. Let's just go out and I'll dance with you. I promise."

No one will hear me if I scream. The music is too loud.

He laughs, knowing I'm just telling him this to get him to leave.

He doesn't even respond to my words. Instead, the hand on my face moves to my throat. "I'll make your first time memorable. I promise."

Oh no. This is not happening. Not after the fun I've had tonight. Chase does not get to ruin it for me.

Act without thinking. Killian's words come into my mind as if he were here, whispering them to me.

I only have one chance to get out of this and I need to do it now.

Don't be afraid, Capri. That girl you saw in the mirror moments ago is who you are now.

With every ounce of strength I have, I bring my forearm up and ram his arm to the left, dislodging his hand from my throat and then bring my knee up into his groin, hard.

He howls with pain, doubling over so I don't wait another second. I bolt for the door, unlocking it and racing out. I don't stop. With my purse slung around my torso where it's been all night, I run down to the living room and out the front door, not caring about my friends in the games room.

People hover on the porch, glancing at me as I hurry across the lawn, desperate to get away.

I don't care where I'm going as long as it's not here. I weave around cars, the sounds of the party become quieter, the further away I get, until I'm stumbling through the large iron gates, which remain open, onto the road.

Snow has fallen again. Not enough to whiten the grass, but enough to feel the icy fingers dancing on my face.

With a quick glance back to make sure Chase isn't following me, I keep running down the road until I can't see the house anymore.

It's only then, do I stop and grip onto a tree lining the street and burst into tears. What a jerk! Why did he have to ruin my night? Why did he have to ignore me when I asked him to stop? Probably because he wasn't expecting me to fight back. After all, I didn't get my nickname at school for no good reason.

My stomach roils to let me know I'm going to be sick, so I hunch over and empty the contents onto the grassy verge, watery alcohol emerging. My head is spinning, the lightweight that I am, taking the full brunt of the drinks I've had.

Ugh. Drinking doesn't feel like a good idea anymore. I'm not sure if I'm sick from that or from Chase cornering me in the bathroom. Probably a combination of both. Now that I'm outside, my breathing steadies.

Once I feel like I'm not going to throw up any more, I move away from the mess I made, wondering how the hell I'm going to get home. All I want to do is crawl into my bed and sleep.

Digging my cell out, I dial Atlas' number and curse when it goes to voice mail.

It's midnight. He's either asleep or out with Coby.

Not knowing who else to call, I see Kill's name on my cell, in two frames of mind on whether I should call him. I could call an Uber. Will he be angry if I wake him? Or maybe he's up playing a video game.

I don't have my own key to the house yet. What if he's out too? If I get an Uber, I may be stuck outside until one of the brothers return.

Deciding to bite the bullet, I dial his number. It rings four times.

Pick up. Pick up.

"Capri?"

His voice sounds sleepy. Shit. I have woken him.

My voice is husky from throwing up. "Kill, I need you to come get me."

"Where are you?" He's on high alert, I can tell.

"I'm at the party." I manage to give him the address, but don't tell him what happened. "I'm outside the gates along the road a bit."

"Are you on your own?" He sounds mad.

"Yes."

"Fuck. Don't move. I'm on my way." And then he's gone. Relief has my legs buckle until I'm sitting on the cold, whitening grass. I put my head in my hands, going over the last half hour. The night had been going so well. I should have known something would happen to kill my fun. One night. That's all I wanted. Am I destined to be a magnet for trouble?

The idea of Chase's hands on me or anywhere near me makes me gag again, but nothing comes out. How dare he do that to me? Drunk or not, I should report him. That doesn't give him any right to come on to me when I told him no.

My hair is sticking to my face, and I'm sure my

mascara has bled into my cheeks by now. The wind picks up, causing me to hug my knees, the scent of my vomit drifting over.

Snowflakes continue to feather down, so I lift my face up to it in the hopes it'll help sober me up some.

I sit like this for ten minutes until the sound of a bike gets louder. A bright light rounds the corner and I know it's him.

It almost has me sobbing with relief.

When he pulls up beside me, he's off the bike in a second, having kicked the stand down.

In a run, he's on me, bending down, lifting the visor of his helmet. His face is filled with concern.

"Little kitten, what the fuck happened?"

He's lifting my chin with his gloved hand. I don't even flinch. Not like I did with Chase. Kill's touch is different and familiar. His very presence calms me, even though he looks like he wants to murder someone.

"I… someone…" And then I break.

Killian rips his helmet off and is pulling me into him, my face mashed against his leather jacket. It's like a balm that soothes. You know that soon, some of the pain will dissipate and you'll be able to breathe again. Just the smell of him is like returning home.

"Shhh. You're okay. I'm here. I've got you."

He's cradling my head against him, letting me cry. His large body warms me until I'm not shuddering anymore and the sobs ease.

When I feel as if I've gathered myself, I pull back.

"Who did something to you?" he growls. He's coiled tight, his jaw looking so sharp it could cut glass.

"Chase. Just a guy from school. He was drunk." I attempt to cover for the guy because Kill has death in his eyes.

"Did he rape you?"

"No! He wanted to take my virginity and when I told him no and he kept touching me, I kneed him in the groin."

Pride enters his widening eyes and his jaw ticks. "You did?"

A quick nod and he's full-on smiling. "Good girl." His thumb rubs my cheek, and he kisses my forehead with such a softness, I close my eyes and relish it. Why is his touch okay but no one else's is? I don't fully understand it.

"I'm going to put you on my bike, okay? And then I'm going to teach this douche a lesson. He can't force himself on you."

The scent of my puke drifts over, and he turns to find it not far away. "You get drunk too?"

There's no judgment, just interest.

"I was onto my third, I think. Something like that. I'm not drunk. Just... happy. At least I was. It's the first time I've touched alcohol, so between that and Chase, I guess my body couldn't handle it."

He picks me up and sits me on his bike, taking the spare helmet and placing it on my head, tying it in place.

I don't like the idea of violence but if Kill doesn't put him in his place, he could try it again. I've never had anyone stick up for me like this. It makes me feel worthy for the first time.

"I'm going to turn the bike around and return to the house, okay? But I want you to stay on the bike."

"Okay. Thank you."

He starts the bike back up and we turn, riding down the road and then heading up the long driveway. Nothing has changed at the house, and everyone is carrying on as if I didn't have a meltdown because of Chase. I briefly wonder how his groin is, but then I dismiss it. He deserved whatever I gave him.

Kill stops the bike and kicks down the stand again. "Are you okay?"

"Yeah, just make it quick. I don't want to be here. What if he comes from the backyard while you're inside?"

He scans the vicinity before turning back to me. "You'll see him coming. If you do, call me immediately. I'll come running."

The idea of seeing Chase again isn't pleasant. He'll be angry for sure and there's no telling what he will do. But I give a curt nod and watch as Killian hurries inside, ignoring the students out front.

They look at him and then back at me, probably wondering why I'm not following him.

I pull my cell out of my purse and hold it ready. Should I need it, checking the yard for any signs of Chase. Maybe he's passed out from all the alcohol. I can only hope.

My cell pings with a message. I see it's from Carly.

Where are you?

I type out a response: *I left. Wasn't feeling it and I think I drank too much. Called an Uber. I'll talk to you on Monday.*

Her reply comes a minute later. Okay. *No problem. Talk then. I'll let Steph know. x*

I'm not in the mood to explain more tonight. It can

wait until Monday. There will be some questions for sure, asking if I'm feeling better. Me lying again to protect myself from relaying the event. It's what I'm good at. Hiding the truth. Keeping things to myself. I know friends are meant to confide in each other, but what can they do by me confessing? I don't want pity.

Waiting for Kill feels like forever, until finally he appears out the front door, looking like an avenging angel. My angel.

Stop it, Capri. He's not yours. He's simply doing you a solid.

It doesn't matter though. I'm grateful he's here for me tonight.

When he stops in front of me, I see the knuckles on his right hand are bright red. Otherwise, he looks unscathed.

"He won't be bothering you again." He grabs his helmet and climbs on before I can ask him what he did.

The engine fires up and thankfully we're leaving and heading home. I don't care if I go to another party for a long time. If Chase hadn't hit on me, the night would have been entirely different. It's sad that one bad drunk has left a sour taste in my mouth.

I snuggle up to Killian's back, feeling safe. He's proven himself tonight. There's no doubt in my mind that he'll always protect me.

FORTY-ONE

Killian

Getting the phone call from Capri had me immediately thinking the worst. Had her father been released and found her? It's the first thing that crossed my mind. That he'd intercepted her at the party. Waited for her outside. When she explained it was someone else, my rage was no less.

I hadn't thought for a second before throwing on my leathers and racing out the door. My need to be the one to save her was pure instinct and one I'm thankful I acted on.

Now, as she's pressed into me on the back of my bike, I feel a shred of relief but mostly volatile anger like no other.

Chase is unconscious with a broken nose and a missing front tooth. He's lucky he was so drunk and probably didn't feel what I did to him. But he's going to be in a world of pain when he wakes up.

I'd had to ask numerous people before someone told me where he was. Out back, attempting to hit on another unsuspecting girl who looked just as pleased that I'd stepped in and saved her as Capri had when I'd showed up on my bike.

After dragging him around the side of the house, I left him in a pathetic heap on the grass, where he'll no doubt stay until the sun comes up. If someone doesn't stumble upon him first.

As if Capri hasn't been through enough already. I can't think straight.

Atlas is on a date, so of course I'm the only one left for her to call. I'm not sure if she tried my brother first, but it doesn't matter.

When we pull into the driveway of our house, I switch the bike off and remove my helmet. Once the stand is down, I peel Capri's hands from around my waist and get off, watching her jerk upright as if she's fallen asleep.

Carefully, I take her helmet off and gaze at her blood-shot eyes. "You with me?"

"Yeah. Just tired." She yawns so I pick her up, noticing how light she is. I don't bother putting her on her feet. I carry her inside and head straight to her bedroom.

"Do you need to take a shower?" I ask, setting her on the bed.

"No. I just want to sleep and forget tonight happened."

She lies down, watching me with heavy eyes.

I turn to leave but she cries out, "Wait. Don't go. Please?"

My heart kicks up a notch, and my eyebrows rise. What is she asking?

"Stay." She moves over against the wall, leaving room for me.

My hand automatically grips the back of my neck, squeezing. She wants me to stay with her? Me?

Noticing my apprehension, she gives me a small smile. "To sleep. I don't want to be alone."

Is she that trusting of me? I can't describe the emotion that washes over me as I step forward and throw my jacket onto the floor before removing my boots. This girl is something else.

"Here. Get under the covers." I pull them aside, helping her climb under. I do the same, keeping enough distance between us so that we're not touching, even though I want to pull her into my arms and whisper words of comfort to her.

Since when have I become *that* guy? Capri Lennon has turned my world upside down in more ways than one. She's under my skin deeper than any girl ever has been, and it confuses the hell out of me.

Not even a minute later, I hear her even breathing and know she's out.

Turning my head, I watch her, bringing my hand up to brush strands of hair from her face, noting how fragile she is. She's already broken once. I'm not going to let it happen again.

Her face is that of an angel. Porcelain skin like the finest China. Lips so kissable that I physically hold myself back from meshing them with mine. I've already had a taste and I want more.

The biggest question is, why has she allowed me in when she clearly has an aversion to the opposite sex? Me, of all people, who made it perfectly clear I was going to have nothing to do with her. And yet, here we are. In her bed. She begged me to stay with her, so she feels safe.

I've already proven it to her. Twice now. A girl with her history doesn't trust easily, so for me to be the one she's chosen to do that lights me up within.

I allow time to study her while feathering my fingers across her forehead and cheeks, listening to her fall deeper into sleep, her mouth opening slightly.

I take a long time to drift off while still caressing her as I realize not only am I comforting her, but she's comforting me.

When consciousness finds me, the sun is peeping through gaps in the blinds. I'm shackled to a bed, the weight of limbs across my legs and torso.

With a glance down, I find Capri wound around me like ivy. My head falls back to the pillow, the sensation bringing a smile to my face. In the night, she's sought further comfort from me, and I must admit, it's not unpleasant. Not at all.

I imagine waking up like this every morning, knowing she's mine. Greeting her with warm kisses, my hands roaming all over her body.

Everything south of my navel hardens as dirty images fill my mind.

Don't go there, Kill. She's innocent. A bud that hasn't opened yet.

Still, the possibility of being her first and teaching her is a nice idea.

I stroke her hair but pull back when she stirs. I don't want her to think I've taken advantage of her in the position we're currently in.

I lower my chin and watch as her eyes slowly open. It takes a moment for her to register where she is and suddenly, she's throwing herself off me and sitting ramrod straight.

"Oh, I… um… what happened?"

Her cheeks redden beautifully at the realization I'm in her bed.

"You used me as a giant teddy bear." I can't help it. Seeing her eyes widen, a hand coming to her throat has me chuckling.

"Relax, little kitten. Take a minute to remember what happened last night."

She does. Her face falling, eyes screwing tightly shut when it all comes back.

"Oh, God." She drops her face into her hands and I'm not sure if it's because of the party or because I'm in her bed with her.

"Nothing happened. I was the perfect gentleman, promise." Not something I thought I'd ever say to a pretty girl.

She's still not looking at me, so I coax her. "Hey, look at me."

Slowly, her hands come down and she turns her head. Even with dark mascara eyes and bed hair, she's stunning.

"You gonna be, okay?" I mean it. I need to know before I climb out and prepare breakfast. There's no movement in the house, so I'm not even sure if Atlas is home or not. He may have stayed out all night.

"How bad did you beat up Chase?"

"You care about how he is?" I ask, suddenly angry that it would even matter to her.

"Not really, but I have to face him at school. I'm not sure I'll be able to do that."

I sit up and face her, placing a placating hand on her shoulder to see if she'll allow me to. After all, today is a new day and I'm not sure if she even wants me touching her again or if she's taken a step back in her healing.

When she doesn't flinch, I answer, "You don't have to worry about that. He's lucky we didn't go to the police. I told him if he even looks at you again, he'll have a permanent disability. I don't think he'll be in school for a while. I kind of broke his nose and punched out a tooth."

"You did?"

"Yep. The golden boy isn't so golden now."

We're staring at each other, me unable to pull away, her searching for something. The air crackles around us, pulling me in like a magnet.

"Thank you. For picking me up. For putting me to bed. And for being there for me."

Eyes like a portal into another dimension weave their magic on me. So much so that I don't see her hand come up to my face and brush my skin. It's not until the contact and burn it evokes that I realize she's touching me under her own volition. This is huge for her. I can't move. Don't want to.

Her head is moving to mine ever so slowly. Time stops. My fingers are curled tightly at my sides as I allow her to control this. Whatever she needs.

I'm combusting. Each brush of her fingertips heats my skin until I'm sure my face is flaming.

When plump, tentative lips touch mine, I'm gone. Every emotion under the sun floods me. My hand comes up to the back of her head, holding her where I want her while our lips open for each other. I groan into her mouth in relief. As if I've finally found what I've been craving. She mewls in response and it's like music to my ears.

I deepen the kiss, needing her like air. Both of her hands now grip my face, firmer, holding me in the palms of her hands. And it's not just my head but my whole body she cradles. My tongue flickers out and surprisingly she meets it. The kiss is as natural as breathing.

Where has this girl been my whole life?

Testing the waters, I touch her neck, moving my lips down to kiss the sensitive spot behind her ear. She extends her head back, a heated moan dragging from her throat, spurring me on, licking and sucking. I don't want to push her, so I let this be enough, even though I'm so hard right now.

"Kill," she pants.

"Mmm?" *Please don't tell me to stop. Please don't.*

"What's happening?"

Indeed. She's feeling it, too. We're both drowning. Drugged on each other. This is the best kind of high.

"I don't know." It's true. I have no idea what the hell I'm doing, but I know I don't want it to end.

My lips find hers again and she's greedier this time, setting the pace. If she hasn't been kissed like this before, she's a fast learner. The first time with her in the shed was simply a test in the water. Like dipping our toes in. This though? This is entirely different.

There's a craving for this girl. To not only have her physically, but mentally as well.

To immerse myself in her mind, body, and soul.

Pulling back for a breath, I note her fully blown eyes. She's the sexiest thing I've seen. Lips swollen. Breath choppy. Chest heaving.

And then the front door opens and closes, a voice calling out. "Kill?"

Atlas.

As if we've been splashed with cold water, we both separate, me scrambling out of her bed, not bothering to look back as I take off for my room. The last thing I want my brother to find is me in Capri's bed, even if we are fully clothed. He'll be able to tell just by looking at us what we've been doing.

FORTY-TWO

Capri

My entire body still feels him. His kiss marked me like a branding iron. All I can think of is falling into him the way I did. And he caught me. There are no words. Every part of me joined with every part of him and not in the physical sense. There was no beginning or end to us. It's hard to describe.

I'm speechless. I don't even know how it happened. The way he'd been looking at me so tenderly, and the way he took care of me last night, opened my eyes to just who Killian MacKenzie is. All along I thought he was an asshole, when in reality he's my savior who has been hurt in the past and doesn't trust easily. Just like me. We're one and the same. His pain, emotional. Mine both mental and physical.

Minutes ago, he revealed his true self to me.

I touch my lips. His impression is still there. My heart craves for him to come back and touch me again and again.

But I hear Atlas walking down the hallway. How would he react to his brother and me? And was it a onetime thing? Will Kill go back to being distant with me? I can't believe he would do that. We have crossed the final barrier we've had up to protect ourselves from our own pain.

Killian is the balm I need. Am I the same for him? And will things be awkward now?

I climb out of bed and open my bedroom door to find Atlas turn just as he's about to enter his own room.

"Hey. I didn't think anyone was home." He walks over to me.

"How was the party? You look like you've been run over by a truck. No one drugged you, did they?" His face is filled with concern.

What do I say to him?

"No. I'm fine. I had a few wines, but I'm all good." He doesn't need to know what happened. He's had enough on his plate with his dad. Hopefully Kill will keep quiet too.

"Says the girl who doesn't drink." Atlas is smiling, so I know he's saying it in jest.

"Yeah, well, I won't be touching it again anytime soon."

"Ahh, hungover?"

Kill exits his room in a pair of sweats. My attention immediately goes to his bare chest, a hot flush creeping up my neck at the sight of him. Atlas turns, finishing our conversation.

"Brother."

Kill's eyes are on mine, and I can't help but hope he's remembering our mouths fused together.

God, he's got a beautiful physique, if you can call a man's body beautiful.

Atlas turns back to me and then back to his brother, who is still focused on me.

"Ahh, am I missing something?"

"No!" Kill and I both say together, snapping out of it.

"Just heading out to get breakfast." He walks past us, his heat blanketing me, his hand grazing mine as he leaves.

When I turn back to Atlas, he's observing me, carefully. "Did he hurt you?"

Is that what he thinks? Couldn't he feel the thick energy in the hallway?

"Not at all. He's been the perfect gentleman. He picked me up from the party after I called. I uh… tried you first, but you were obviously busy. My friends had too much to drink." I need to turn the conversation back to him.

Guilt mars his features. "I'm so sorry. Yeah, I stayed at Coby's. We kind of had an argument, but we'll work it out."

He bites into his lower lip, forehead creasing, eyes staring off to nowhere in particular.

"Are you sure?" It's still early days for his relationship. The idea of them already fighting isn't good, but I don't say that.

"Yep. All good. I'm just going to get some shuteye. It's been a long night."

Tell me about it. Atlas looks how I imagine I do. Disheveled with bags under both eyes.

Needing to pee and shower, I nod, letting him go before heading to the bathroom.

* * *

The water turns cold before I switch the shower off and step out. I needed extra time under the spray to process everything that had happened last night. The good and the bad. The good outweighed the bad, so I need to focus on that. To take stock of how far I've come in such a short time.

If my mother were here, would she be proud of me? That she's never attempted to contact me gives me my answer. Still, a girl can't help wondering what she looks like now. Where she lives and does she have another family?

I've searched the internet over the years for Katherine Lennon but to no avail. It's as if she is merely a ghost. Snippets of memories destined to haunt me forever.

I need to leave her in the past where she belongs. As much as I envy girls who have great relationships with their mothers, I'm not the only one who must do without.

My head is down as I walk into the kitchen, slamming into a body.

Killian. He grips both my elbows to stop me from falling.

"I'm so sorry! I wasn't watching where I was going." It's obvious.

My breath is stolen from me as I take in the full picture of him. Every muscle he has appears more rigid and defined, his hair a mess, eyes dark and dangerous. As if I didn't see him five minutes ago. When he's standing at his full height, every part of him seems more pronounced. Soft skin over hard steel.

"You were miles away. Were you thinking about last night?"

"No. I was thinking about my mom."

This gets his attention. I've never spoken about her with him.

"Oh. Does she live out of state? I haven't heard you mention her." He lets me go but remains in my space and frankly, I don't want him to move.

"I'm not sure. She left when I was eight years old. Probably because of my father. In a way, I can't blame her, but it would have been nice if she took me with her or called to see if I was okay occasionally."

Why am I blurting everything out to him? He won't want to hear about more of my past. I blink up at him, waiting for his dismissal, but the opposite happens. He utters two words. Two words that are pregnant with meaning.

"Her loss."

Meaning, he thinks I am worth more than her. That I'm worth something. Perhaps to him? I can't be sure. But it warms me all over. This new place we're at as far as our truce goes is nice. He's nice.

He leads me to a dining chair, sits me down and says, "Coffee? I sure as hell need one. We can talk while we drink." Who knew the broody bad boy could hold a regular conversation? He's continuing to surprise me.

"Okay. Cream. No sugar. Thank you."

I very much like this Kill. He's kind and caring, unlike his alter ego, which I hope I never see again.

Things aren't awkward as I imagined them to be.

He's putting off whatever else he needs to do to make me coffee and to talk. It must mean something, right? He cares.

Watching him move around the kitchen is going to become my new favorite hobby. He's lithe, like a panther, his movements fluid.

"Earth to Capri?"

"Huh?"

"Do you want anything to eat? I'm making pancakes."

"Oh, no. Thanks."

He's smirking at me, knowing my full focus was on his body. And rightfully so. I can't imagine any female not taking their fill.

Kill places my mug down and moves to turn some more pancakes over.

"Thank you."

"Sure. You positive you don't want some of these? I've made a gazillion."

My stomach rebels at the idea of eating. "No. I'm good. Coffee will do."

He nods, proceeding to finish making his breakfast. Me ogling him while I can, sipping my brown beverage, enjoying the companionable silence.

Finally, after stacking up a plate high and grabbing some maple syrup from the cupboard, he settles into the seat opposite me, a mouthful of food blowing out his cheeks.

I remember I didn't have a chance to tell the boys about the call with Gina.

So, when he watches me as if prompting me to make conversation, I do.

"The officer who took my statement called with an update about my father."

He stops chewing and gulps down some coffee.

"And?"

"And she said they found evidence at the house to build a case. He'll get two years minimum. Ten max."

He mulls it over, taking in my tone of voice.

"Are you happy with that outcome?"

With a shrug, I tap my fingers on the wooden table. "Yes, and no. I think two years is not enough and hopefully the judge will, too."

He nods. "Well, either way, you can breathe easier, knowing he's off the streets. Hopefully, he'll get what's coming to him in prison." He squirts more maple syrup onto a pancake, folding it up and stuffing half of it in his mouth.

A mouth that feels way too good on mine. There's a crumb on his lower lip I want to wipe off, but he beats me to it by swiping his thumb over it. Not before he catches me watching him again.

"Am I making you nervous, little kitten?"

Yes. Most definitely.

"No. I just… this is nice. To be civil to each other."

"I think we passed that point when we had our tongues down each other's throats, don't you?"

Sheesh. Does he have to be so blunt? The vision of it brings about another wave of longing, causing me to squirm in my chair. His lips are nice, but his tongue? It makes my knees feel weak even sitting down.

"Did you like it?" His voice is rougher than normal. Gritty. Sexy.

There's no use acting dumb. I know exactly what he's referring to.

"Yes." My eyes finally lift to his and oh boy. His pupils are fully dilated. There's only one thing on his mind.

How did we get off the subject of my father? Not that I'm complaining.

He rises, pushing the chair back. In two strides, he's standing in front of me, his erection staring me in the face.

Where do I look? Where do I look?

"As much as I'd like to continue discussing that monster who raised you, we're done with that conversation. He's getting what's owed him. My brother and I will keep you safe when he gets out. That's a promise."

Alright. Way to wrap up our talk. He's taken on a rougher edge. More dominant. I'm not sure what he's doing, but I'm sure I'm about to find out.

"Stand," he orders, and like the little puppet I am, I obey.

A large hand holds my chin and lifts my head so we can stare at each other. He's so much taller than me. I truly do feel like a midget next to him.

"It's all I can think about. The way you responded." He's pushing me gently back until my back rests on the counter and then I'm lifted so he can stand between my legs.

"Tell me, kitten. What do you want me to do? And

don't say nothing. I see it in your eyes. You want me as much as I want you. But I know you're inexperienced, so we'll go at your pace, even if I want to have you screaming under me."

I whimper at his dirty words. He's lit a match and I feel the inferno getting out of control.

"Kiss me. Touch me."

Atlas can walk in at any time, but neither of us care. We're too swept up in this moment. The unconstrained energy zapping between us.

With no warning, he slams his lips onto mine, his large body pulling me into him. I gasp into his mouth, every atom in me exploding in sensation. There is nothing but us. This feeling.

Tongues clash, teeth gnash, lips attack mercilessly. My hands find the rigid planes of his chest with a braveness that's plucked from deep within.

We're breathing the same air. It's euphoric. He grinds himself into me, groaning.

"This is what you're doing to me. You drive me crazy."

Ditto. He's clawing his way under my carefully constructed armor with such a ferocity, I'm not sure it exists anymore.

"Come shower with me." His lips are at my ear and then they are sucking my lobe. Oh my. This brings about a new sensation. Who would have known the ear is so sensitive?

Then I remember there's no hot water left. I took it all.

"It'll be awhile before there's hot water. I kind of used it all."

He pulls back to look at me. "Hmmm. Greedy little thing, aren't you? Well, who said anything about a hot shower?"

An opened mouth kiss to my neck and I can't think. "Okay."

Because what else can I say? I'm throbbing everywhere and if I don't release the valve that's about ready to blow, I'll go crazy.

Kill picks me up and I wrap my legs around his waist so he can carry me down the hall to his private bathroom.

He kicks his bedroom door shut and locks it.

I'm actually doing this. Not having sex. It's too soon, but I'm going to be naked with a guy. He's going to see my scar. Suddenly I'm panicked. Nervous about what he'll think.

I stiffen in his arms, and he stops just inside the bathroom. "What?"

"I've never let a guy see me naked. I have a large scar."

Burying my head into his neck, he places me down on the soft mat outside the cubicle. "I don't care about some stupid scars, Capri. Hell, I've got some. They are okay. In fact, they prove just how strong you are. You don't have to hide from me. Not anymore."

And my heart just melted. Still a little nervous, I nod, watching as both his hands undress me. All the while, his eyes remain fixated on mine.

"We're just going to make out, okay? I won't do anything you don't want me to do."

Relief has my shoulders sag. He's giving me my power back.

Unlike last night with Chase. He's showing me that not all guys force themselves on to a girl.

When he bends down to pull my panties off, I automatically bring my hand down to cover my small patch of hair I keep neatly trimmed. It's barely enough to cover me.

Kill pushes my hands away, glancing up. "No hiding, remember?"

He takes his fill, kissing my thighs on each side before standing. "You're beautiful."

Even though I've never thought of myself as beautiful, and leaned more toward ugly, Killian makes me feel like his words are true because he believes them. There's a two-inch-long scar on my belly where I was pushed down the basement stairs and landed on a piece of glass from an earlier episode of my fathers where he smashed a beer bottle in a fit of rage. His eyes find it, but he doesn't dwell, instead a finger comes up to trace over it, almost reverently, making me feel like he truly doesn't find it ugly.

"Now, take my sweats off so we can shower. I want to wash you. The water will be cold, but I'll keep you warm."

And there he goes again. Being all sweet.

My fingers shake as they pull at his waistband, dragging his sweats down.

Shock at his lack of underwear and the girth of him, make me take pause. My head snaps up. "That's big."

He laughs, tipping his head back. "It's average, but you probably think it's big because you haven't seen one before."

Perhaps, but I've seen videos, and this is way beyond average. Up close, I wonder at the softness of it, even though it's engorged. The head is redder than the rest. A vein pops down the length of it.

He doesn't have any pubic hair. He's shaved it all off, giving me a full view of everything.

My pulse pounds in my ears as he steps out of his sweats and moves past me to turn the faucets on.

With his back to me, I observe his tight ass, watching it clench as he moves.

I'm dreaming or out of my body. One of the two. I must be. This isn't me. This isn't real. And yet, the way my entire body trembles and the clarity of it all lets me know it's very real.

When he turns, he resembles a prince of darkness. Hair wet, body too perfect for words, tattoo almost coming alive. Nipple hoop dripping with water. It's his eyes, though. They burn through me, scorching my flesh.

The cold water isn't bothering him as he stands fully under the spray, letting it rain down. I'm caught in his web. Stuck, gawking at the picture before me.

A hand comes out, motioning me forward. "Don't be afraid of me. I won't hurt you."

And so, lacing my fingers with his, I let him drag me under the too cool deluge, squealing as the temperature steals my breath.

"It's freezing!" Goosebumps rise and spread every-where. I go to pull away, but he's still holding my hand.

He steps out of the shower momentarily, breaking our contact. I wonder what he's doing until he turns on the heat in the bathroom. A vent in the ceiling begins blowing hot air out, in stark contrast to the freezing water.

Kill climbs back in, his erection bouncing. I can't stop looking at it. Wondering.

"You can touch it if you want. You can touch any part of me."

He's offering himself up to me, giving me more power to take control. This is so new for me, to have a choice.

My head shifts up and I find him watching me. I move closer, scared yet intrigued.

Slowly, my fingers lift, grazing his cock. It jerks and I do the same.

Kill chuckles. "That means it likes you. Do it again."

I do, amazed at the soft surface covering the hardness underneath. My hand grips him, causing him to moan.

"That's it. Rub your hand up and down the length."

My eyes meet his half-closed ones, and I can see his pupils are fully blown again, just like when we kissed. It causes a flooding between my legs.

His request has me obeying. "Am I squeezing too hard?"

"That's perfect. Just like that. Squeeze somebody wash on. Get it all soapy and slippery."

The very idea brings about a full body shiver and it's not from the chilly water anymore. I've forgotten about that. The bathroom is heating to the point of me needing ice to put out the fire.

I grab the bottle and squeeze a copious amount into the palm of my hand before coating him in it and massaging it in. My small hand doesn't completely encircle his girth, but I do my best to work the underside as well.

He's getting harder if it's possible. A low growl comes

out of his throat as if he's in pain, but when I look up again, I see his eyes squeezed shut, head thrown back, every muscle and vein in his neck protruding.

"God, that feels so good. Make me come."

Oh boy. Why do I like his dirty mouth? The throbbing between my legs is extreme now. I've masturbated before, so I move my left hand down to ease the pressure, causing me to moan.

Kill's eyes fly open, his attention zeroing in on my hand, rubbing myself.

"You want me to take over? Do you want relief?"

I'm nodding before he finishes and when he covers me, stroking my clit, I almost see stars.

We're standing in the cold shower, burning up, my hands working him and his me.

The only sounds are the water hitting us and our moans and groans as pleasure takes over.

When he uses a finger to penetrate me, I cry out. "Kill!"

"Kiss me."

So, I do. I unleash everything locked away. Pain. Heartbreak. Disappointment. My vault opens and I give him everything I am. I put everything into the kiss. It's frenzied.

A hand grips my head, pulling me closer as if I'm still too far away.

He's unraveling with me as we tear at each other, my pace increasing to bring him to orgasm.

"God, Capri. You're like the tightest of gloves, squeezing my finger. Mmm. You feel amazing. I'm imagining my cock in there."

It's the first time he's called me by my name. It means

something. He's not just seeing the little kitten he refers to. He's seeing me. With all my faults, scars, and baggage. He's accepting them all. Just the same way I'm accepting him.

And then I'm coming apart. Detonating further when the heel of his palm pushes on my clit.

My voice is deep and delirious as I ride the glorious wave of pleasure. Seconds later, Kill is coming too.

"Fuck! Fuck!" He's groaning as if in pain and the sound is music to my ears. Because I know it's ecstasy. From me. I've done this to him.

Ropes of semen coat me but quickly get washed away by the shower spray. It seems as if he'll never stop. To watch porn and experience it are two totally different things.

My body shudders from aftershocks. His finger is still inside.

Then he's crowding me, withdrawing his finger, and placing it in my mouth.

"Open."

My lips part for him to push inside and allow me to taste myself. When I wrap my tongue around his finger, he hisses.

"My turn."

He pulls his middle finger out and penetrates my wet center again before bringing it to his mouth and sucking.

"Mmm. Even better than I imagined."

Even though my body feels like a pool noodle, I'm still turned on watching him.

In a sudden bold move, I wait for him to pull his finger

out and then I'm pulling his head to mine, needing his mouth on mine more than anything else in the world.

It's primal and raw as he eats my face.

I've been to Hell, and now I've stepped over the threshold into Heaven. Killian is that Heaven and I never want to leave.

Forty-Three

Atlas

I sleep for an hour and then I'm awake, my brain overthinking too much to switch off.

The last few days have been hard. I'm attempting to process the fact that even on his deathbed, my father still never accepted me for who I am.

It cuts deep. I feel myself drifting into a dark space. I've been there once, and I don't want to return, but I can't seem to drag myself out of this funk. Given the fact Coby and I had a huge fight about something so trivial, I can't even remember what triggered it. My head is a mess.

I'm partly to blame because my mood is so shitty, but he knows about my visit with my dad. Can't he understand how deeply it's affected me? It's not just that one visit, though. It's my whole life and how I've had to pretend with my parents. To act as if I'm someone else and not me. I just wanted acceptance. Nothing more. Even if they didn't care for me but were okay with my sexual orientation, I could have handled that. But my father has always made me feel like something ugly. A stain on society.

Some parts of me believe that. I'm not the norm. I was cut from a different mold. But to have it shoved in my face time and time again leaves a person mentally drained.

I'd been doing so well, too. Or maybe I've been pretending to be okay when, deep down, I'm simply attempting to be happy when, in actual fact, I'm sad. So fucking sad.

My cell pings with a message and upon finding out it's Coby asking if we can talk, I ignore it and switch my phone off. I know how this ends. He's going to break up with me. I can feel it. The way we left things. The tension is still there. He's realized we're not compatible. And it's probably a good thing this early on. Before we both get attached. I thought maybe this relationship might be different. After losing Jayden, I didn't think I'd ever feel for a guy again. But Coby changed that. He's fun and silly and likes the things I like.

Well, fuck him. Fuck everyone.

The house is as silent as when I arrived earlier. It's not common. Kill is normally up early, and Capri is not one to sleep until mid-morning.

I push my covers off and head out, needing to use the bathroom. My brother has the en suite which leaves Capri and I to share, which I don't mind. She's clean and tidy and keeps the clutter to a minimum.

As I move down the hall, I notice Kill's bedroom door open and hear the shower. Well, at least I know he's home.

Capri's door is shut, so I go relieve myself and walk to the kitchen to put coffee on.

Even though two people are still in the house, I feel alone. My eyes are gritty from lack of sleep and my body is running on vapors.

I slump over the table, waiting on the coffee, my heart in pain. Everything feels gray, the color gone. Figuratively, not literally, but it's enough to have me wondering what I'm freaking doing. What am I here for?

I'm a fraud. Everyone thinks I've got my shit together. I don't. It's all a facade. My head is barely above the water. I've been treading for a long time. And now, I'm spent.

Rather than wait for the coffee, I remember about a bottle of Jack Daniels sitting unopened in the cupboard above the stove. It's sitting unopened from when I'd wanted to get wasted on the anniversary of Jayden's death. But Capri appeared on the bridge that night, stealing my attention away from my grief.

I'd been planning on coming home and drinking the entire bottle until the girl with the sad eyes happened.

I'm quick to open the bottle now, taking a swig, enjoying the burn. It's been a while since I've been plastered, and what better way to drown my sorrows than in my own home on a Sunday?

Why has Kill been in the shower for so long? He's going to use all the hot water.

Sitting in my slump, thoughts swirling, memories surface.

"You okay, man?" I ask Jayden, noticing him withdraw from

me lately. He's quiet and always seems to be zoned out. He's been ostracized by his family because he's gay and it's hit him hard. We've found comfort in each other because I'm in the same boat, except my brother is and always has been by my side. I'm lucky to have him. Jayden has no one besides me.

"Yeah. All good." *He's not even looking at me.*

"You know you can talk to me, right?"

It's then his gaze clashes with mine. It's also then that I realize how lost he is. There's an emptiness in his eyes I've never seen before. It scares me.

"I know. I just need to be left alone right now."

Hours later, they find his body washed up on the shore of the river. It destroyed me.

I wonder if he's finally at peace. Perhaps he didn't take the easy way out. Perhaps he took the only way out.

FORTY-FOUR

Killian

We dry off, clean and sated. Capri gifts me with her shy smile as she walks into her room and closes the door to get changed.

I throw on a pair of jeans and a shirt, before swaggering to the kitchen, feeling better than I ever have. That shower? Holy crap. Hearing her come apart like that, knowing no other guy had fingered her to orgasm, filled me with ego boosting adrenaline.

There is no turning back now. I can't stay away from her, even if I wanted to.

My brother turns when I enter, a half-empty bottle of Jack in his hands.

What the hell? He never drinks in the day.

"Atlas? What's going on?"

He stares at me blankly. "Just having a drink. You want one?"

"No. It's eleven in the morning. Why are you drinking?"

Something is going on with him. He's been different lately. It has a lot to do with our father's words to him. They seem to have cut deeper this time.

I sit opposite him.

"Talk to me, Bro."

He takes another long swig. "Nothing to say."

Okay, now he's worrying me. This is not my brother.

"Don't you think you should put that away now? I think you've had enough."

He swipes his mouth with the back of his hand. "I'll decide when I've had enough!" His voice is louder. Angrier.

Something is wrong. I don't know what to do. What to say.

Before I can speak, my cell rings.

I glance at the screen and see Mom is calling.

"Hi, Mom."

She's sobbing and I know exactly what has happened.

"Is he gone?"

"Yes. A half hour ago" Loud wails fill the line.

"We'll be right there."

My eyes find Atlas. He knows. But his face is blank, just like I know mine is.

We knew it was coming. We welcomed it, even.

"Get yourself together. We need to go."

"I'm not going anywhere. You go. I don't want to see her."

It's not an option. She needs her sons. We're all she has and even though she supported that ass with everything he said and did, she's still our mom.

"I'm not asking, Atlas."

I rise to find Capri, leaving him to heed my words.

She's dressed and brushing out her damp hair when I knock and enter her room.

"Hey," she greets me, obviously sensing my mood. I'm not smiling. I'm not anything as I move closer to her.

There's a strange sense of relief washing over me to know the man who caused my brother and me the most pain is no longer breathing.

"What's wrong?" She's up off the bed, standing in front of me.

"Mom, just called. Dad passed."

Her face falls. "Oh, Kill. I'm so sorry!" Both her hands cradle my face. "Are you okay?"

Normally, it would be a silly question to ask someone who has just lost a parent but, in my case, I nod and answer truthfully.

"Yeah. I'm good. Atlas and I need to go to the hospital, though. You going to be okay here?"

"Of course. You go do what you need to."

She's amazing. I touch her lips with mine, softly, needing to feel her before I leave. Her scent soothes me. With my forehead to hers, I whisper, "See you soon."

"See you soon."

And then I'm dragging my brother's drunk ass out the door to his car, where I drive us to the hospital for the last time.

FORTY-FIVE

Capri

They're gone for a couple of hours. I didn't realize Atlas was drunk until Kill messaged me from the hospital to let me know he'd caused a scene in front of their mother and hospital staff.

I'm not sure he's talking about the same guy we live with. I know Atlas has been a little off lately, but to be drunk in the day and to cause a scene just isn't in his nature.

There must be more going on with him than he's letting on. Worry settles low in my gut.

I need to try to talk to him. After all, I wouldn't be here today if it weren't for him. Of course, I'm going to be there when he needs me. Hopefully Kill can find out what's going on.

The idea of him suffering alone saddens me. I can

relate. It's not a nice feeling to have people around you, but still be so alone.

I attempt to call him, but it goes to voice message, so I offer him my condolences and tell him we'll talk when he gets home.

When I finally hear the garage door open and the car pull in, I'm up off the couch, waiting for them.

Kill enters first, his attention drawn to me in an instant. He smiles slightly, walking to me and pulling me into his arms.

"How did it go?"

His cheek rests on the top of my head. "Eh. It wasn't good, but it's over now."

I can only imagine after his earlier message.

Noise behind him alerts me to Atlas walking in, head hung low. He looks terrible. Shoulders hunched. Hair messy as if he's just got out of bed.

"Atlas?" I pull away from Kill and move closer to the boy who saved me.

His head raises and I gasp at his red eyes. Not from crying, but from booze.

He's carrying the empty bottle of Jack.

I look to Kill in question. He nods, letting me know his brother has had the entire bottle.

"Why didn't you take it off him?" I ask, anger rising. How did he let Atlas drink it all, and in the car none-the-less?

"I tried. He refused to go unless I let him take it with him."

"The fucking bane of my existence is gone," Atlas yells,

slurring his words. "Time to celebrate. Any beers left, Kill?"

Before Killian can answer, Atlas shuffles to the fridge, opening the door, but his brother is moving fast, slamming it shut again.

"Enough! That's enough! You're going to pass out or get alcohol poisoning. Whatever is going on with you, let us help you. Booze isn't the answer."

Kill is yelling. He's scary when he's pissed. His brother isn't fazed though. If anything, I can see there's about to be a showdown.

Oh, how the tables have turned.

The brothers I first met have done a complete three-sixty.

I can't do anything but watch the train wreck. It's not my place to step in. All I can do is to be here to pick up the pieces.

"Nothing is the answer. Don't you see? There's nothing to help me. The gay fuck up. Did you see Mom's eyes when she saw me? I've seen that look so many times before. And it wasn't because I was drunk. She's just as disappointed in me as *he* was. Do you have any idea how that feels? Do you?"

He's moved into Kill and is pointing a finger in his chest.

"You know I do," Kill grinds out, his whole-body stiffening.

"Yeah right. Because people judge you every second of the day. You who has never had to worry about people's reactions when you tell them you like guys. Their eyes go from accepting to disapproving in an instant. They judge you even if they don't fucking know you. And for what? Because of whom I am? Don't tell me you know how I feel."

"I know how it feels to have the one person who should love and support you, pick you apart because you haven't followed in his footsteps," Kill counters, but it doesn't matter.

Atlas is too far gone. He's got to a point where he's going to explode.

I can't stand by another second. I'm going to try to reach him.

"Atlas?"

He pivots to me as if he forgot I was even here.

The absolute pain I see in his expression kills me. I move across the floor.

"Hey. It's okay. Let's go sit in the living room and we can talk. I can help."

He laughs. I don't know where Atlas has gone, but this person is a stranger.

"Help? You think you can help me the same way I helped you?" He sways, so I grip his arm to stop him from falling over, but he shrugs out of my hold.

"Yes! If you'll let me in. Don't shut us out." My voice is desperate.

"Leave me alone."

Kill takes my hand, which Atlas notices. He looks between us and then again at our joined hands.

"Well, well. It seems you two are over your differences. Isn't that nice? You have each other."

I go to draw my hand away, but Kill grips it harder. "Yeah, we've worked out our differences. I thought you'd be happy."

For a moment, I see a sliver of the old Atlas as his eyes soften. "I'm glad you're not fighting anymore. You continue to surprise me, Brother."

Then he moves out of the kitchen and down the hall. His voice calls out on his way, "You should have jumped when you had the chance, Capri."

His bedroom door slams shut.

I look to Kill to find his face distraught. I'm feeling the same.

You should have jumped when you had the chance, Capri.

Does he not want me here anymore or is he meaning life is so hard I should have taken the out?'

"He'll be alright. He just needs time to process everything." His words fail to appease me. Nausea rolls in my stomach. I'm so worried.

"Hey." Calloused fingers lift my chin. "I know my brother."

Does he? Truly? Because when I looked into Atlas' eyes, I saw the same haunted expression staring back at me I'd seen in myself.

But I need to trust Killian's words and hope he's right.

"Come on. Let's go give him some space. Do you want to go for a ride?"

"Maybe we shouldn't leave him on his own."

Will he be okay? Does he really need space or is he silently crying out for us to stay?

Kill puts his arm around me and says, "Come on. We'll let him sleep off the alcohol, go for a ride, and then we'll all order pizza and watch a movie."

My shoulders sag. "Okay. Fine. But I get to pick the movie."

* * *

The exhilaration of being on the back of the bike helps me settle. I still can't help but worry about Atlas. I haven't seen him like this. It brings back haunting memories of not so long ago when I looked like him.

He's always been so strong. But I guess we're all only human and at some point, we break.

We wind through the stunning Maine countryside until we pass the sign for Moosehead Lake, a destination I've only heard about.

Momentarily, my anxiety eases and I take in the surrounding beauty. An array of color paints the perfect landscape with pine trees joining the mix. I lift my visor to breathe in the pure, crisp air, letting it fill my lungs fully.

We slow and pull into a rest area with picnic tables overlooking the water and all I can do is stare in wonder. I've never seen anything so breathtaking.

Once we're stopped, Kill switches the engine off and removes his helmet, climbing off and motioning for me to do the same.

I take his outstretched hand and let him remove my helmet.

"Welcome to my favorite place," he smiles genuinely, his eyes alight with a new kind of happiness I don't get to see.

"It's stunning." There are truly no words.

A car is parked nearby, a family sitting at one of the tables, eating.

Kill grabs my hand as if it's the most natural thing in the world, and in this moment it is. His large fingers entwine with mine, evoking emotions I don't have time to question right now. My belly is upturned and my chest flutters.

"Come on, let's sit and soak in the atmosphere."

Peace envelops us as we sit at a table. It's as if we've stepped into another world filled with color, beauty, and serenity.

"How do you know about his place?" I ask in awe.

"I'd heard about it through people I've spoken to. Customers who own bikes. I started coming here a couple of years back."

My head tilts upwards, my eyes closing as I inhale until my lungs are full. "I love it."

When I lower my head and open my eyes, he's watching me. "What?"

"Just looking at you experiencing it for the first time." His smile appears almost shy, the corners of his lips upturned, eyes bright.

"I didn't realize how much I needed this." The weight of all that has happened these past weeks is strikingly clear. A sense of regret that I'd almost ended it all washes over me, but I quickly push it back, thankful that I am still here to enjoy this.

Something occurs to me as I move my attention to the glass lake with its mirrored finish, trees reflecting on it.

Killian never talks about friends or has people over. Atlas doesn't really either, but at least he has Coby.

Is he a loner like me? Or have I simply never met anyone else close to him? He's always either working or at home.

With more bravado than I normally have, I ask, "Do you have friends you come here with?"

His gaze finally leaves mine, a tic in his jaw appearing.

"Nah. Friends are overrated." With a quick side-eye to me, he breathes out through his nose on a sigh.

The words answer my question. Why does the idea of him having no friends sadden me? I've got Carly and Steph. No one deserves to be alone.

But I don't push. The subject is painful, I can tell. All I do is take his hand and squeeze hard, once again surprising myself at my ability to touch him without thinking.

At the contact, he spins to look at me, as if he still can't believe it either, even after what we've done together.

"Well, you have me. I'll be your friend." It's true. Even if I want to be more. He needs to know. There's someone besides his brother who will be there for him.

"I…" he falters, then unlaces our fingers and brings his hand to my cheek. "I don't know if I can be friends."

My breath stalls, hoping he doesn't push me away again.

"I like you too much to be just friends." The softness of his touch and the way he's searching deep inside me with his penetrating stare brings my body alive.

I lift my hand and place it over his. "I like you too much to be just friends, too."

His face moves slowly to mine, as if he's giving me

enough time to accept his touch. Only, I don't need time. I've already accepted it. I crave it.

Our lips collide and I finally breathe again, needing his connection to me as if it's the very oxygen keeping me alive.

I don't care that we are in front of others because when we kiss, it's just the two of us. The world narrows to where his lips meet mine.

We've crossed a line. One I most certainly can't come back from. I'm not sure about Kill. I'd like to think I'm more than a little fun for him, but who knows?

When he pulls back, we're nose to nose. His eyes crinkle at the corners. "You're getting under my skin, little kitten."

I light up at his words. It's as if he heard my internal dialogue and he's confirmed my doubts.

"You're getting under mine too."

We kiss again, this time less passionate and more sweet.

"Come on. Let's walk around the lake for a bit."

The rest of the day flies by. We talk about our lives, mine sounding like a morose horror flick and his more like an angst-ridden drama. But somehow, we connect through our pasts, both of us having dealt with selfish fathers who failed to see us for who we are.

The sun is going down when we decide to head back home. Atlas should have sobered up and be awake now.

"Let's grab pizza on the way. I for one am starving," Kill confesses just as my stomach rumbles.

We both chuckle and climb back onto the bike, taking

one last look at our piece of paradise before we drive
away.

Forty-Six

Atlas

My head is throbbing, and my mouth feels like it's coated in concrete when I walk into the kitchen after passing out for a sizeable chunk of the day.

Where the hell are my brother and Capri?

The house remains empty, loneliness seeping through my pores once more. I need company and feel my anxiety kick back in from this morning as silence greets me.

My mind is filled with chaos, though, loud enough to break through my exterior reality.

Dark thoughts swirl like an eddy, dragging me under. I'm so fucking tired. Mentally. The constant fight to prove my worth to my father. It's as if even in death, I feel him judging me. Throughout school, my classmates teasing me because my voice didn't drop as deeply as other boys my age. The fact I didn't date girls had me being called gay from the get-go. Back then, it confused me I liked boys. I wanted to be normal like everyone else.

Meeting Jayden had been the turning point for me. He got me. Understood what it was like to be different. To finally find someone who I could be myself around.

But he struggled with his identity too and in the end, it all got too much. God, I miss him. More than I let on to anyone.

My heart aches. I'm sick of being sad inside. To the outside world, I'm happy because I've learned to plaster on a fake smile and lift everyone else up. To be the dependable one. The one who tries to save everyone. Everyone but me. Who will save me?

I haven't switched my phone back on. I don't want to hear Coby tell me he doesn't want to see me anymore. I just can't deal with it. Another rejection. My head lowers as I grip my hair and curse. "Fuck!"

I need to get out of this house. The walls are closing in on me. But where do I go? I don't feel like being around strangers. I need my brother, but he's gone AWOL.

Grabbing my keys, I exit the house and climb into my truck, driving to God knows where.

I end up at the bridge where Jayden took his life, and Capri found hers. I haven't visited it since that night I talked her down from the edge. The sensation of being back is strange, as if I almost wait for her to appear as she had that night.

I park at the edge of the span and climb out into the chilly night. The sun has only gone down. It's not pitch dark. Just enough light to guide my way to the middle.

The rushing water below stands out in the otherwise

quiet. My breath billows out in front of me as I climb onto the railing and sit. A sudden calm settles over me as I breathe in the scent of nearby pine trees.

Is this how Jayden felt before he stepped off the edge? Did the water call to him the way it suddenly calls to me? My chin lowers to the dark, angry swirls rushing underneath.

It wouldn't take much.

FORTY-SEVEN

Capri

We're almost home, with three pizza boxes in the new bag attached to the side of Kills bike. He attached it for me, so I don't have to wear my backpack when riding from school. It's a thoughtful touch and a useful one tonight. As we round the corner to our street, a profound sensation hits my chest. It's a feeling of doom and I can't place it. All my senses are on high alert as I glance around the now familiar neighborhood. It stays with me for a minute and then it's gone.

When we pull into the driveway at home, we both notice Atlas' truck is gone. I hope he hasn't gone to drown his sorrows again.

Inside, the house is in darkness, so Kill flicks the light switch on, bathing the living room in a warm glow.

"Maybe he's with Coby, sorting things out. They had a fight, which is probably why he got shit faced."

I hope he's right, because the uneasy feeling that something isn't right comes back and hovers.

I place the pizzas on the coffee table and turn to him.

"Maybe you should call and check in on him. He wasn't too happy this morning."

Kill nods, digging his cell out and dialing his brother's number.

He waits and, with a frown, disconnects the call. "Hmm."

"What?" I swallow hard, sensing all is not okay.

"His phone's switched off. Odd. He always has it on."

I turn away and begin walking toward his bedroom to try to shed light on why I'm suddenly feeling panic rise. My gut is screaming at me to listen to it, but I'm attempting to calm it down and think rationally.

Upon opening the door and turning on the light, I immediately see his cell on his bed. My heart climbs in tempo. His bed is unmade, clothes scattered around. So unlike him. His room is usually immaculate.

"Kill?"

Footsteps sound down the hallway until he's standing in the doorway. "Yeah?"

I point to Atlas' cell.

His features pinch hard. In two long strides, he's beside me, picking up the cell and switching it on.

Dozens of messages ping through as if he hasn't checked it in ages. A sick dread filters through my body.

"They're all from Coby. He's trying to contact Atlas. What the fuck?"

When Killian's eyes find mine, I see the same panic in him I'm feeling.

"I'm worried. Should we go look for him?"

"I should have been here. I should have waited until he woke up and then talked to him."

My hand finds his arm. "You weren't to know. He may have just gone out somewhere. We shouldn't be panicking."

"He doesn't have friends like me. He wouldn't go out on his own."

I sit on the bed, attempting to quieten the pulse in my ears. The whooshing. The same open wound inside me that hasn't properly healed.

"Check his messages from Coby." Maybe there is an answer why Atlas is out without his cell.

Kill clicks on the messages, his silence almost undoing me.

"What do they say?"

"Apologies. Asking Atlas to call him. Asking where he is and why he's not messaging back."

Shit. The guy must be worried, too. "Maybe call him?"

Kill looks at me as if unsure. "What will that do?"

With a shake of my head, I don't really know, but we have nothing else to go by. "It may provide answers as to Atlas' state of mind."

A quick nod and then he's dialing. Coby answers almost straight away. Kill's put it on speaker so I can hear.

"Atlas? Where are you?" There's concern in the poor guy's voice.

"It's Killian. Atlas' brother. He's not home and has left his cell here with your messages unread. Any idea where he might be?" It's a long shot, but what do we have to lose?

There's a long pause before, "We had a big fight. He's been… distant. I called him out on it and asked him to let me in, but he shut me out. Something about his father and feeling like a failure. I told him if he wasn't going to talk, then maybe we should put some distance between us so he can sort it out. But…"

"But what?" Kill growls. He's every bit the dark knight right now. Ready to snap. Wound so tight, every sinew and muscle on his hands and arms protrudes.

"But I felt bad afterwards. I've been calling him to apologize. Well, you saw some messages. I really like him. I don't want to fight. I want to be there for him in whatever way I can. He told me about Jayden. To be honest, I don't think he's ever got over his death."

Kill is squeezing his fist over and over. Squeeze. Release. Squeeze. Release. I don't think he even knows he's doing it.

Something hits me. Hard.

I don't think he's ever got over Jayden's death.

You should have jumped when you had the chance.

Oh God. No.

"Kill?"

He spins to me at the sound of my frantic voice. I'm on my feet. "I think I know where he is. Coby, meet us at Wilson's Bridge."

Kill drops the phone and we're out the door.

Being on the back of the bike now isn't exhilarating. It's scary because as fast as we're weaving in and out of traffic, running red lights, it can't get us there fast enough.

I hope I'm wrong, but everything in me is screaming that he's gone to the bridge. To end his life.

My chest aches as I squeeze Kill hard, the only lifeline I have.

What must he be feeling? Are we too late? The idea of him jumping is horrifying. My mind slides back to the night it was me, in his position. The way he coaxed me down just by making me feel like I mattered.

We all need to feel that. Even in the darkness, we all need a sliver of light. I had no idea the boy who saved me needed saving himself. Have I been so selfish that I haven't seen the signs all along?

The very idea of him not being around fills me with premature grief.

As soon as the bike turns onto the abandoned road and we're pulling up next to Atlas' truck, I'm off, tearing my helmet off and throwing it on the ground, not caring if I damage it.

The moon is a small crescent in the sky, making the surroundings almost pitch black. But I know the way. I'll always know the way.

I scramble over broken bitumen and weeds, Killian's feet behind me, praying he's here.

When I get to the edge of the bridge, I see a lone figure sitting on the railing in the middle of the span.

I call out, and his head pivots. "Atlas!"

He stands teetering on the edge.

"Wait! Don't move!" My voice almost gets lost among the sound of the rushing water below.

"Brother!" Kill is yelling. Out of his mind.

"Stop!" Atlas cries. "Don't come any closer."

We immediately freeze, not knowing if he's going to take that step over the edge or not.

"You don't need to do this. Come down and we can talk. I love you, man."

Killian creeps closer, so he's beside me. I glance at his profile and break at his desperation.

"You're the only one. I don't have anyone else. I have no one," Atlas cries. He sobs. Frantic.

I feel like I'm teetering on that edge with him, only I can't tell him I'm jumping with him because I'm too far away.

"You're wrong. You have Capri. Coby."

A choked laugh. "Coby doesn't care. He's going to break up with me."

"That's not true, brother. I read his texts. I called him. He's worried about you. We all are. He wants to make things right with you. He loves you."

If it wasn't so dark, I could see his expression. All I see is him staring back at us. Have Kill's words registered?

"If he's so worried, then where is he? Huh?"

The sound of feet slapping against the ground in the distance has me turning. A figure is closing in at full speed. Coby.

"I think you have your answer," Kill shouts, shoulders sagging only a fraction.

When you're in a dark head space, words are meaningless. Until they penetrate and make sense. Until they make you feel something other than despair.

"Atlas!" Coby yells, out of breath. He stops just in front of us, assessing the situation. "I've been calling you."

Atlas looks down at the water and then back over at

us. My breath falters. We're all hanging on by a thread, not knowing what the next second will bring.

"You were going to break up with me!" It's a broken cry filled with pain. Another blow to his already fragile state of mind.

I know what loneliness feels like. I've lived it most of my life.

"No! I wasn't. After our fight, I felt terrible. I've been trying to contact you to apologize. I'm so sorry. I want to help. To be here for you. To be your person."

He's listening. He's still with us. He hasn't jumped yet. I decide to try.

"If you jump, I'm coming in after you. Don't think I won't. Remember? You jump, I jump. I won't let you do it alone."

Kill grips my arm. Hard. "Are you fucking insane?" There's a new horror written on his features.

"It's okay," I whisper. "I'm not going to do it. It's the reverse psychology he used on me."

"You won't do it." Atlas moves, facing us fully, his foot slipping slightly, causing him to grab the railing tighter.

We all cry out, automatically moving closer. "Atlas!"

I don't think I've breathed fully since we got here. Both of his hands come up to stabilize him. I remember him telling me, of the five students who jumped, none survived. Not good odds.

"We've got pizza at home. We got your favorite," Kill tries, as if food can bring him back from the brink.

Atlas laughs. "He died, knowing I'm a joke." His father. A man who ultimately led his son here tonight. All because of his own archaic beliefs and an unwillingness to accept his son the way he is. Well, I hope he's watching this train wreck happen, knowing he played a big part in it.

"You're not a joke. Dad was the joke. He wasn't man enough to step up and be the father we needed. I've got your back, though. Always have. Don't do this. Don't leave me. It'll destroy me."

It will. I know it with every fiber of my being. He'll never be the same again.

"I'm nothing. Just a waste of space. A blight on society." He's weeping openly and my tears are welling too. I don't know how to help him.

"Come down, Atlas. Please. We can go away. Just the two of us. I know we haven't been dating long but I feel you. I see you. I've got you." Coby tries, holding out a hand. I don't want to imagine how this will affect him if things go south.

We wait with bated breath.

Somehow, we've all crept forward without even realizing it. We stand at the first part of the metal structure. My eyes have adjusted to the darkness, and I can now see the sheer agony on Atlas' face. His eyes are wide with fear. Not fear of dying, but fear of living.

I lift my hand and hold it out. "All you've got to do is take this lifeline, Atlas. You gave me one and now I'm returning the favor. Do it for me. Do it for Kill and Coby. But more importantly, do it for yourself. There are so many amazing things waiting for you to experience. I know you can't see it now, but the darkness always clears. Always. I'm proof of that."

I'm a mess of cries with snot dripping down my face. I

wipe it away as I feel a comforting hand on my shoulder. I quickly look up to find Kill's eyes wet like mine.

He's losing it.

Atlas appears to decide. A quick nod of his head and he's taking tentative steps toward us.

But he's not looking where he's going. Not watching his feet. He's staring at us. As if in slow motion, he loses his footing, causing him to be pulled from the safety of the railing. His left hand loses its grip. My eyes find his alarm shining back at me like a torch. And then he falls.

There's two seconds after he's fallen where the world stops. All we hear is Atlas screaming. None of us move. We can't process what's happening until our brains catch up with our eyes.

And then mayhem erupts.

We all shout at the same time, sprinting to the spot where Atlas just fell from, my heart dropping with him. Words play in a loop in my head.

That could have been me. That could have been me.

Seeing it happen to someone I care about puts everything in perspective. Except if Atlas hadn't found me, I would have had no one screaming my name.

Kill is roaring as he sprints forward. "Atlas! No! No! No!"

The splash is barely audible as we peer down at the choppy water.

I grip my hair, shattering into a million pieces.

Coby cries out into the night, slamming his hand down onto the railing. "Fuck!"

Kill is already turning and running off the bridge.

"What are you doing?" I scream.

"I'm going to get my brother!"

He's insane. I can't let him do it. "No. Stop! You can't go in there." It's as if I'm talking to deaf ears. He's already scrambling down the steep incline, Coby hot on his heels.

"Call 911." It's the last thing I hear as silence descends again.

My fingers pull my cell out of my pocket, shaking as I connect with the operator. I relay all I can with our location, out of my body as if this is all happening to someone else. I'm on autopilot.

All I can do is wait and pray.

FORTY-EIGHT

Capri

The ambulance arrives ten minutes later, a flurry of sirens and madness. Ten minutes of anxious waiting to see if any of the three guys appear. I'm pacing.

The three paramedics, including the driver, are firing questions at me, which I attempt to answer the best I can. Two of them scale the huge drop to where Kill and Coby went. God. This is a nightmare. If I lose them all, then what?

My eyes squeeze shut, my chest aching. I'm sure I got through to Atlas. I'm sure of it. I could tell he wanted to come to us. But maybe he was never meant to be saved. Maybe fate knew all along how his story ends.

Waiting is driving me crazy. I feel helpless. The idea of Kill dying with his brother has me bending over and retching. Nothing comes out because I haven't eaten anything for most of the day.

A soft voice from a woman asks, "Are you okay?"

I rise and find her face pinched in concern. "Yeah. I'm just sick with worry."

"What were you all doing on this bridge?"

"Our friend, he… ah… we thought he was going to jump. We tried to talk him down and then he just… slipped."

This can't be happening. The shit that is my life keeps playing repeatedly. I can't catch a break. It's one thing after another.

Trapped emotions I've buried from my own trauma. Pain. Regret. Sadness. It fists through my psyche. I thought I'd purged most of it but obviously not.

I fall to my knees, not feeling them hit the unforgiving ground as I retch, again and again, bile coming out.

A voice comes out of a walkie-talkie, muffled. The woman walks away from me, leaving me to purge. My life was improving. Because of Atlas. Because of Killian. What is the irony that I should lose both when I'm only beginning my healing journey? They'll never get to see the impact they've had on me.

It hurts. It hurts so bad. The idea of being all alone again.

When my stomach decides it's had enough, I sit up, listening as a chopper sounds in the distance. It's coming closer. Have they found Atlas? Is he alive? Or are they going to be lifting three bodies from their watery coffin?

I can't bear to look. So instead, I bury my head between my knees, taking deep breaths to cope.

The chopper is close. It almost sounds like it's going to land beside me. But still, I don't raise my head, silently praying over and over.

I don't want to see lifeless bodies hanging precariously from a rope and then winched on board. Ignorance is bliss. I'll deal with the outcome when it's time.

Until then, I continue to push breaths out between my lips and suck air in through my nose. In. Out. In. Out.

The icy air penetrates my clothing and settles in my bones, causing me to shake uncontrollably.

"Come on. Let's move to the ambulance. I've got a nice warm blanket with your name on it." The nice lady is back.

My head lifts as if it's weighed down. She's holding out her hand. "You're going to freeze out here."

Will it really matter though if Atlas and Kill are already gone? I want to tell her that, but I stand on shaky legs and allow her to pull me into the ambulance, where I sit in the front seat with a thermal blanket over me. The shudders ease but don't disappear altogether. I think I'm in shock.

"Have they found them?" I ask, not wanting to know but having to at the same time.

"We're working to get them out of the river."

That's all she says, which provides no comfort whatsoever. She either doesn't know or she's sparing my heart for the time being.

"Can I call anyone?" The woman asks. When I find her name badge, I see her name is Joanne. She looks like a Joanne. There's a teacher at school with the same name and has a similar mannerism to her. Friendly. Caring.

"No. There's no one. Everyone I care about is in the river."

She gives me a pitying look as her radio goes again. Upon answering it, I zone out until she finishes talking and turns to me.

"We're heading back to the hospital. The chopper is air-lifting all three."

That gets my attention. "Are they alright? Did they say?" It means they've found Atlas and the others. But she doesn't answer me.

She's walking around to the driver's side. There were two men with her. Where are they? Perhaps they're with the guys. I'm hoping so because the more medics assisting them, the better.

I make small talk with Joanne, not really wanting to speak but not wanting to be rude either. She has a job to do, and I appreciate the work she does. I don't even know if I'm ready to find out how the boys are. Not yet. I need to remain ignorant until we get to the hospital.

She asks me about school. My family, which I overtly avoid by changing the subject. My voice isn't my own. I'm shooting things out of my mouth way too fast.

The siren isn't going, so we're having to deal with traffic like everyone else. Some people pull over and let us through, but others continue on their merry way. Why isn't the siren going?

I count down the minutes until we're pulling into the ambulance bay at the hospital. I throw the blanket off me and follow her inside the back entrance, desperate for news of the boys.

"You can sit over here, and I'll go find some information for you. Can I get you a coffee?"

Not even caffeine can calm my heart rate. "No, thank you."

She smiles and turns to the busy desk, where nurses and staff are racing around frantically to deal with two other ambulances prior to ours.

A voice comes over the PA system. "Code Blue E.R. Code Blue E.R."

Then things really get hectic. It's a whirlwind of activity. Every atom inside me prays that it's not one of the guys.

Please, if there is a God. I'm begging you. Save them. Keep them alive.

Joanne walks back over to me. "The boys are alive. The guy that fell off the bridge is in surgery for a broken pelvis and ribs. All three have suffered hypothermia. I can take you through to see your friends."

I'm standing. "They're alive? All of them?" My voice is trill. I'm not believing what I'm hearing. How did Atlas survive when others haven't?

I'm not questioning it for long though because once we're through a set of double doors and my eyes zone in on Kill, layered in a blanket and sitting on a chair beside Coby, I'm running.

As soon as he looks up, he's on his feet, the blanket dropping to the floor, bracing for impact. I plow into him, unable to contain my tears. "You made it."

His face presses into my head, his arms bracketing me as if he never wants to let me go. "I made it, little kitten. And so did Atlas."

My sobs keep coming as I glance at Coby, who's still seated, but he's watching us and smiling.

I pull away from Kill and lean down to Coby, throwing my arms around his shoulders. "I was so scared. I didn't think any of you would make it."

His hair is wet against my cheek, but I don't care. He helped save Atlas, and for that I'll be eternally grateful. "Thank you."

Standing up straight, I see his own eyes welling up. "Just glad we acted so quickly and could get him. He got snagged on a tree branch down the river. We had to let the current take us. He was unconscious when we found him."

"How did you know he'd floated there? He could have sunk to the bottom."

Coby finds Kill, and he smiles. "Because Killian never lost sight of him, even in the darkness. I guess it was just lucky Atlas had on his puffy red jacket."

Relief doesn't describe what I'm feeling. What I imagine we're all feeling. I walk back to Kill and wrap my arms around his waist. My front is soaked, but I don't care. "You're incredible. I've now seen firsthand how close you both are. You'd risk your life for him. That's what family means."

"I just hope he realizes the lengths we'll all go for him. He doesn't need our father anymore. He has us."

When the boys are allowed to leave, Coby heads home to shower and dry off with the promise to return to wait out Atlas' surgery.

Kill and I get an Uber back to the bridge to pick up his bike. It's a somber scene. I'm not sure I will be returning here anytime soon. There are too many bad memories.

We've decided to do the same as Coby and get changed, then go back to the hospital. It's now 4 a.m. so there's no point in attempting to sleep.

Kill drags me into the shower with him and I'm honestly too tired to care. It'll save time and hot water.

Once in the cubicle when we're both naked, he pulls me against him once more. His embrace is beginning to feel like my safe place.

"I know how worried you were. I didn't think. I just ran. I'm sorry for what you went through." Both hands grip my head and pull back so he can see me. His long lashes are dripping, mouth red and tempting. I can't help myself. I lean up and mesh our lips together. He drags out a moan, his shoulders sagging. I daresay he wasn't sure if he'd be coming home or not either. And for that unwavering loyalty to his brother, I've fallen a little more.

Yes, that's right. I've fallen for this tall, dark, broody guy who tonight showed me just who he is.

He might not have many friends, but those he lets in, he's loyal to the death.

It shows his character even with all he's gone through.

Our kiss deepens for a minute, and then Kill draws back. He brushes water off my face, eyes an array of emotion.

"I couldn't lose him. It would have killed me."

"I know." I do. I've seen it since I came to their home. Their twin bond. It's unbreakable and I only wish I had a family like that.

His lips find my forehead, nose and then lips again.

"Just you being here is helping. I… don't let people in. Especially girls."

My mouth moves to speak, but he places a finger over it to stop me.

"You? I don't know what you're doing to me. You've managed to crawl so deeply under my skin, I can't get you out, no matter how hard I've tried."

I place a hand on his cheekbone. "Then stop trying."

We're staring at each other, drinking each other in, so much being said without words.

"Atlas is going to have a hard road ahead. I don't think I can do it without you."

"You won't have to. I care about him too. He saved me, remember?"

Kill nods. "Can you stay? With us. For a while?"

My eyebrows raise. He's asking me to move in permanently.

A smile graces my lips and I know there's a twinkle in my eye. "You want me to live with you?"

It's his turn to smile, and it totally undoes me. His face is breathtaking.

We're only touching with our hands, nowhere else. It's hard to contain all I want to do with him when we're both naked. But now is not the time. There will be plenty of time for that. We need to get back to Atlas.

A cheeky grin. "Think you can put up with me, little kitten?"

"I know I can. Give me any sass and I'll take you down."

The laugh that rumbles up from him is priceless and makes my legs tingle. Things are going to be okay. More than okay. I think I've finally found my place in the world. My home. Family isn't always blood. It's who steps up for you and is there for you, not only in the bad times, but the good too.

We might have had a rocky start, but nothing comes easy. Not for the likes of us. We're fighters and will continue to be so. But we've made a vow to do it together.

Forty-Nine

Capri

Two weeks have passed and thankfully, Atlas is healing. He's been in a wheelchair and now is on crutches, but his spirits have lifted.

He mended bridges with Coby and found out that the text messages he thought were to break up with him were to apologize.

Coby has been around here every day, and they appear closer now.

Kill has had to keep the repair shop running, but I've been taking time off school to help him as much as I can. If I'm not in the office, I'm handing him tools and learning things about cars I never would have.

We're fast approaching Christmas and my eighteenth birthday. The latter not being as important as spending the day before opening gifts and drinking eggnog. I have no idea what to buy for my new family. Kill says he doesn't want or need anything, but I'm not buying it.

Everyone needs something.

It's 6 p.m. and the three guys and I are sitting around the kitchen table. Kill whipped up a delicious roast dinner with all the trimmings. We've been sharing the cooking and sometimes preparing meals together. There's such a great energy here.

"Sooo, what do you all want for Christmas?" I ask, swallowing my last mouthful, placing my knife and fork down, and taking a sip of water.

"Don't buy for me," Coby offers, but I'm shaking my head.

"Of course, I'm buying for you. You're a part of this family now. It can either be something you really want or some lame ass gift you'll never use."

His eyes widen at my brash attitude, but then he's smiling. "You've come out of your shell lately."

I glance at the two brothers. "I guess this is who I've always been, but was too scared to show it. You've all helped with that."

Kill grips my knee under the table and squeezes. It's been so nice between us. He's not the snarky dick I first met. He's attentive and kind to me. My heart melts whenever my eyes meet his. We've become each other's person, which is great because Atlas and Coby are joined at the hip.

"Just get me a voucher. That way, I can think about what I truly want, although…" His eyes find Atlas's. "I think I have already found what I want."

They ogle each other, causing Kill and I to chuckle. It's sweet though too. To see both guys happy.

"What about you two?" I ask, pointing to the MacKenzie brothers.

"You." Killian replies, his eyes darkening.

I whisper, "You already have me. Pick again."

Atlas clears his throat. "If you want to know what to get me, how about the new C.O.D game?"

"Okay. That I can do. Done. You other two, think about it and get back to me."

After dinner, Coby leaves, and Kill is going to the shop to finish up a BMW that's getting picked up tomorrow. It's just me and Atlas in the living room, finally getting to watch a movie that had been planned the night everything went to hell.

The pizza ended up getting eaten two days later, which between hospital visits and work was a godsend.

Fast and Furious blares from the speakers but I've got something on my mind. I haven't been able to truly talk to Atlas because the others have been around, or I've been working.

The one time we spoke, it was about my father getting locked away, to which he held me and told me he'd always protect me. Just like Kill. My heart expanded at both boys' declaration.

I press pause on the movie and see him pivot his head to me out of the corner of my eye.

"Atlas?"

"Yeah?"

"Are you truly okay? I mean, do you think about it still? Ending it all?"

The silence that ensues bothers me, so I look at him.

He's already watching me. "No. I wanted to end it all so badly until you showed up with Kill. It was you."

My breath stops. "What do you mean? I didn't do anything."

A lazy smile forms on his lips. "Oh, but you did. Don't you get it? As I stood there and saw you, the first night we met came flooding back. My words to you. How your life has changed so much for the better. And then what you said to me…"

Memories of the words I spoke in desperation are fuzzy, so I ask the question. "What did I say?"

"You jump. I jump. I won't let you do it alone."

I'm still a little confused and he must realize it from my expression because he continues, "It sunk into my brain that you'd follow me into death just to keep me company. No one's ever said that to me. Well, apart from my brother. But you understood exactly what I was going through. You saw me as I saw you that night. Having one person who knows how dark the mind can get is a lifeline in itself. To not feel alone. Sure, Kill and Coby have my back, but it was you. You've been there. The despair. The need to not feel."

He reaches over and squeezes my hand. "Thank you. For being here. For just being you."

The fact that I offered is all that matters. Sometimes words are louder than actions. Sometimes they penetrate our thick walls we put up to keep ourselves safe.

The same as when I thought Atlas was there to jump the night I was. Even if he hadn't been in my most vulnerable moment, he made me believe I wouldn't be alone. That's what we all want, right?

I'm astounded by his words. The depth of them. "I'm not going anywhere. You always have me and Kill and Coby. We're family now."

Primrose Series

By Tanya Renee

Prairie Sky

Prairie Nights

Prairie Fire

Prairie Hearts

Prairie Sound

Prairie Rain

With The Band Series

By Tanya Renee

Finding Direction

The Spring of Love Series

By Virginia Taylor

Forever Delighted

Forever Amused

Forever Heartfelt

The Tooth Fairy Chronicles

By Victoria Rocus

Tooth Decay With A Side Of Fae

Toothaches And Wedding Cakes

Baby Tooth And Tangled Roots

Wisdom Tooth And The Awful Truth

A New Page

by Aimee MacRae

It Happened in Paris

By Michelle Beesley

For more information visit:

www.serenadepublishing.com

About the Author

Amanda is a multi-genre author from Australia who loves to write about broken characters who find their way out of the darkness. She's an avid reader who hopes to make writing her full time career. With twenty books to her name, there's no slowing down.

When she's not reading she's spending time with her three cats and her family and pursuing her latest junk journaling hobby.

Acknowledgments

Firstly to my family and friends who have always supported me. You know who you are and I can't thank you enough for always believing in me.

Secondly to my readers. It still blows me away that I get to share my stories with the world. You have no idea the joy I get at hearing from a reader who connected and loved one of my books. I truly appreciate all of you.

Serenade Publishing for taking a chance on me. It's nice to live in Australia and have an Australian company represent me and my work. I look forward to an ongoing, wonderful relationship.

Lastly, and I know this might seem a bit strange but I'd like to thank myself and my belief that I could achieve the mammoth task of writing my first book. It all started with a word processor around twenty six years ago when I had an idea and a lot of inspiration. While it took me many years to get my book into the hands of readers, I never gave up on the dream and always believed in my writing. If you are considering writing a book and don't think you're good enough, just start! Don't put it off. Write the first draft. Scribble down whatever is in your head and then worry about it making sense. If I can do it, so can you!

Much love. Xx